The Birth of a Gangster 2

Delmont Player

Lock Down Publications and Ca$h
Presents
The Birth of a Gangster 2
A Novel by *Delmont Player*

Delmont Player

Lock Down Publications
Po Box 944
Stockbridge, Ga 30281

Visit our website @
www.lockdownpublications.com

Copyright 2022 by Delmont Player
The Birth of a Gangster 2

Lock Down Publications
Like our page on Facebook: Lock Down Publications @
www.facebook.com/lockdownpublications.ldp
Book interior design by: **Shawn Walker**
Edited by: **Tamira Butler**

Stay Connected with Us!

Text **LOCKDOWN** to 22828 to stay up-to-date with new releases, sneak peaks, contests and more…

Thank you.

Submission Guideline.

Submit the first three chapters of your completed manuscript to ldpsubmissions@gmail.com, subject line: Your book's title. The manuscript must be in a .doc file and sent as an attachment. Document should be in Times New Roman, double spaced and in size 12 font. Also, provide your synopsis and full contact information. If sending multiple submissions, they must each be in a separate email.

Have a story but no way to send it electronically? You can still submit to LDP/Ca$h Presents. Send in the first three chapters, written or typed, of your completed manuscript to:

LDP: Submissions Dept
Po Box 944
Stockbridge, Ga 30281

DO NOT send original manuscript. Must be a duplicate.

Provide your synopsis and a cover letter containing your full contact information.

Thanks for considering LDP and Ca$h Presents.

Acknowledgments

First and foremost, I have to acknowledge Allah for his beneficence and his mercy, for he could have, and had every right to, wiped me from existence, due to the way I was living. On the level of a Beast, being controlled by my lower desires for money, fame, and power. None of which gained me anything in the end. Unless, of course, you consider the hurt, pain, prison time, and self-destruction.

But, all praise be to Allah, that he speaks to man through man! I can't thank Allah enough for his coming, in the person of Master Fard Muhammad, nor can I thank him enough for the Most Honorable Elijah Muhammad and the honorable Minister Louis Farrakhan, for without these three great men of God and their life-giving, life-saving teachings, I would still lack true knowledge of self, wisdom, and understanding. And I could never thank Allah enough for seeing something in me worth saving. For raising me from the dead, back unto the living. Al-Hamdu Lillahi Rabbil-'Alamin—Praise be to God, Lord of the Universe.

A special thanks to all the family: one love, Jasmine, Latonya, De'Bre'Anna, Ta'Nyah, Detaunn, Antaunn, Uncle Natler Lomax, Anthony 'Nolf' Nilson, Chanae A. Temple, Tineeka, Yolanda, Cassandra Stanback, Sha'Kia Mayo, fat Max, Uncle Earl, Aoama fatiu, Michelle Bronn, Terry Hill, Cousin Jamal, G.S. Daniel Carter-El, Bro. Stud. Minis. Warren Muhammad.... To name a few friends and programs who showed up or showed out in support of my second birth and vision with letters, emails, phone calls, speeches, job offerings, re-entry assistance, Facebook posts, etc., Mr. Stanley Mitchell (no struggle no success), Kermit Fonlers (Focus Movers), Urban Reads Bookstore, Living Classrooms Project, Dr. Stanley Andrisse, MBA, PhD (Johns Hopkins), all my North Branch detail officers who submitted a comment or inmate evaluation form on my behalf, Sister Arlene "Lady Blue" Major (50 Shades of Blue, Domestic Violence Initiative), Nation of Islam, Mosque #6, Behind the Wall Mentors, Mr. Dren Leder (Loyola University Maryland), and Bro. Cash and the entire Lockdown staff. Thank you all for your trust, faith, and continued support. When it's all said and done, you won't regret it!

Dedication

A'myiah C. Johnson, the best thing that's ever happened to me!
My mother Linda O. Player for her faithfulness!
Grandma Wilhelmina Player for her grace!
Aunt Priscilla Carter for her wisdom!
Aunt Barbara Carter for her lesson!
Mom Jacqueline Shakir for her prayers!
Mrs. Dorothy Alexander for her blessing!
Mom Creola Truesdale-Barnes for her 'G'!
My Susan Kerin for her unconditional love!
My nieces/ribs for their inspiration!
Chanae A. Temple for our bond and her example!
Momma Mary Moore for her light!
Godmother Jane Davis for her encouragement!
Ms. Lea Green for her commitment!
Saprina Edwards for her dedication!
Samone Jones-Player for cracking the code!
Sara Felder for her hard work!
Erika C. Brown for her understanding!
My M.G.T. SISTERS for setting the standards!
Tineeka and Yolanda Player for their loyalty!
Melissa Powell for her undying support!
Tia Hamilton for her guidance!
Tiphani Glover for our b-day connection!
Octavia Bowman for her realness!
Attorney Elizabeth Franzoso for her fight!
The Honorable Judge Melissa Phinn for her courage!
My sisters for the player's future!
And finally, Sis, Tamika D. Mallory for carrying the torch!

Delmont Player

Chapter 1

The Good, the Bad, the Gangster

I was finally discharged from the hospital, only to be transported right to the Central Bookings Intake Center for processing and stuffed into a holding cell like a sardine, with a gang of older cats who wanted to know what I was in for. But, I just found an empty spot and sat my ass down to gather my thoughts and wait for my free five-minute phone call.

I wasn't stupid, I knew all that "Ahhh shorty, nephew, you're a baby" shit was just a trick to help them nosey niggas get some information so they could jump on my case and help the state throw a young nigga in the Crisco and fry my ass in some hot grease.

"Hello." My attorney, Elizabeth Franzoso, picked up the phone on the third ring.

"Hello, Miss Franzoso?" I questioned to be sure.

"Yes, with whom am I speaking?" she inquired.

"Uh, this Dakaron," I confessed, deciding to add my last name. After all, she did have a lot of clients. "Dakaron Truesdale."

"Eh, yeah, hey, good morning, Dakaron," Ms. Franzoso perked up. "I spoke with your mom this morning and she informed me that, ummmm, you were being moved."

"Yes, ma'am, they already moved me. I'm at Central Bookings now. That's why I called," I explained, looking around.

"Good, good," she said. "This is a step in the right direction. Now we can get this ball rolling. I'll be over to the city lockup to see you this week so we can began preparing our defense."

"Defense?" I repeated, looking at the phone in anger. I didn't know how many times I had to tell her ass that I hadn't murdered this nigga. "I didn't do it, that's my defense."

"Unfortunately, Dakaron, we're going to need a better tactic than that, because that won't hold up in court," Ms. Franzoso assured. "As I explained, at this stage, we have two choices. Either we accept the state's deal or we fight."

I thought about my and Elizabeth Franzoso's last visit. She'd told me that the state prosecutor had contacted her with an offer. She would drop the first-degree and handgun charge, in exchange for a second-degree guilty plea if I testified against Frank. I'd gone off on Ms. Franzoso. There was no way in hell that I would plead guilty to a murder I didn't commit, let alone snitch, testify, or whatever on anyone. Ms. Franzoso had said the prosecutor owed her a favor, but twenty-five years didn't sound too sweet to me. In fact, twenty-five years sounded like life to me.

"I ain't taking no deals," I declared firmly, wondering how many good men had been sold up the river doing all these 'favor for a favor' negotiations. "Them bitches gonna have to bring it," I added, ready to go to war. Shid, I hadn't survived this long by laying down when the cards weren't falling in my favor.

"Then, we fight," Ms. Franzoso exclaimed.

"One minute!" the guard signaled, getting my attention as he uncuffed the next guy for the phone.

I quickly gave Ms. Franzoso my ID number and asked her to pass it on to my mother and them. "Make sure you don't talk to anybody except me about the case. No friends, no cellmates, nobody, Dakaron!" Ms. Franzoso instructed, making me laugh. "I'm serious, I don't know how many times some scorned woman or old cellmate showed up in court."

"I got you," I assured.

"And stay out of trouble, Dakaron, that's the last thing we need right now, okay?"

"Look, I have to go." I nodded to the guard, ignoring Ms. Franzoso's trouble statement. There was no way that I could agree to that. The jail was a breeding ground for trouble. It actually thrived on that shit.

"Okay, take care of yourself."

"You do the same, bye." I hung the phone up and strolled on down the hallway to the holding cells as instructed. "Ay, how long does it usually take to get over the jail?" I asked nobody in particular, walking into the holding cell. After taking three slugs and being laid up in the ICU for over two months getting my weight back up, the last thing I wanted to do was be stuck in a holding cell all night. Honestly, I'd wanted to stay at the hospital. Saprina had even tried to get the doctor to stop the court order. But, once the judge found out that I was gaining weight and the shit-bag had been removed, she agreed with the detectives that I should be moved to the city jail for security reasons.

"It depends on what time we see the commissioner tonight," one of the older cats explained.

Damn! I thought, tossing my shirt on the concrete bench to stretch my ass out. How the fuck did I end up in this shit? I mean, I had always been the stand-up type. There wasn't a whole lot that could stress me and I would never fold under pressure. But still, to be charged with a murder I was absolutely sure I didn't commit was fucked up.

"Don't worry, young blood, you'll be there soon enough," a tall, slim, Morgan Freeman looking old head assured from over in the corner he sat in with his partner.

It was around 5 o'clock when the bail reviews were being called. We fell out of the holding cell like livestock and lined up on the wall to listen for our names. Then, we were ushered down the hallway into a room full of empty seats and ordered to fill them in as the first person's name was called. I already knew that I wasn't going to be fortunate enough to receive a bail, not with a body. Especially not after the nigga who went before me was caught with the dead body of his witness locked inside the trunk of his car while out on bail.

I'd never seen no shit like this in my life. They were putting everybody's business out there. One sucker started snitching right there in the bail review hearing. Then, there was the sick mother fucker who niggas threatened to chop up once we hit the jail because he had 'allegedly' touched his own daughter. When it was my turn, I stood up, trying to fix my clothes. I wanted to at least look a little presentable. But, just like everybody else, after I was identified, I stood there in a daze as the prosecutor painted a better picture of my case than Picasso before convincing the old ass judge to deny bail.

"That Devil, full of race hate brother," the old head who'd been sitting with Morgan Freeman inside the holding cell mumbled as the judge continued to add his two cents.

After seeing the commissioner, we were all separated into three groups. Those who had received bail, those who were given their own recon, and, finally, those who'd have to fight it out in court. Then, we were lined up and marched over to the Baltimore City Jail for better or worse. There was a lot of small talk about who was going where and what not because of their charges. And a lot frustration surrounding the fact that the sick nigga who'd touched his own daughter had gotten a bail.

"I was going to put that knife in that nigga, square business!" the older guy walking in front of me told his friend.

"I wanted to put that dick in him!" his friend retorted, making me shake my head.

"Okay, gentlemen, most of you know the routine!" One of the guards who was escorting us turned around. "But, for those that don't, this is where the game stops!" he added with a sinister laugh.

"Don't pay that clown no mind, young blood," the Morgan Freeman look-alike whispered as we walked through the doors of the city jail. "He's trying to scare you."

"You smell that?" the guard continued, and for whatever reason, I sniffed the air. "Yeahhhh, that's the smell of danger, blood, and shit, baby!" he declared, smiling. "But, if you got a real good nose you can smell the fear on some and the hungry on others. This is where your real gangster gets measured. "

I carefully took in the scenery as I thought about what the guard was saying. I knew it was easier to claim to be a gangster than it was to actually be one. But, I was a born gangster and I wasn't tripping about proving it. I felt like I was seeing the city jail for the very first time. It felt different, darker, more serious even. Maybe it was because I was charged with a career-ending offense.

Another thing I instantly noticed was that, there were some fine ass bitches working over the jail. *That's probably how they keep a nigga calm*, I thought as a sexy redbone strolled past in the opposite direction.

"What you know about that R and R? And I ain't talking about rest and relaxation, baby!" he warned, and I believed I knew exactly what he was referring to.

We were led to one of the bullpens just across the hall from intake and told to wait by a cute ass female guard with the prettiest honey-brown eyes I'd ever seen. I flirted with her as she took my ID, but all she did was play shy and blush. I did catch her name though.

It took about two hours for everybody to be seen and given a bed location. It had been so much easier going on the hopper tier. "It's a bunch of bitches down there, soldier," one of the old heads spoke up after it was determined that I was going to G-section because of my barely healed wounds. "That joint a check-in spot for rats, for real!" he added, giving me a strange look.

"Yeah, well, I don't give a fuck about none of that!" I assured, knowing that I was as solid as they came. "I just wanted to know how the section was," I informed, going to sit back down.

"Nah, soldier, I didn't mean nothing like that," he explained as I took my seat on the bench. "I can look at you and already tell that you're a monster, shorty."

"All is well, yo." I took a deep breath and tried to collect my thoughts.

"Take the game from me, young blood, don't sleep on them G-section cats. They're playing with that hospital steel up there," the Morgan Freeman look-alike cautioned, walking over with his partner, patting his miniature bush, before taking a seat beside me on the bench. "Their knives coming straight off the doctor's table."

"What's your name, yo?" I questioned curiously, because he always had something slick to say.

"Jim Bean," he revealed without hesitation. "And this here's my main man, Muhammad." He gestured toward the short, darkskin, baldheaded brother he'd been hanging out with all day.

"Dak," I confessed.

"Dak, huh?" Muhammad smiled. "What does your mother call you?"

"Dakaron," I admitted.

"Okay, Brother Dakaron. I respect how you carried it back there, when dudes started asking about your case," Muhammad commended.

"Yeah, my brother told me a long time ago to never trust a man always looking for a story, because he probably didn't have a problem telling one," I explained.

"That's good advice," Jim Bean spoke up. "I like that."

"So, what's y'all situation? I mean, like I don't want no details or nothing." I couldn't help but to smile. Especially since I'd just said that slick stuff about being nosey.

"Nah, I know what you mean, young blood." Jim Bean laughed himself. "Mister Charley got us on a trumped up bank job," Jim Bean professed.

"Mister Charley?" I repeated, confused. "Who the hell is Mister Charley?"

Jim Bean and Muhammad looked at each other, as if to see if I was serious, then burst out laughing. "I can dig it, young blood." Jim Bean smiled. "Mister Charley is the white man. Uncle Sam's brother."

"Or just the devil," Muhammad seconded.

I stole a look at Muhammad. He was throwing me off with all the 'devil talk.' "So what now?" I questioned. Understanding that once you got booked, there weren't too much options.

"Well, I got twenty-five no pussy to back up for another bank robbery, so I can't do nothing but go to trial, if I can't get this shit dropped," Jim Bean explained.

"And them devils already know that they're going to have to take me to war, because I don't take no deals," Muhammad declared.

"Especially from a system of devils that refuses to give my people freedom, justice, and equality."

"Man, what the hell is a devil?" I fired, unable to hold my tongue any longer. "Is that the white man?"

"Yeah and no," Muhammad replied, confusing me even more. "I mean, I don't really have the time to explain." Muhammad was starting to sound crazy. "In a nutshell, though, a devil is a mindstate, not a color. So, any wicked-minded person can be a devil," Muhammad continued, probably reading my facial expression. "That's why—"

"Okay, gentlemen, listen up, because I don't like having to repeat myself!" a guard ordered, unlocking the grill, interrupting our conversation. "If I call your name, step out! Because trust me when I tell you, if you miss your ride, your ass will be stuck down here until next shift." He pulled the grill open and looked sown at his clipboard. "Darryl Hill, Montray Muhammad, Kevin Richardson, and James Suber! Let's go! N-section run!"

"That's crazy," I fired, realizing that Jim Bean and Muhammad's names had been called when they began moving. I was actually interested in what Muhammad had to say.

"A'ight, young blood, stay up." Jim Bean got to his feet and began to cross the bullpen.

"If you ever get the opportunity, Dakaron, see if you can get up to the gym on Friday for the Nation of Islam service." Muhammad exited the bullpen.

"Ayo, Jim Bean," I called out, standing up. "Give me a piece of advice before you bounce," I continued when he turned around.

Jim Bean seemed to consider his words carefully before he spoke.

"A first impression can only be made once, young blood. Remember that, and you'll be okay no matter where you land."

"I heard that." I smiled, sitting back down to ponder on what Jim Bean had said, but for some reason, it was Muhammad's words that stuck with me.

Chapter 2

Welcome to 'G' Block

G-section was a totally different atmosphere than the hopper tier. There was loud music playing on the tier, everybody was out running around, the cell doors were open, etc. The tier officer informed me that I was assigned to cell seventy on the westside. I ended up in the cell with the tier representative, a dude named Fat Relly from over East Baltimore, who was locked up for an attempted murder on a police officer, after having opened fire on the ghetto bird during a high-speed chase on his dirt bike. Fat Relly put me down with what was what and who was who. He also gave me all the information I needed concerning visits, packages, and commissary.

I'd just finished making my bed, when our neighbors came over to kick it with Fat Relly and introduced themselves. Meat and his cousin Hyme were both from over Chaple Hill. And before long, we were all tripping like old friends. We went in the dayroom and played some spades. Then, I jumped on the phone real quick to call Chanae and let her know about the visits and clothing packages.

After getting Monique on the three-way and lining things up for a visit, I hopped in the shower and locked in for the night to finish straightening up, while Fat Relly ran around doing the tier-rep thing, which basically consisted of moving around the entire section or meeting up the gym with the other tier reps to be the go between for the men and guards when there was an issue.

Fat Relly and I smoked some weed and got to tripping off his pictures. Fat Relly had pictures of everybody, including a few niggas I knew personally. "Who is this?" I asked showing him a photo of a bunch of bad bitches with blond hair.

"Oh, that's my bitch Netta and them 'Knock 'Em Down' Girls," Fat Relly confessed with a smile. "I was running through all them bitches." He continued, "See shorty right here." He pointed out a fine little red, bow-legged bitch. "That's Bunny, she got the best head in East Baltimore."

"You was hitting all of 'em huh?" I questioned as I continued to flip through the pictures. Fat Relly definitely knew how to pick 'em.

"Damn near. Hold up, give me that." Fat Relly reached for a photo that appeared to be out of place. "That's my little cousin, Beama. That's not supposed to be in there."

I checked the photo of Fat Relly's cousin out as I passed it to him. *Damn, she bad*, I admitted, eyeing the smiling chocolate drop in the skimpy white bikini and heels with the buck teeth. But, I kept my thoughts to myself. After all, shorty was his cousin.

In the morning, I called Chanae to make sure everything was set up. Once Chanae told me that everything was good, I told her that I loved her and went to get ready for my visit. "All is well?" Fat Relly inquired as I stepped into the cell to grab my shower grip.

"Yeah, my folks will be down here later on."

"Say no more." Fat Relly continued to lotion up and prepare for his own visit.

I was tripping off Relly's fat ass. The nigga had about fifteen pairs of brand-new tennis up underneath the bunk and a good twenty different outfits hanging from a makeshift clothes rack. All the latest, high-priced shit at that. He was probably the slickest fat nigga over the jail.

When Chanae strutted into that city jail visiting room with her hips swaying in some low-riding, skintight, hip-hugging jeans with a yellow Polo shirt tied just above her navel and a pair of fresh butters, all I could do was lick my lips and shake my head. I missed her so much. She had the nerve to have her newly red, dyed hair cut boy short like the rapper bitch Eve too. Then, her sexy ass, lip-glossed lips looked so delicious that I got angry for a moment, wondering who the hell she was getting all dressed up for.

I slowly scanned the visiting room, mugging a few niggas until Chanae finally took her seat and niggas' attention went elsewhere. I was so focused on Chanae and all the attention that she was getting that I almost didn't even notice my mother walk in behind her.

"Oh, hey Ma!" My face lit up like a Christmas tree at the sight of my mother.

"It took you long enough to see me," my mother teased.

The visit seemed to fly by and before I knew it, I was back on the tier going through the clothes and shit. "Now you aren't the only nigga who can get fresh around this bitch," I joked, fucking with Fat Relly as we both went through the gear we'd just gotten.

"I see you," Fat Relly acknowledged.

"What's up with y'all niggas?" Meat walked up and stood in the doorway of the cell.

"Nothing," I replied, folding one of my Polo t-shirts. "I'ma have something nice for niggas later on too."

"My man." Meat seemed to zone out for a second, looking up the tier. "Oh, you got them new J's too, huh?"

"Come on now, you know I gots to stay fresh over this bitch," I arrogantly said as Hyme came up and tapped Meat on the arm.

"Let me see them joints, though." Meat stepped inside the cell. "I been trying to get my girl to grab them joints for me." Meat continued cutting his eye at Hyme as I handed him one of the Jordan's. "What size you wear, Dak?"

"Eight and a half, nine," I disclosed, instantly feeling some tension as Fat Relly got up off of his bunk.

"I'ma 'bout to go jump on the phone real quick." Fat Relly walked around Meat and dipped out of the cell.

"Yeah, me too," I seconded, feeling a little bit uncomfortable, before moving to follow Fat Relly.

"Nah yo, hold up, let me holler at you for a minute," Hyme spat, suddenly blocking the doorway. "I want all that shit you just got off the visit."

"Come on, yo, stop playing." I laughed nervously. "Watch out."

"Do he look like he's playing, bitch?" Meat fired, pulling out a big ass piece of sharpened steel that resembled a butcher's knife. That was all I needed to see. I mean, I wasn't no dummy.

"Y'all niggas tripping, that shit ain't about nothing. Y'all can have it!" I submitted, putting my hands up in surrender.

"Fuck is you doing, Meat?" Fat Relly snapped as my heart began to beat out of my chest.

"This ain't got nothing to do with you, fat boy," Hyme looked over his shoulder to explain, and I made him pay.

I hit Hyme with a nasty right that sat him on his back pockets, and quickly excited the cell.

"Bitch!" I stole him again before he could recover and spun around to square off with Meat. After all, the greatest weapon in the world was heart. And I had a lot of it.

I tagged the hell out of Meat as he rushed out of the cell with the sharpened joint. Hyme grabbed my leg and made me stumbled into the grill. That's how Meat's slimy ass got on me with the joint.

"Ahhhh!!!" I screamed out as Meat caught me in the arm. I didn't know if I felt the knife going in or not. But, I saw that motherfucker cut into my flesh before Meat drew back to stab me again and broke down the tier. I wasn't just going to stand there and let that nigga stab me to death.

Hyme got up off the ground and shook my blows off as I begged niggas on the tier for a joint. Then, he and Meat advanced. I placed my back up against the grill, threw my hands up, and got ready to touch everything on the tier.

Hyme got to me first and we got to clutching. Going blow for blow up and down the small tier to the point where Meat couldn't really swing the knife without stabbing Hyme also.

"Tier wet! Tier wet!" someone alerted us to the fact that the CO was about to come onto the tier to make his rounds. Meat and Hyme ran down the tier into their respective cell with me hot on their heels. Hyme's blows had me jive dazed. But, I wasn't about to go out like no bitch.

"Don't do no hot shit, yo," Fat Relly warned, grabbing my arm to stop me from entering Meat and Hyme's cell.

"What?" I looked at him sideways. "That nigga just stabbed me," I argued.

"I know, but if you run in their cell while the police making rounds, niggas are going to say you pulled a check-in move," Fat Relly explained.

"What the fuck am I supposed to do then?" I questioned honestly.

"Wait until we come back out and see them niggas like men, or check in," Fat Relly replied.

Checking in wasn't even an option. I was a fucking Truesdale. I came from a line of certified gangsters. So, inside the cell, I begged Fat Relly for a knife as I tried to clean myself up. I wasn't big enough, nor strong enough, to go up against Meat and Hyme alone. But, Fat Relly kept playing the, 'he didn't want to get involved' card. This was until, I offered his fat ass the smoke I'd just gotten off the streets.

"...just grab that joint and I'm good," I pleaded a moment before the CO stopped outside the cell to talk to Fat Relly about trash being all over the tier.

I zoned out for a moment as Fat Relly and the tier officer continued to talk. I was thinking about what the old head, Jim Bean, had said to me back in the bullpen about 'first impressions.' City jail was no different than the streets. Representation was everything. It followed you everywhere, be it for the good or bad. Sometimes it was all you had. So, once you damaged it, it was over.

"Somebody bleeding?" The CO began looking around. It was more of a statement than a question. It was like once the guard spotted the first drop of blood, he morphed into inspector gadget. The next thing we knew, there were COs all over the section like bloodhounds.

It wasn't long before they started pulling us out of the cells to do a body check. At which time, they discovered that I was leaking and rushed me down to medical. About ten minutes later, they brought Hyme in to have his split lip looked at. After that, we were both placed on administrative lockup. However, the guards ended up finding a knife in Hyme and Meet's cell during the cell search while they were packing up Hyme's property, so Meat was sent to lockup also.

Chapter 3

When a Gangster Evolves N2 a Monster

"Truesdale, pack your shit! You're moving in five!" the lockup tier officer yelled from the front of the tier, and I smiled. I had been waiting to hear those words ever since I'd finally gone up in front of the review board and been recommended off two days ago.

I got up, banged on the wall to put my neighbor on point, and waited. A few seconds later, my neighbor knocked back on the wall, and I reached my hand out the grill, in between the bars, to grab the murder weapon he'd manufactured for me. All my other property was already packed up. I retrieved the knife, unrolled the cloth it was wrapped up in to test the sharpness of the blade and check the rubber handle, for obvious reasons. Then, I stashed it inside my property and waited for the cell door to open.

What the prison administration didn't know was that, although Meat and Hyme would remain behind the door, I was still going to tear the fur off somebody's ass as soon as I got back in general population. I mean, niggas had tried to rob me, and somebody had to answer for that. And now, thanks to my neighbor for helping me put two and two together. I knew exactly who the puppet master was who was pulling all the strings on the section, and I had the right artillery to stop the show. It all made sense, though, when I considered it. I should've known better. You could never trust a motherfucker who could be bought. It didn't matter who they were, family, friend, or foe, because their interest always changed with the conditions. And that was why I planned on barbecuing a nigga's ass.

"Heads-up, Dak!" my neighbor warned as the lockup officer came down the tier, but I had already heard the keys.

"I'm straight," I assured, letting him know that I was good to go.

"Truesdale, you ready?" The lockup officer appeared in front of the cell, holding the radio mic in his hand.

"Yeah, I'm ready." I nodded, itching to go put in some work.

Stretching the extension, he brought the mic up to his mouth and pressed the button. "Open cell, twenty-one!" he commanded a second before the cell door clicked and slid open. "Step out, so I can pat you down real quick," he instructed, and I complied.

"You know you're going back on G-section, right?" he informed as I turned my back to him and raised my hands in the air to be searched for weapons. I kind of got the impression that he was trying to scare me. But, I was smiling inside. The news couldn't have been better. I'd honestly thought that I would end up on another section and have to find a way to get over to G-section, so that I could get my get-back and let niggas know that I hadn't pulled no slick check-in move.

"You don't got no problems with that, do you?" he questioned, running his hands around my waist and down my legs.

"Nah, I'm good." I looked over my shoulder as he began to bring his hand up between my legs. "Whoa, yo!" I jumped, turning around the moment he threatened to touch my nuts. "Ain't nothing up there!" I shouted, wondering if he was one of them undercover male correctional officers, using his job to feel and see nigga's dicks.

"I'm just doing my job." He straightened up, backing off.

Over the last two weeks, all the jail staff had come to respect how I'd carried it when I'd gotten stabbed. I'd kept my mouth shut for real. I didn't even do none of that yelling up and down the tier, 'dry snitching' shit dudes loved to do, knowing that the guards were listening. And that really seemed to impressed them. Especially since so many niggas got behind the door and started spilling their guts to whomever would listen.

"Yeah, a'ight." I turned back around to see what was next. I was ready to hit the section and lay my 'g' down. I was sure violence was equated to bravery over the jail just like it was in the streets. Whoever was the most vicious and aggressive got the most respect. I had been getting up early, every morning before the shift changed, to sharpen my steel. Because when the time arrived, I wanted to be able to tear up or tear off everything I hit with the blade of my knife.

I needed niggas to know that I didn't do no bullshitting when I was playing with that bone chipper.

After grabbing my bag, the tier officer led me to the dayroom and locked me inside. I began pacing the floor, thinking, wondering if niggas knew that I was on my way back to the section. More importantly, I wondered if the puppet master knew that I was coming for that ass.

"Let's go, Truesdale, your ride's here." The lockup officer unlocked the dayroom door.

I carried my bag out into the hallway to see that my escort was the fine little, thick, peanut-butter complexioned, sexy female CO with the intoxicating, honey-brown eyes, I'd been sweet on since hitting the jail. I couldn't do nothing but smile.

"How you doing, Miss Glover?" I broke the silence, slowly licking my lips.

"Oh lord, you again?" She shook her head, smiling, probably loving the attention. "Truesdale, right?"

"You better know it," I declared, dropping my bag to strike a pose, jive kind of happy that she even remembered a young nigga. Especially considering the fact that she crossed paths with hundreds of men on the daily basis.

"I told you, you were nothing but trouble the day you came in the jail, see." She gestured toward lockup.

"How you just going to give me a charge?" I looked at her questionably. "Whole time, though, I been set up like Roger Rabbit."

"Whatever." Miss Glover rolled her pretty eyes. "Can you pick your stuff up so we can go?"

"Yes ma'am," I flirted, making her blush as I grabbed my bag and slung it over my shoulder. It had to be flattering to have a young, slick nigga like myself chasing her. Especially since she knew I really found her attractive.

"Didn't I tell you about calling me ma'am?" she reminded, glaring at me with those pretty ass eyes. "I ain't that old."

"I'ma get you before this is all over with, watch," I assured.

"Yeah, in your dreams," she teased, walking off.

"Dreams come true," I reminded, following behind her, watching her ass and hips move. Miss Glover was plain, but bad. She didn't do the heavy makeup thing like most of the female guards, but that only made her more appealing to me. She also didn't wear her uniform tight to the point where you could see her panty line and pussy print, but any nigga   with eyes could tell that her thick ass had a body up underneath her uniform.

On the way to the section, I continued to flirt with Miss Glover, asking her all types of questions. I wanted to know everything there was to know about her. Age, first name, neighborhood, panty color, etc. But, she kept bucking the system, refusing to give up any information.

"I'm serious, I won't tell nobody," I promised, trying to encourage Miss Glover to tell me her first name.

"Boy, I'm not telling you my name. I know how y'all niggas do around here," she rationalized, refusing to give up the goods. "I tell you and you tell everybody else."

"See, you're used to dealing with them lames," I argued, knowing that only a lame would have niggas all up in her personal business.

"But, I'ma 'G,' I always keep motherfuckers on the need-to-know basis."

"Let you tell it." She twisted her sexy, juicy lips up as we approached the section. "What?" she inquired curiously as I continued to stare at her.

"I ain't say nothing." I smirked. If she only knew the thoughts that were running through my head right now, she'd probably mace me.

"Can you at least tell me the color of your eyes?"

"Hazel." She glanced at me.

The fact that she answered, caught me off guard. So, it took me a second to regroup. "Come on now, any nigga who looks at you can see that. Tell me something that nobody else knows." I decided to try my hand again.

"They change colors in the spring." She smiled, and I didn't know if she was joking or not. "They also change colors when I see bullshit too," she added, giggling.

"Oh, you got jokes, huh?" I fired, loving her sense of humor. "What about your birthday?"

"Why? So you can tell everybody that too?" she teased, still smiling as we came to the grill on G-section and she checked the volume on her walkie-talkie. "See, you just can't be happy with knowing the color of my eyes," she continued, before using her radio to notify the section officer that we were at the grill.

"I told you that I want to know something that nobody else knows," I challenged.

"Give me one good reason why I should tell you my birthday."

"Because, I want to buy you something nice," I explained, making her smile. She had to respect that.

"February sixteenth," she whispered. "And if you repeat that shit, you're cut off, I'm serious."

"Hell no!" I exclaimed, holding up my ID card. "I knew I was on your pretty ass for a reason. You're an Aquarius!" I handed her my ID.

"Oh, lord." She read my ID and smiled. "Why did I tell you that?"

"Don't worry, your secret's safe with me." I winked at her, knowing we now had something in common, as the G-section tier officer came down the tier to open the grill. *I bet her pretty ass won't forget me now*, I thought, smiling to myself. I was going to hook her fine ass, if it was the only thing I ever did before I left the jail. "I'll see you around, Miss Glover."

"Bye, Truesdale." She smiled, showing off her pretty teeth as she watched me closely with those honey-brown eyes.

"I got him from here, girl," the female tier officer assured, unlocking the grill, requesting my ID as I sat my bag down in front of me. "Truesdale?" she questioned with a pause, looking me up and down. "You the one had all that shit going on down here while I was on vacation, huh?"

"Don't believe everything you hear, shorty," I warned, looking inside the dayroom as niggas began to notice that I was back. But, my mind was on one thing, and one thing only. Retribution.

"Shorty?" she repeated, almost as if she was offended, but I could tell that she wasn't. "The name is Officer Christian," she corrected.

"Calling somebody shorty." She checked my ID again. "You're barely off the hooper tier."

"My bad, Officer Christian," I apologized, reading her name tag. T. Christian, COII. Officer Christian was nice and thick too. Her eyes weren't as magnetic as Miss Glover's, but she had that smooth, dark-chocolate skin that I loved so much. *These women are going to fuck around and get a nigga caught up over here*, I thought, accepting my ID back.

"Mmmmm hmmmm," she mumbled. "Make sure you remember that," she warned.

"I will," I vowed, checking out Miss Glover one more time.

"You're going in cell forty-seven on the eastside," Officer Christian revealed.

"Nah," I challenged, needing to hit the westside. "They said that I was going back on the westside," I lied, stuffing the ID inside my pocket.

"Well, traffic got you assigned to cell forty-seven on the eastside. So, that's where you're going today," Officer Christian promised. "Grab the bedroll and mattress by my desk. You can work everything else out with the sergeant." She dismissed me and went back to talking to Miss Glover.

"Man, that's crazy." I peeped in the dayroom again and saw niggas looking at me all leery. So, I just snatched my bag up off the floor and carried it up the steps to the other side of the section, because I didn't want to make a scene while I was riding dirty. I'd heard the whispers, and I was ready to make niggas stand on what they'd said. The good thing was, I was back on the section and I'd already laid eyes on my man.

After carrying my bag up to the cell and coming back down to get my mattress and bedroll, I tossed everything on the bunk and headed for the dayroom. Though not before quickly getting my murder weapon out, tying it around my wrist, and slipping it into one of my hoodies to make sure it wasn't so noticeable. When I walked into the dayroom and posted up near the phone, everybody just looked at me as if I'd lost my mind. "Ayo, hold me down on the phone," I requested, walking up behind a nappy-headed dude in a wife-beater.

"Oh shit, Dak, what's up?" Burnze went off the moment he turned around and saw me. "Baby, hold on for a second. They just brought my niece's father on the tier."

"Damn, yo, I didn't even know that was you with all that hair and shit." I embraced SweetPea's brother.

"My sister told me you were over here," Burnze admitted, breaking the embrace. "I didn't know that was you that got caught up on the other side though."

"Yeah." I shook my head looking around. "But, you know I'm not about to let that shit go."

"What's up? What you got in mind?" Burnze questioned, ready to pick my brain.

"Fucking up a nigga's future and making everybody question his past," I replied sincerely. "You strapped?"

"Come on now." Burnze grinned like I should know better. And maybe I should've. Most niggas in prison were usually the same niggas they were on the streets. And on the streets, Burnze kept that pistol on him. "Hold up, though." Burnze held up a finger. "Let me get off the phone," Burnze requested, always down to get into some dumb shit.

Once Burnze got off the phone, I told him exactly what and who I had in mind. Turns out, my main target had niggas shook because he was hooked up with all that 'inmate counsel' shit, and them nig-gas could go anywhere in the jail. So, a lot of niggas on the section just stayed out of his way because they were afraid to stand against him. But all that was about to change.

"You already know I don't give a fuck," Burnze assured. "I'll go at any of these niggas with you."

"I'ma hold you to that." I smiled, knowing how Burnze got down. "How often we get to see that nigga?"

"Every day for real," Burnze confessed. "Sometimes it depends on who has the tier. But you know your man back over there too?"

"Who?" I questioned, confused.

"Meat," Burnze revealed.

"Oh yeah?" I couldn't believe my luck. I hadn't even known Meat and Hyme had gone up for their infractions yet.

"Yep, he came off admin Tuesday."

"That's even better," I admitted, perking up. Meat had my blood on his knife, so victory couldn't truly be gained until I got his blood on mine.

"You not going to be able to get to that nigga until gym day. And that's if he goes to the gym," Burnze explained.

"What day we got gym?" I questioned, because there weren't enough guards employed inside the city jail to keep me off Meat's ass. I'd sneak over to the other side and catch an out of bounds ticket to get that nigga, if I had to.

"Sunday," Burnze stared at me.

"Sunday it is then," I vowed, reaching for one of the phones. I had to call the home front.

***

When the tier officer screamed down the tier for us to get ready for gym, I threw on a black Russel sweatsuit, some black, leather 996 New Balance, and a black soldier rag. I heard the doors began to open on the top tier and got ready.

"You ready to do this nigga?" Burnze hopped down from the top tier, directly in front of the cell.

"What you think?" I replied, lifting up my sweatshirt to reveal the handle of my murder weapon as I stood at the grill waiting for the grill to open. I was ready to chop something up.

"Let's go tear these niggas up." Burnze stepped back as the cell doors opened. When the grill opened, I stepped out on the tier ready for whatever. I'd never let my guard down again. Not after niggas had almost tricked me out of my life.

I fell in line beside Burnze, behind my cell buddy, and headed toward the gym with the rest of the section. Everybody in the crowd seemed to know that something was about to go down. The tension was so thick, you could almost taste it. Niggas wanted to see a show. They wanted something to talk about. But I planned on giving them a whole lot more than that. When Burnze and I got to pushing them joints up in that gym, niggas wouldn't have nothing else to talk about. At least, not until somebody could outdo us.

As we neared the gym, I began getting myself mentally inclined. I was going to really put Meat's gangster to the test. I knew that any nigga could go with the gun, but a lot of niggas got their minds right when them knives came out or it was time to go with the hands, because it was up close and personal. I knew this because I'd been outnumbered a time or two and pulled the knife to even the odds.

After beating the pat down, Burnze and I entered the gym ready for war. It was time to finally make my first impression on a large audience.

"So, how you wanna play this?" Burnze questioned as we made our way across the gym to post up and wait for the other side of the section to arrive. "You wanna go straight at these niggas?"

"Nah." I shook my head. "Let the police roll out first. I don't want them niggas to have no excuses."

"Man, Dak, fuck them niggas, ain't no rules to this shit!" Burnze spat. "Let's get on them niggas as soon as they come through the door."

Burnze was right. There honestly weren't no rules to war once blood was drawn. And we knew that Meat was out for blood. He'd been sending me kites all week, by the nigga I wanted the most at that. It had been so hard to fake the funk with the nigga that it was almost painful. But still, I wanted both of them niggas in the gym when we got to slinging them joints, and I wasn't about to chance fucking that up.

"You're right, but if them niggas don't come through the door together, it will all be for nothing."

"They're coming in now," Burnze said, getting my attention. We stood there and watched the other side of the section spill into the gym. It seemed like everybody was out. Meat and Fat Relly were the last two niggas to enter the gym. I saw Meat post up on the other side of the basketball court as Fat Relly made his way over.

"What's up, Dak?" Fat Relly strolled up and attempted to give me a handshake.

"That's what I'm trying to figure out." I eyed Fat Relly's hand and left him hanging.

"Meat trying to see you head up, one on one with the hands," Fat Relly confessed.

"What? Mannnn, I ain't trying to hear none of that! I ain't doing no more fighting. I want blood, that bitch ass nigga stabbed me," I snapped, looking in Meat's direction.

"Yeah, I'm hip, but niggas trying to get uptown too," Fat Relly rationalized, almost making me laugh.

"Nigga," Burnze began before I waved him off.

"Honestly, yo, I ain't got no more rap," I fired, staring Fat Relly down.

"Little Dakaron?" someone called my name, almost as if they were unsure.

Turning around, I saw my man, Willie Bates, walking toward us.

"Oh shit, what's up, big homie?" I gave Willie Bates some love.

"What the fuck is up, jack? I'm hearing some niggas about to get it in over this bitch! And look up to see you, what's going on? You ain't got nothing to do with nothing, right?"

"Yeah," I confessed. "Niggas tried to rob me on the section about a month ago, and I ended up getting hit."

"Niggas what? Tried to rob you?" Willie Bates questioned, surprised. "Who?" Willie Bates turned to Fat Relly. "Ayo, Relly, who the fuck tried to rob my little brother?"

"Niggas didn't know shorty was your peoples, Willie Bates," Fat Relly assured.

"That's not what I asked you, jack," Willie Bates challenged. "I asked you who tried to bring my folks a move."

"One of 'em right there," Burnze volunteered, pointing Meat out. "The brownskin nigga with the cornrows, leaning up against the wall with his foot on the basketball."

"Meat?" Willie Bates seemed surprised.

"You know that nigga?" I questioned curiously.

"Yeah, that's his fucking homeboy!" Willie Bates gestured toward Fat Relly, and that was all I needed to hear. I was already going to chop his fat ass up anyway. But, Willie Bates had just put the nail in his coffin. "All them niggas from the same neighborhood." Willie Bates turned his attention back to Fat Relly. "Y'all niggas still running that bullshit ass robbery game. I done told you before, Fat Relly, that shit was going to bring unnecessary drama and attention to the fucking inmate counsel, because you're a tier rep."

I peeped over at Burnze while Willie Bates was checking Fat Relly, and began easing my joint out. Fat Relly was just beginning to explain himself when I got my knife completely out. "Come on, Willie Bates, you know how that shit goes, man." Fat Relly smiled. "Shorty a soldier, though, he held his own. But now—"

I slammed the knife into Fat Relly's chest, catching him off guard as he tried to get Willie Bates to play umpire, referee, or something, but nobody could speak for me. Especially after somebody harmed me. I was my own man. I carried my own weight.

"Ahhhh," Fat Relly screamed out and tried to break across the gym, but I was on his big ass. I stabbed him in the back repeatedly as he continued to call out for Meat. Burnze clipped Fat Relly near the top of the key on the basketball court, and we started butchering his big ass.

"Nah, bitch, don't cry now! Your whore ass been breaking bad on the section for months," Burnze taunted, like his beef was personal.

I looked up and saw Meat running across the gymnasium toward us with a vicious ass knife in his hand as Fat Relly began to recover, and met him at half court with my adrenaline still running.

The most important thing that a man could take into battle, was a legitimate reason, and I had two. Meat and I stood off for a second, as if the half court line was the scratch line. Everybody had their eyes on the showdown. If Meat wasn't ready to die, now would've been the best opportunity to take flight. But, Meat committed himself to hand-to-hand combat, and the die was cast.

I was the first one to swing my knife. I brought the joint overhand and tried to stab Meat in his head, but he took it in the shoulder and damn near let the air out of me with a chest wound. I stumbled backward as adrenaline appeared to jolt through my entire body. I could still hear Burnze and Fat Relly going at it. I stabled myself and went at Meat again.

It seemed like Meat and I were going at it like Lebron James and Michael Jordan, shot for shot. Both of us held our own once the slinging got started. And truth be told, by the time the COs began to rush in, we'd gone up and down the basketball court and left it a bloody mess. There were inmates, correctional officers, mace, and blood everywhere. In the end, we all just lived to die another day.

Chapter 4

Weight up with My Gangster

After about three and a half weeks, I was placed on K-section, or killer-K, as most people referred to it. Nobody came forward to volunteer any information about the gym incident, and none of the CO's could put a weapon in my hand, so the prison administration only issued me a simple assault infraction, for which I basically received time served because it was my first actual write up. Everybody else got ninety days or better on lockup because of their prison jackets.

When I hit killer-K, I could literally feel the respect as I strolled down the tier to toss my shit in the cell before heading for the dayroom. Turns out, a lot of dudes didn't really fuck with the Chaple Hill boys and only stayed out of their way or stood with them, because they were afraid to stand against them. I guess men still recognized men, gangsters still did what they wanted, and suckers still got what their hands called for, no matter where you were. Frank had been sending me over and keeping me up to speed my entire time on lockup. He told me how the jail was buzzing about the gym situation and how niggas were saying, I was a monster with that knife in my hand. I mean, not to take no credit from Meat or nothing. The old head was definitely a vet. But, I was all heart and guts and probably a little ego.

In the dayroom, dudes laid out the red carpet for me and basically handed me the tier. I got the only TV remote, they flipped one of the phones upside down for my convenience, and asked my opinion about everything. Not to mention, every time I got up to do something, niggas parted like the Red Sea. It kind of made me smile inside, because I'd always been the type of nigga to rise to the top of whatever environment I was in. I jumped on the phone and burnt it down.

First, I called Chanae. Then, I got SweetPea and Delmonte on the phone. Of course, she cursed me out about getting Burnze caught up. I hadn't realized that Relly's fat ass had managed to get his knife out and stab Burnze a few times. But, I just told her to hook-up with Jamaine and come see me, because I didn't want to talk reckless on the jail phone. Before I hung up, I played a guessing game with Delmonte and talked to her about cartoons for about ten minutes. Then, I told her that I loved her like ice cream and hung up.

"Ayo, you watching this?" A tall, brown-skinned, wavy haired old head in a yellow Phat Farm sweatsuit and some black and yellow Nike Airmaxes walked up beside me as I sat on the dayroom table, drying off after having gotten out of the showers.

"That joint watching me for real," I admitted as he moved to change the channel without considering anyone else.

"What's up, though?" He walked back over, extending his hand. "Sha'wayne."

"Dak," I responded, shaking his hand.

"Yeah, I'm hip to you, slim." Sha'wayne nodded. "I respect how you carried that shit with Fat Relly and them on G-section. You ain't got too many niggas who are going to hold their own like that against them Chaple Hill niggas. Let alone carry that mail with the knife."

"I heard that," I replied, all nonchalant, like what Sha'wayne had said wasn't effecting me, as I squirted lotion into the palm of my hand. But, the truth was, that honestly, deep down inside, my ego was eating that shit up like a motherfucker. *These niggas respect my gangster for going up against Hyme and them!* I thought, lotioning my legs up. Sha'wayne and I went on to rap until it was time to lock in for the evening.

Sha'wayne confessed to me about throwing hands with Hyme up in the square when he'd first hit the jail on his drug case. "Them niggas weren't letting nobody get on the phones. This was when we were all on M-section though," Sha'wayne revealed. Besides the fact that Sha'wayne was a project nigga, Murphy Homes at that, he was cool as shit, stupid funny too.

Inside the cell, I finally got to cleaning up. Wiping the cell down from top to bottom with a bleach concoction the tier runner had given me. I was so glad that I was in the cell alone that I didn't know what to do with myself. "Truesdale!" I looked up to see none other than my jailhouse crush, Miss Glover, with mail in her hand.

"Now, I'm starting think that you're stalking me." I smiled, inhaling her attention-grabbing fragrance.

"Oh lord, why didn't I recognize your name?" Miss Glover shook her head.

"What you got, the tier?" I questioned, praying she did.

"This is my regular tier, yes." She eyed me before continuing. "And I'm telling you now, Truesdale, if you start some shit down here, these old guys got something for you."

"You just really think that I'm a troublemaker, don't you?" I ignored the little threat, warning, or whatever it was.

"Are you related to Wallace Allen?" Miss Glover questioned with a curious look.

"Who?" I replied, just as curious.

"Wallace Allen," she repeated.

"Never heard of him!" I confessed.

"Well, anyway, his crazy tail got caught up in two murders in one month over here. Now, he's sitting over the Baltimore City Super Max, looking dumb," she declared.

"What that got to do with me?" I wondered. "I haven't gotten caught up in nothing yet."

"You keep on, you will," Miss Glover assured, staring at me with those pretty eyes. "You know what? Never mind."

"What time is it?" I smiled, standing at the grill. I had been laid back, zoning out so much that I hadn't even realized that the shift had changed.

"Three thirty-five." She checked her watch.

"You gonna give me my mail now? Or are you going to stand here stalking me all day?" I teased, instantly seeing Miss Glover's face tighten up.

"Truesdale, please." Miss Glover rolled her eyes. "Get your ID. You got some legal mail too." She waved an envelope back and front.

"Oh, you don't know who I am now?"

"Do you want your mail or not?" she questioned with an attitude.

"Of course," I replied, folding my mattress back to grab my ID.

"Then, come on. Plus, these letters came up from lockup. Your cell location should change tomorrow as soon as the mailroom officer comes in and sees the paperwork," she explained.

I tossed my regular mail onto the bed. Then, I signed for my legal mail and stood at the grill as Miss Glover carefully opened the envelope right in front of my face and handed me all the contents. Which was nothing but Elizabeth Franzoso informing me of my arraignment date. *Damn, she smells good*, I thought, licking my lips as she strutted off the tier. I sat down on the bunk and tore the uptown addresses off all three envelopes, tossed them into the toilet, and laid back on the bunk to read my mail.

The first letter was from Detauwn. I ripped it open, sat the photos to the side, and began to read. *What's up little brother? I miss you already. Just lay low and stay out of trouble. The case straight-up bullshit! And them folks know it. Here are some butt-naked flicks of some freaks from up the way and a few dollars to hold you over for a minute. The family is good. The kids are getting big and everybody's praying for you. I talked to Antauwn last night. He said, keep your head, stay Truesdale strong, and watch out for them snakes. Well, love you shorty. Walk slow, but think fast. Love big brother, Detauwn.*

I flicked through the photos and almost lost my mind. There were photographs of at least two freaks from up the Heights that I'd always wanted to fuck, but out of fear of SweetPea, they never let me hit.

Next, I busted open SweetPea's letter. The first thing I saw was a scribble-scrabble crayon letter and picture from Delmonte. I smiled from ear to ear. SweetPea always knew how to melt a gangster's heart. I unfolded SweetPea's letter and read it.

Dear Dakaron, I wanted to let you know that I am always here for you. NO MATTER WHAT! I got your back. Me and Delmonte, just remember that. I will always love you, don't drop that soap, though, nigga! You know my daughter's father a gangster (smile).

N-E-way, keep your head up and fight them bitches all the way if you have to. And when Chanae falls off, oops! I mean, if she falls off. I'll still be here. Don't get me wrong. She's cool and all, I like her, just not for you. OXOXOXOXOXOXOX Love always, your trooper and gangster bitch, SweetPea. P.S. I hope you like the pictures (smile). I thought I would give you something to think about, nigga!

SweetPea was something else. I stared at the photographs she sent to me for a good ten minutes. She was going to get a nigga in trouble. Even after having Delmonte, her body was still crazy tight. I shook my head and tucked her photos off because I felt my dick getting hard. *Man, a nigga got to get back on them streets*, I told myself. I checked out Delmonte's letter one more time before taping it up on the wall above my head, next to a picture of her mother and Chanae. Then, I opened the last letter, which I knew was from Chanae—Mrs. Truesdale, according to the envelope. Chanae had always had that pretty handwriting. Reading Chanae's letter was different. It was almost like I could hear her talking to me. Like her words came up off the page. Almost as if she was right in the cell with me.

After I finished reading Chanae's six-page letter, I decided not to go out for recreation. Besides, I wanted to mess with Miss Glover every time she made her rounds. But, she had a trick for my ass. She kept sending this lame ass CO nigga around. So, after a while, I just said fuck it.

Stashing Chanae's latest photo underneath the bunk, grabbed my earphones, threw the Love Zone on, and laid back staring at her until I dozed off.

***

I shot straight to my regular phone as soon as the cell door opened for recreation. I'd received a kite from my rap buddy, Frank, last night concerning Jamaine, and I needed to find out what the fuck was going on. I walked into the dayroom and jumped right on the phone, as usual. A nigga had to keep his ear to the streets. I pulled the kite with Paul-Paul's new number on it out of my pocket and called him.

Once Paul-Paul's phone began to ring, I turned around so I could observe the entire dayroom. I'd learned a lot over the last couple of weeks. The main thing being, the power and influence dudes locked up actually possessed. I mean, it was crazy how more often than not, niggas behind the walls had their hands in shit. I mean, people would really be surprised if they knew just how many murders and stuff were sanctioned, orchestrated, stopped, or, in some cases, solved from behind prison walls. Sometimes dudes in the joint actually knew who was behind the mask before the blood was dry. Why? Because, most of the time, they were the teachers, mentors, or puppet masters who used their personal mistakes to train others on how to plan and successfully carry out crimes. That's why it was said that, "if you have a good name in prison among the right men, then, you had less to fear than those in the game who didn't."

"What's up, nigga?" I fired after Paul-Paul accepted the collect call.

"Ain't shit, out this bitch, getting it how I live," Paul-Paul replied.

Paul-Paul put me up on what was what and gave it to me real when I questioned him about the situation with Frank and Jamaine. Paul-Paul said, Jamaine was out there fucking up. Blowing money, chasing bitches, and partying all day. Running around playing big shot with Monique. I just sat there on the phone listening, trying not to get upset because Jamaine hadn't told me none of that. In fact, he gave it to me like he was making sure Frank was good. I mean, every time I'd talked to him on the cellphone when I was still in the hospital, he'd told me that Frank was good.

"Try to call that nigga on the three-way real quick," I requested, shaking my head. I'd thought Frank's lawyer fees had been taken care of. After all, we'd been arrested months ago now. Paul-Paul called Jamaine's phone twice, but he never picked up.

"That nigga got that caller ID shit, so he sees my number. He's just not answering. You know him and Frank got into it the last time they were on the phone."

"Call my house," I instructed, hoping to catch Chanae or Shaun at the apartment. I knew Shaun had put Jamaine out for cheating. But, I figured I may get lucky since Jamaine had a way of always talking his way out of some shit. But again, we got no answer. *They're probably at school*, I thought, when the answering machine picked up the phone.

"Hang that shit up!" I ordered, hoping that Jamaine showed up with SweetPea for my visit. One thing was for sure, two things for certain, whenever I put SweetPea on a mission, I could always expect results. They may not always be the results I wanted. But, SweetPea always delivered. "You gotta stay on top of that nigga about Frank's lawyer," I continued, knowing from experience how easy it was for a good nigga to turn bitter behind prison walls. I didn't know what I'd do if Frank went home on some Quincy shit.

"I got him, yo," Paul-Paul assured, and I prayed that he was able to get a hold of Jamaine. "But, at the same time, Dak, I'm not going to be out here babysitting dog about no lawyer money. When he knows he's supposed to be on top of that shit!"

"I respect that," I admitted honestly, still needing him to stay on Jamaine. Niggas' freedom was on the line and I had to make sure Frank was good. "Just ask him about it."

After a long pause, Paul-Paul finally spoke, "A'ight yo, I got it."

"Thanks, yo," I said, knowing the phone was about to click off.

"One," Paul-Paul said before the line went dead.

I left the dayroom and dipped down the tier to Sha'wayne's cell real quick. I wanted to holler at him before I hopped in the shower to get ready for my visit.

***

"Truesdale, visit!" It was around twelve o'clock when the tier officer came to the cell to inform me that I had a visit. I was already dressed and ready to go. I had on a fresh pair of New Balance, some Maurice Malone Jeans, and a button-down shirt. So, I grabbed my ID, took my visiting pass, and headed for the visiting area. I was a little nervous walking into the visiting room to see SweetPea, because we hadn't laid eyes on each other in about four months. I strolled in, found my seat, and sat down. Then, I waited for the visiting room officer to call SweetPea's name. When SweetPea walked into that visiting room, I was all smiles. I just couldn't help myself. SweetPea was still bad. She had on some skintight jeans that revealed her red thong and made her pussy print resemble a balled-up fist. *Damn! I wish I could hit that right now*, I thought, as other niggas began taking SweetPea in as she strutted through the visiting room, goosing right in front of their own women. But, unlike with Chanae, I loved the fact that niggas wanted what I had. It made me feel proud.

"You look good, as always," I admitted, remembering how I had eaten her pussy the first time I got a look at her body.

"I know." She smiled confidently.

"Turn around, let me get a real good look at you," I requested, wanting to see that ass up close.

SweetPea slowly turned around as I took her in from head to toe.

"You miss that, don't you?" she teased, looking at me over her right shoulder with her whole butt on full display. I could literally see her phat pussy hanging from the back.

"Girl, ain't nobody looking at your ass," I lied, catching the dude sitting next to me chick giving SweetPea the evil eye. Probably because SweetPea had her man's attention too. "I wanted to see what kind of jeans you had on."

"Mmmmmm hmmmm." SweetPea took her seat.

"Where Jamaine at?" I questioned, concerned.

"He never showed up. He said he was coming through this morning. Supposed to have met me at Ms. Nenny's on Jefferson Street for breakfast, but he never showed up," SweetPea explained. "I tried calling him, but he never answered."

I sat there in silence for a moment, trying to figure out what the fuck Jamaine was up to. Why the fuck hadn't he taken care of Frank's lawyer fees? He, of all people, understood how victory only favored niggas who made the best moves and the least mistakes.

"That nigga bluffing, Dakaron," SweetPea added.

"Nah, Jamaine good," I assured, not wanting SweetPea to think that my niggas weren't real. Plus, I'd always been the type to show faith, even when I didn't have none.

"I'm telling you, I know a phony nigga when I encounter one. And your boy is as phony as they come," SweetPea fired. "I could instantly tell that he was the selfish type," she continued.

"Why you say that?" I was curious.

"Because the whole time I was talking to him on the phone, all he kept talking about was himself and how he gets money, trying to get me to hook him up with somebody. For real, he was cracking on me on a sly tip."

"Cracking on you?" I twisted my face up.

"Yeah, cracking on me," SweetPea clarified. "Trying to show off, but you already know that I hate weak, phony ass niggas who talk too much."

"So, how my princess doing?" I asked, needing to change the subject. One thing I knew about SweetPea, she did not bite her tongue for nobody.

"Bad as ever, missing you, thinking she's grown." SweetPea smiled. "She always talking trash too."

"Just like her mother," I reminded.

"You mean, just like your ass," SweetPea retorted with the quickness. "Detauwn came by yesterday to get her for his daughter's party."

"Yeah, my niece Ta'nyah turns one Sunday." I remembered. "What's up with him though?"

"Nothing, you know how Detauwn is." She paused, and I knew something that I wouldn't like was about to follow. "He don't think Chanae's built for no bid, if you end up getting one."

"Man, we're not even going to start that shit." I waved SweetPea off, shaking my head. *This nigga Detauwn, man!* I thought. *Now he's poisoning SweetPea.* "I don't know what Detauwn got against Chanae," I confessed honestly. From the first time he'd met Chanae, he told me that she wasn't ready for who I would become, because of the roads I had to travel to get there. He assured me that she would bail if I ever went to prison or shit got hard. But, I hoped that I'd never have to prove him wrong.

"Well, you already know that I'm built for whatever!" SweetPea bragged. "The question is, what about Chanae?" SweetPea questioned, making me wonder for a moment. "Look, you ain't got to answer that," she coached when I remained silent. "Just know that I'm always here when, I mean, if she rolls out and leaves you for dead."

"Man, SweetPea, go ahead with that shit," I fired, having no plan of going to prison. "I don't know who's worse, you or Detauwn's ass. Y'all be talking like y'all want a nigga to go to jail to prove a point."

"Never that! Nigga, you know I love your black ass too much," SweetPea argued. "On another note, I'ma have something nice coming your way in the next day or two."

"What?" I raised my eyebrow. "How you pull that off?"

"Don't worry about it." SweetPea smiled. "Just let me know when you get it. It's that new hydro from up the way."

I just shook my head and let it go. SweetPea and I talked about everything under the sun. The lame nigga from Park Heights she was dealing with, our daughter, and the affects the jail shit was having on my relationship with my daughter. I promised SweetPea that no matter what happened, I'd always make sure she and Delmonte were good as long as I had breath in my body. We ended the visit talking about Delmonte's future.

Chapter 5

Gangster Roll Call

"....I'm telling you, Dak, that shit was funny as shit. That nigga, Scooty, fat ass, fast as shit!" Sha'wayne explained while we sat in the dayroom after dinner, high as shit off some hydro, laughing at everything.

I still couldn't understand how SweetPea had gotten that shit to me. But, I wasn't asking no questions.

"How the fuck them niggas get into it, yo? They don't even be fucking with each other." I was really curious how Scooty fat ass and No-Limit had started fighting. They were from two different parts of the city, East and South Baltimore, and they didn't roll in the same circles.

"You know how Scooty fat ass is, always joking with mother-fuckers he don't even deal with," Sha'wayne replied. "At first, they were going back and forth. Then, they started getting serious, disrespecting each other. Talking that Harford Road, Westport shit! Who was really getting it in. Scooty had the whole dayroom laughing at No-Limit. So, he started calling Scooty stupid and shit. So, Scooty was like, don't forget I got a rack of bodies, homie."

I pictured Scooty's Biggie Smalls-looking fat ass and laughed as Sha'wayne continued to paint the scene for me. Scooty was the only Baltimore nigga I knew who looked like one of the most famous rappers on the East Coast, yet sounded like one of the most popular ones from down South.

"No-Limit started saying the only reason he was locked up for all them bodies was because he was an amateur. Mannnnn, Scooty fat ass went off and No-Limit smelled blood." Sha'wayne shook his head. "He started riding Scooty, telling him that only fools got jammed up for all their murders because they didn't know what they were doing. He didn't care who told. And then, he said, Scooty wasn't dangerous because he could put in work and got away with it, but because he was dumb enough to shoot a nigga anywhere and wasn't scared to go to jail for it. Mannnn, that was it. Scooty cracked the fuck out of No-Limit. I didn't know his fat ass hit that hard. His fat ass quick too...." As Sha'wayne began telling me the part about how No-Limit's pants slipped down around his ankles, I couldn't help but to continue laughing. "Scooty started getting the best of No-Limit until he flipped Scooty fat ass over and they began going at it."

"Now, that's crazy," I said honestly after Sha'wayne finished. "If a nigga ever got out on me like that, I'd go home, fuck his mother, and make him my son."

"Yo, you stupid as shit."

"I'm serious, go uptown and make him a nigga your son," I spat, laughing again. "But think them niggas though."

"Why you say that?" Sha'wayne appeared curious.

"Cause both of them niggas play too much," I replied.

"Truesdale." Miss Glover poked her pretty face inside the day-room real quick to get my attention. "Can you come here for a minute," she continued when I looked up at her.

"Excuse me for a second, yo," I requested, hopping up off the table to go see what Miss Glover wanted.

"I keep telling she's on you, nigga," Sha'wayne teased, but I refused to feed in. The jail wasn't nothing but a big ass soap opera. Everybody was in everybody's business, trying to find out who was fucking who, what had happened earlier, when the next pack was coming in, and why somebody had gotten carried a certain way. But, unlike most niggas who wanted to be somebody, I wasn't dying to be the topic of discussion when it came to my personal business.

"What's up, Tiphani?" I questioned in a whisper, looking around.

"Boy, what I tell you about calling me by my first name?" Miss Glover warned, scared to death. "I'm not playing, Truesdale, if the wrong person hears you say that, I'll get in trouble. And I don't want to be caught up in none of these little rumors going on around—"

"A'ight, my bad!" I cut her off. "I was only messing with you. It won't happen again," I promised wholeheartedly. I definitely wasn't trying to get her into no trouble or make her apart of rumor-ville. I just wanted her to know that when I was on something, I made it my business to find out everything there was to know about it.

"That's kind of what I want to talk to you about," she confessed.

"What's up?" I got serious, hoping she wasn't about to get on no bullshit.

"Nah, it's nothing really." She paused to take a deep breath. "I just need you to do me a favor."

"I'm listening."

"When you're out for work at night, and you see the officer from J-section at my desk or floating around, please don't say nothing to me, like how you be playing and stuff, making me laugh," she pleaded.

"Why? That's your boyfriend or something?" I asked, already knowing the answer.

"No," Miss Glover lied, getting defensive. "I don't mess with my coworkers," she assured, but the truth was, I was already hip to the foreign, insecure lame with the Haitian name and accent. He was one of them fake tough types, running around, hiding behind his uniform, playing gangster. When the fact of the matter was, he'd missed his calling as a 'swung dog.' "I just don't want to start no shit."

"I got you Ti—I mean, Miss Glover." I smiled devilishly. Now, I knew why the lame was always acting like a bitch whenever I came around. He must've felt threatened. And the only time a man felt threatened, was when he wasn't on his job.

"Thank you." She seemed to relax.

"Can I still talk to you when ol' boy ain't around though?" I tested the water.

"Yeah," Miss Glover replied without hesitation. "You be making me laugh." She giggled like a shy little schoolgirl, and that was all I needed to hear. Laugh now, give me that pussy later, I thought sizing her up, licking my lips.

***

"Are you ready for court, Truesdale?" The CO popped the cell door about five thirty in the morning.

"Huh?" I rolled out the bunk, half asleep, wiping the cold out of my eyes, looking at my watch.

"I said, get ready for court!" the CO repeated.

"Nah, I thought you said something else," I admitted, before shaking my head and stumbling over to the sink to wash my face with cold water. "Man, I was having a good ass dream," I said to myself out loud. I had been getting some bomb ass head from a bitch whose face I couldn't even remember.

After washing my face, brushing my teeth, and taking a quick birdbath, I got dressed casually for court. I threw on a three-button, two-tone Polo shirt with dark slacks and soft-bottom Rockports. I wasn't trying to walk up into the courtroom looking thugged out.

"Let's go, Truesdale!" The same CO from the midnight shift showed up again. *Damn! This nigga on my top*, I thought as he tried to rush me along.

I stopped at Sha'wayne's cell for a moment to let him know that I was finally going to court for my preliminary hearing. He wished me luck and told me that he'd rap to me later on 'if' I came back. A picture on his wall got my attention, but before I could inquire about it, the CO chump ran down and rushed me off the section. It took about three to four hours to go through all the normal processing at the city jail and courthouse before Frank and I finally got in front of the judge. The courtroom was packed too. The entire hood was up in that bitch, wall to wall. It made me feel good and sad at the same time.

"There go Jamaine right there," Frank whispered to me as Jamaine and Monique slipped into the courtroom just before the bailiff got everyone's attention.

"All rise, the honorable Judge Octavia Bowman, residing," the bailiff ordered as the judge strolled in from her chambers. "You may be seated."

"Call your case, Miss Shakir." The judge got straight down to business after getting comfortable in her seat.

"Thank you, Your Honor." The state prosecutor began going through her folders as I sat down beside my attorney. "Good morning, Your Honor, Jacqueline Shakir, for the State," she informed, looking toward us.

"Morning, Your Honor." My lawyer shot to her feet. "Elizabeth Franzoso, for Mr. Truesdale."

"Chip Johnson with the Baltimore City Public Defenders Office, for Mr. Lace." Frank's lawyer stood up, adjusting his eyeglasses.

"Okay, the floor's all yours, Miss Shakir." Judge Bowman leaned back in her chair.

"Your Honor, this is the State of Maryland verses Dakaron Michael Truesdale and Franklin Boolidge Lace. Case number 1-9-8-2-6-1-0-1-2, dash 1-4. Mr. Truesdale and Mr. Lace are both charged with first-degree murder and handgun violations in the death of one, Darryl James Diggs...." The prosecutor began laying her case out for the judge under very few objections. Elizabeth had already explained to me how preliminary hearings went. The state presented a summary of their case and the judge decided if there was enough evidence to send it downtown, before the circuit court. "....request that the case be sent downtown due to the overwhelming evidence."

"Objection! Your Honor." My lawyer was on her feet. "Miss Shakir keeps mentioning this overwhelming evidence. But so far, the only thing she has managed to reveal is the fact that the state refuses to produce this so-called eye witness," Elizabeth fired, on top of her game. "If this alleged witness is so credible, where are they?"

"This is not a trial, Miss Franzoso," the judge scorned. "But, if you have a motion, I'll hear it."

"Well, yes, Your Honor." Elizabeth pushed a few files to the side and began flipping through the pages of a thick law book. "According to Supreme Court case Anthony Fields versus Washington, where there is insufficient evidence, that undermines the integrity of a case, the court shall dismiss all charges," my lawyer cited the law.

"Mr. Johnson." The judge turned her attention to Frank's public defender. "Would you care to make a motion?"

"Well, Your Honor." He slowly stood back up. "Seeing as that I was just given the case this morning, I would like to refrain from entering my own motion for dismissal on Mr. Lace's behalf. But, I would like to go on record to second Miss, Fran-yo-so, is it?"

"Fran-zo-so," Elizabeth corrected. "Z-O-S-O. Don't worry, you'll get it."

"Well, I would like to second Miss Fran—" He took his time and spoke very slowly. "Zo-so's motion."

"Your motion is noted," Judge Bowman declared. "Do you want to respond to that, Miss Shakir, before I make my ruling?"

"Yes, Your Honor. As I said before, there is no lack of evidence in this matter. We have an eye witness, who will testify to the fact that both Mr. Lace and Mr. Truesdale drug the victim into an alley-way, where they continued to beat and assault him before Mr. Truesdale executed him." Jacqueline Shakir was just as tough as Elizabeth said she would be. "And as you're well aware, Your Honor, with the high rate of witness murders, we have to protect this witness as long as we can."

Judge Octavia Bowman didn't even retire to her chambers before declaring that there was enough evidence for my case to be sent downtown. "We kind of knew that was coming," Elizabeth leaned over and whispered. "But, it was still worth a shot," she added as we all stood up again as the judge exited the courtroom.

Once the judge was gone, Frank and I turned around to face the family. I thanked them for their support, told my mother and De-tauwn I loved them, and blew a kiss to Chanae. Frank's attention was on Jamaine. He wanted to know what the hell was going on and why his lawyer wasn't paid yet. Jamaine kept trying to calm Frank down, but I felt him. A good lawyer was the difference between life and freedom.

"I got you nigga, damn!" Jamaine snapped on Frank, embar-rassed, as we were escorted from the courtroom.

Before being transferred back over to the jail, Frank and I got a chance to really chop it up about the case. I wanted to know if he had, in fact, killed this dude. Because, I mean, at the end of the day, he was my nigga and I'd stand and blow trial with him if I had to. But, Frank gave me his word that he didn't put the dirt on Darryl Diggs, and neither one of us could remember where we were on the night in question. "Fuck!" I snapped, pacing the bullpen. "Somebody's setting us up."

Once I got back on the section. I jumped straight on the phone. I had to try to figure out exactly what the fuck was going on. This shit wasn't a joke no more. The case had been sent downtown. That meant that the state really thought that they had enough evidence to convict us at trial, and that was a problem.

Chapter 6

Gangster Disciples

"Ayo, did you get on top of that shit with Frank's lawyer yet?" Paul-Paul looked over at Jamaine as he drove Monique's Benz through Sandtown.

"Yeah," Jamaine lied.

"Who you get?"

"Ahhh.... the little bitch downtown," Jamaine stuttered. "Ummm.... I forgot her name. I gave Frank's sister the money to handle it. But, them niggas ain't going to trial anyway, watch," Jamaine assured confidently. "As soon as Monique and I find out who's telling, it's a wrap. That's why I don't know why Frank tripping. That's what he needs to be focused on. Who's snitching and not dropping the soap," Jamaine joked, but Paul-Paul didn't find the situation funny. Having done a light bid himself, he knew that having a person that you could depend on while you were behind the wall was more valuable than gold.

"Yeah, but they done sent the case downtown now, so anything can happen," Paul-Paul warned. He wanted to say something to Jamaine about partying all the time but held his tongue. After all, Jamaine was supplying him with the work. So, despite how he felt about the shit with Frank, he wasn't out there to make sure he got coke when he needed it, Jamaine was.

"I'm telling you yo, I'm all over it." Jamaine fast talked Paul-Paul before changing the subject. "You feel like taking a ride with me?"

"Where at?" Paul-Paul asked inquisitively.

"Out this bitch house in Essex," Jamaine disclosed with a smile. "It's a party and it's going to be mad bitches there."

"That's a bet," Paul-Paul agreed, turning the volume up on the music.

Delmont Player

Chapter 7

Gangster, Gangster, Read All About It!

Over the next several months, the nights seemed to go on forever and all the days began to run together. It got to the point where I started questioning everybody's dedication to my freedom. Even my lawyer's. Especially after we discovered that only one of the lead detectives on the case had, in fact, testified in front of the grand jury, and Elizabeth told me that we had to wait on the state's disclosure to find out who the witness was.

Jamaine kept telling me that China Doll was nowhere to be found, but I wasn't trying to hear that shit. Not as long as he was running around partying, living life, while Frank and I were fighting for our lives. On top of that, this nigga still hadn't paid for Frank's lawyer. Things were getting crazy, but nobody knew what was about to happen. Nobody could have guessed the chain of events that were about to hit home and make niggas realize that the moment you stopped thinking like a hunter, you would soon become the prey.

The only good thing that had taken place in the last few months, was the fact that I'd finally gotten Miss Glover to let her guard down, and although I still hadn't hit yet, she'd jerked me off and let me kiss and play with her pussy a few times, which was real tight and wet. Just the way I loved it.

"Ayo, go to channel thirteen real quick!" requested a light brownskin, bumpy-faced nigga named Lil' Ray, with small plates in his head. "My brother just did some gangster shit!"

Everybody looked to me. "Go ahead." I nodded, and this old head changed the channel to thirteen. And sure as shit, there were two dudes' faces, plastered across the screen.

"Somebody turn it up for me, yo!" Lil' Ray requested from the phone. "I see it now, baby! That's my hood right there!" Lil' Ray spat, fired up.

There were some things about prison I would never understand. Like how niggas got over the jail and fell in love with court and cop shows. Or how nobody wanted their homeboys to go to jail, but the minute they made the local or national news, we would be pumped up like a motherfucker. Almost as if to say, 'look what my hood breeds.' However, we were just as quick to disown a snitch. I mean, no respectable neighborhood wanted to be associated with a rat. At least, not one everybody knew about.

"....if you're just joining us. This is Sha'kia Mayo with Fox News, standing just outside the Westside Shopper Center strip mall with breaking news," the cute little news reporter said. "Where less than an hour ago, city officials discovered the bodies of two federal informants, stuffed up inside the ventilation system, behind Western Autos." The cameraman zoomed in for a close-up. "Authorities are seeking any information leading to the capture and conviction of Kenneth Williams and Don Pulley, both shown in the above photographs. The pair are wanted in connection with at least six other homicides, dating back to the spring of nineteen ninety-four. When then state witness, Dietrich Fortune, was found shot to death in a project building staircase to prevent his testimony in an ongoing drug investigation. We will continue to update you on this case as information becomes available. I'm Sha'kia Mayo, reporting live from Fox News. Back to you, Tasha Nelson...."

"Them niggas off the chain!" Lil'Ray hollered into the phone to whoever he was talking to, as a pretty, dark-skinned chick popped up on the screen. "I hope they split that nigga Keith Mickles' head like that, for all that telling he out there doing."

"Ayo, turn the movie back on!" I ordered.

"Chill, man." Sha'wayne tapped me on the leg, probably reading my mind. He knew that I didn't really go for Lil' Ray. His bumpy face ass was too loud and too sneaky for me. Always creeping around, stealing niggas' commissary and shit. Plus, I wasn't too fond of the looks he gave me from time to time. But, Sha'wayne had bidded with him before and said that was just how he was. "That nigga don't mean no harm, trust me, I know. I was up the farm with his chump ass," were Sha'wayne's exact words concerning Lil' Ray.

"Them the type of niggas I need in my corner right now," I admitted, because Jamaine was out there in the streets playing.

"You and me both," Sha'wayne seconded.

"Hold up, yo!" I tried to stop Lil' Ray before he began fucking with the TV socket, trying to use a pencil and some toilet paper to light up a wick so he and Sha'wayne could smoke some weed. "Wait until the news go off," I snapped. Because I was now lusting over the chocolate news lady Tasha Nelson.

"I got it!" Lil' Ray assured a second before sparks shot out of the socket and burnt his hand. "Shit!" Lil' Ray cried out in pain, fanning his toasted hand.

"I told your silly ass, you didn't know what you were doing," Sha'wayne spat, laughing.

"Man, I knew y'all niggas were going to do that shit!" I snapped as the TV screen went blank. It was almost count time and these geeking ass niggas were in the dayroom, trying to smoke a blunt. But now, somehow, Lil' Ray's dumb ass had fucked around and blown the power.

"Stick your finger in there and try to remove the lead," I ordered, thinking about what dudes did when they blew the power, while trying to bang the stinger.

"Nigga, I'm not sticking my finger in there fucking with that electricity," Lil' Ray retorted, still waving his hand. "That shit just burnt the fuck out of me."

"Nigga, you the one blew the power!" I argued, feeling some type of way that I was missing the end of the pretty news chick's segment..

"Why don't you stick your fingers in there and get it out?" I heard somebody mumble with an accent, and looked up to see Miss Glover's cornball ass boyfriend and the tier officer who'd been working since she'd taken a vacation.

"Stick your bitch ass fingers in there and get it, nigga!" I challenged, standing up. One thing I couldn't stand, was a wild, hating ass lame who kept faking.

"You think you're tough because you keep going back and forth on lockup," he fired, moving toward me.

"Nah, nigga, you think I'm tough because I keep going back and forth on lockup," I corrected, meeting him the rest of the way.

"Truesdale, you need to step back out of that officer's personal space," the tier officer warned, snapping the button on his mace holster. "I won't ask you again."

I took a few steps back, smiling and put my hands up. "Whoa, man, you ain't got to pull the nine out, baby," I joked. I knew Miss Glover's bitch ass boyfriend didn't want the type of drama I could bring to his life. Square ass nigga, probably grew up playing soccer or something on the beach. But, I was straight from the streets that ate lames like him for breakfast. Hence, the occupations. "I'm backing up," I submitted.

"Yeah, he's good," Officer Lame repeated, eye fucking me. Wasn't nothing worse than a jealous ass nigga who couldn't handle his woman.

"That's what they tell me." I winked at him and grinned.

"Dayroom closed anyway!" Officer Lame spat, looking at his watch.

Everybody got up and started collecting their things. I could feel Miss Glover's lame ass boyfriend's eyes on me as I grabbed my shower bag and food off the table and headed for the door. "Step to the side, Williams," the tier officer ordered, and Lil' Ray complied as I stepped around him and kept it moving.

I was strapped up and wasn't about to go down bullshitting. I peeped back to check on Sha'wayne. He had the blunt literally behind his ear in plain sight. But, dumb and dumber were so focused on Lil' Ray that they let Sha'wayne walk right past them. "Man, y'all on some bullshit," I heard Lil' Ray say as the tier officer directed him to place his hands on the wall. I gave Sha'wayne some love and beelined to my cell.

I had already put my joint up and kicked back, when the cell door popped open a second before the tier officer and Miss Glover's lame boyfriend showed up. "Shakedown, Truesdale," the tier officer explained, pulling the grill open so the lame could enter the cell. I sat up, reaching for my tennis, but the lame kicked them out of my reach and pushed me into the wall as I stood up.

"Let me put my tennis on, bitch!" I requested, ready to rumble if that was what he had in mind.

"Nah," he replied, pulling out a razor-sharp ice pick with a shoe-string handle. "You're tough, right?"

I'm not even going to front, I froze straight up. I mean, what the fuck was I supposed to do to a correctional officer with a knife? That was like a police with a gun. "Nah, nigga, run your mouth now!" he dared. "Mister tough guy! Say something!" he challenged, but I remained silent. Honestly, I was trying to figure out what his angle was and what the fuck my next move was going to be.

I shot the tier officer a curious look. But he only hunched his shoulder, as if he was just along for the ride. "Go ahead, say something now, bitch!" He stepped so far into my personal space that I could actually feel and smell his hot ass breath on my cheek. "And watch me stab myself and give your punk ass the charge!" he threatened as I just stared him down, silently vowing to make him answer for his sin against me one day.

"You got that," I whispered, humbling myself as he continued to hold onto the ice pick, uncertain. "You got that," I repeated, ready to accept defeat. At least for now anyway.

"Yeah, I know I got that, nigga!" He peeped over his shoulder at the tier officer before leaning forward to whisper in my ear. "If I hear about you hanging around Tiphani again, I'ma come back up here and put that knife in your bitch ass, you hear me?"

I just nodded. Not so much in agreement, but more so in the sense that I was going to finish his ass the first chance I got. Miss Glover had his ass turned out. I mean, I knew firsthand how good her little pussy felt, tasted even. But still, only a pussy-whipped fool would threaten a gangster and not finish the job.

Delmont Player

Chapter 8

2 Good 2 B Gangster

It had been about a month since the shakedown incident, when Lil' Ray's man, Don, hit the section. The news said they had cornered him over some female's house near Jefferson Street. Pussy got a nigga every time in one sense or another. It was just something about that lava between a woman's legs that made a nigga knowingly and unintelligently jeopardize his health, life, and freedom.

Jamaine had finally taken care of Frank's lawyer, but the lawyer was so cheap and bullshit that Frank decided to just keep the bread and stick with the public defender, Chip Johnson. Sha'wayne was a few days into trial for his drug beef, and things weren't looking to promising.

SweetPea told me that Burnze was off lockup, but I didn't know what section he'd been sent to. Miss Glover kept asking me questions, trying to figure out if something had happened between the lame and I, but I played it cool and just continued to play with that pussy every chance I got. Shid, if he wanted to continue to tell her shit, that was on him. Because as far as I was concerned, it wasn't nobody's business but ours. So there wasn't no one to talk to and nothing to talk about. When the time was right, he was going to stand on what he'd done.

"Truesdale! Grab a broom and sweep the catwalk before you lock in!" Miss Glover ordered as I mopped past her desk, just before lock time.

"Come on, Miss Glover, it's already nine thirty!" I bucked.

"Okay, since you said that, you can sweep the entire catwalk. The west and east side," Miss Glover informed, looking at me as if daring me to challenge her. "Or you can just quit!"

"Yeah, I heard that," I mumbled for show and kept doing my job. Miss Glover knew damn well that I wasn't going to quit no time soon. Next to the tier reps and paint crew, I had the best job over the jail. I was the closet man. Simply meaning, I was the first one out to get the supplies ready and the last one to lock in, after I put the supplies back up. I had access to the best steel and the greatest hiding spots.

I took my time getting to the catwalk, waiting until after everybody had locked into their cells before I even began. I got Miss Glover to open up the gate that allowed you to walk completely around the section and come out on the other side. I swept all the way down the catwalk and around the back until I was behind the tier in a blind spot. Then, I waited. Five minutes later, Miss Glover came from the eastside, that way the nosey inmates who'd seen me sweeping around the catwalk from the westside of the section, and the stalkers who'd clocked Miss Glover, would assume that we'd gone all the way around to the other side.

The moment I saw Miss Glover, it was on. I pushed her sexy ass up against the wall and started tonguing her down as my hands traveled to her wide, thick ass cheeks. "I missed you so much!" Miss Glover inhaled, squeezing my dick.

Breaking the kiss, I stepped back and yanked my sweats down. "Who you missed the most?" I teased as my dick jumped out of my boxers, already hard. Miss Glover bit her bottom lip and gently took me into her soft hands.

"I don't know," she admitted, cupping my balls, slowly running her hand up and down my length. "It's something about the hook in this black motherfucker that I love."

"Arghhh," I threw my head back and groaned. Miss Glover's snug hand continued to leisurely glide back and forth across my dick. I knew exactly what she was trying to do, but I wasn't having it today.

"Hold up, baby," I pleaded, on the verge of succumbing to that familiar urge. "It's your turn today."

Today, I had other ideas, other plans. Today, I wasn't just going to settle for no hand job. I didn't care how good it felt. Today, I wanted more than just a simple taste or feel of Miss Glover's wet pussy on my fingers. Today, I was going to eat the lining out of that motherfucker and knock the bottom loose.

"Dakaron, we can't," Miss Glover warned, putting up a half-hearted fight to stop me from unbuttoning her uniform.

"I know, baby. I know." I continued to disrobe her. I crushed my lips back into Miss Glover's mouth as my hands continued to work. "I got you," I assured in between kisses. Once I started on Miss Glover's neck, it was over. I watched her girly features crinkle up as I sucked, kissed, and licked on her neck, ear, and shoulder before making my way to her nice size breasts. Miss Glover's breasts were gorgeous, just like the rest of her, soft too. So soft, in fact, that they made her nipples seem harder. I rolled my tongue over Miss Glover's nipples extremely slow as she shivered and moaned in my arms. Then, I began working on her uniform pants.

Once I got Miss Glover naked, I was no more good. I had to step back and take her in from head to toe. *Damn, her old ass is bad! Nice and thick too*, I thought, licking my lips. No wonder why that wild, bitch ass, Haitian nigga from J-section running around acting crazy. Of course, I knew that Miss Glover wasn't no more than twenty-nine, thirty, but still. To an eighteen-year-old who was used to fucking bitches his age, Miss Glover was a grown woman and I knew that I had to treat her like one.

I knelt down front of Miss Glover and carefully guided one of her baby-soft, thick thighs to my shoulder as her pretty, phat little pussy opened up right before my eyes. "I knew the first time I saw you that you had a pretty pussy," I mumbled more to myself than Miss Glover, before leaning forward to get my first real taste of that pussy.

"Mmmmmmm," Miss Glover cooed as my tongue snaked out and began to saw back and forth between her juicy pussy lips. I paused to blow on her clit before forcing my tongue in and out of her tasty pussy. Miss Glover rotated her hips in a way as to feed me more pussy. And I didn't disappoint. I ate all she was willing to give. Going to work on that pussy. Slowly teasing her clitoris, gently kissing her pussy lips, all the while using my fingertips to toy with her pussyhole.

After a while, I laid Miss Glover down on an old, paint-covered blanket so I could really get to that pussy and do some damage. I held Miss Glover's legs back by the ankles and ate that pussy like it was my last meal. I ate her pussy so good that she forced her legs down and locked her thighs around my face until she was about to come. The thrill I provided couldn't be ignored. "Ssssssss, boyyyy, I'm going to—ohhhh!" Miss Glover's entire body began convulsing as she damn near ripped my head off from the shoulders.

I slide up between Miss Glover's legs and rubbed the head of my dick between the soft, juicy folds of her pussy lips before opening that pussy up in one long thrust. "Oh my god!" Miss Glover whimpered as I hit that spot. "Right there, Dakaron. Just like that," she begged, looking as if she may faint. "Gosh, that motherfucker thick," she whispered again, in her own little world. Miss Glover lifted her head back up to look down between our bodies as my dick slipped in and out of her tight, snug pussy. "Oh my god!!!!!" Miss Glover began shaking her head like she couldn't believe that she was absorbing all of a young nigga. "Boyyyy," she cried out, squeezing me tightly as I hit bottom. But, like I said, today, I planned to show off.

I hooked Miss Glover's legs over my forearms and slowly got to my feet. Then, I planted my feet and hoisted Miss Glover's lust-plagued body up and pent her against the wall before stroking that pussy balls deep again. "Oh my god, I'ma cum again!!!!" she moaned in my ear, locking her arms around my neck. "Please, Dakaron, please don't drop me."

"I got you, baby," I managed confidently, keeping Miss Glover's body suspended in the air. I repositioned myself to where I was able to tuck Miss Glover's legs completely over the folds of my arms so that I could hit that pussy nice and deep standing up.

Once I got to long stroking that pussy, it was over. Miss Glover started moaning so loud and breathing so hard that even she thought somebody might hear. So, our mouths met, and our tongues connected as I pounded away like I was trying to nail that pussy to the wall. *I know that lame not hitting this good pussy right,* I thought as Miss Glover's pussy muscles rippled over my dick, hot and wet. It was no doubt in my mind that Miss Glover hadn't ever had that pussy knocked out the park like this.

"Damn," I spat out loud. I couldn't believe how tight and wet Miss Glover's pussy was.

I looked into Miss Glover's pretty face as she stared back at me with those beautiful, intoxicating, hazel eyes, and I couldn't take it anymore. Good, wet, bottomless, snug pussy around my dick. Baby-soft flesh pressed up against my body, nails firmly dug into my back, passionate moans in my ear, hot breath on my neck, and submissive pleas to make her cum again. "Oh my god, Dakaron. Please, I can't cum again. Please don't make me cum a—" Miss Glover bit down on my shoulder as the all too familiar feeling began to jolt through my entire body like electricity too.

I went balls deep one more time and nutted as Miss Glover clamped up on me. It was like for a moment, we were both super strong, locked up in mid-air. And then, all of a sudden, we crumbled to the ground laughing.

"Boy!" Miss Glover slapped my shoulder. "Didn't I tell you not to drop me?"

"My bad," I apologized sincerely. "That pussy made a young nigga weak," I admitted, making Miss Glover smile.

"Come on, before we get in trouble and I end up losing my job."

Miss Glover give me a quick kiss on the lips and played with my dick, like she couldn't help herself.

"You got to do something for me first," I demanded, grinning.

Miss Glover's girly features crinkled up again as her pretty eyes beamed at me. "What?" she questioned, still playing with my pussy-wet dick. "You want me to suck your dick, don't you?"

"Next time." I smiled. "Right now, I want you to tell me who's the best," I challenged. "Me or that old Haiti nigga?"

Miss Glover remained silent, watching herself continue to play with my dick. For a moment, I wondered if she even heard me. Then, she finally looked up and admitted that she was not only dealing with the lame, but that they had recently moved in together. "I don't want you fucking that lame no more."

"Dakaron, we live together," Glover tried to justify.

"So! That's my pussy now!" I declared, thinking about how his old ass had tried me. "And I don't want you fucking him, okay?"

"Okay," Miss Glover agreed, shaking her head.

"Good girl." I slapped her gently on her soft cheeks and watched them jiggle before kissing her again. "You go ahead of me. I'll wait for a few minutes."

I helped Miss Glover get dressed and made sure she looked presentable before she walked out the other end of the catwalk with a new pep in her step and exited the catwalk. You couldn't tell me that I wasn't that nigga. Not at that moment. Not after I'd just gotten finished fucking what could probably be considered the baddest thing over the jail and making it mine.

Chapter 9

G's up, Hoes Down

"That's probably him right there." Paul-Paul pointed as he and Jamaine sat on the hood of his car outside the Baltimore City Jail.

"Which one?" Jamaine questioned as a group of guys spilled out of the city jail gates, looking around.

"The one with the bright yellow sweatsuit on," Paul-Paul revealed.

Dak had asked Jamaine to pick up his new friend, Sha'wayne, and show him a good time because he'd just beaten his drug case in a jury trial and Dak wanted to welcome him back to the streets. Jamaine knew that Dak was disappointed in him because he hadn't been carrying things the way he should've been carrying them. But, partying with bitches and shit was his MO, so he planned to show Sha'wayne a good time to let Dak know that he could count on him. Jamaine straightened up as the dudes made their way toward them.

"Sha'wayne?" Jamaine questioned cautiously.

"Nah." The dude in the yellow sweatsuit walked right on past Jamaine, looking at him strangely.

"You Maine? Dak's people's?" Another guy stepped out of the crowd.

"Yeah," Jamaine admitted. "Sha'wayne?"

"Yeah," he confessed.

"Okay." Jamaine smiled, extending his hand. "What's up?"

"Ready to hit these bricks and get some pussy," Sha'wayne replied honestly, shaking Jamaine's hand.

"That's why Dak sent me to pick you up." Jamaine's smile widened. "Because if I know anything, I know how to bring a nigga home to some bitches."

Jamaine and Sha'wayne climbed back into the car behind Paul-Paul and pulled off. "So, how long you been sitting over the jail?" Paul- Paul broke the silence.

"Almost two years," Sha'wayne replied.

"Almost two years?" Jamaine repeated, surprised, taking his eyes off the road for a moment to look back at Sha'wayne. "Damn," he continued after Sha'wayne nodded. "They can hold niggas that long?" he inquired, thinking about Dak and Frank.

"Yeah," Sha'wayne admitted. "Plus, I waived my Hicks."

"Your what?" Paul-Paul turned around.

"My Hicks," Sha'wayne repeated.

"What the fuck is that?" Jamaine fired over his shoulder, slowing down for a construction worker.

"Well, you have the right to a speedy trial. That basically means that the state has to try your case within one hundred eighty days. Unless you sign a Hicks waiver," Sha'wayne explained.

"Well, Frank and Dak better not sign that shit!" Jamaine argued.

Jamaine, Sha'wayne, and Paul-Paul talked about jail, rights, and Dak a little longer before changing the subject.

"Oh, you're going to love this bitch," Jamaine guaranteed. "Tweety's right all the way around the board. Her sister, Tamara, though, the baddest thing up Edmondson Village, hands down," Jamaine bragged before going on to describe her in detail. "I'm telling you, yo, ain't nothing fucking with shorty."

"Why the fuck you didn't hook me up with her then?" Sha'wayne questioned.

"Because her red ass is mine, nigga, that's why!" Jamaine laughed. "But, I'm telling you, you're not going to be disappointed. All these bitches bad."

Jamaine wasn't lying. Tamara Nickleson and her sisters, Tweety and Kia, were some fine ass motherfuckers who lived on the corner of Edmondson Avenue and Edgewood with their mother, Debra, an older, fine, chocolate thing who could've easily passed for their older sister. When Jamaine, Paul-Paul, and Sha'wayne got to the house, everybody went their separate ways. Jamaine dipped off with Tamara, Paul-Paul slid down the base with Kia, and Sha'wayne and Tweety's fine ass got busy right there on the living room floor.

Chapter 10

Starin' at a Gangster Through the Rearview

Everything was going good until one of Paul-Paul's spots was hit and he ended up getting shot. The way it was explained to me was that Sha'wayne, Paul-Paul, and one of his Sandtown homeboys were inside one of Paul-Paul's spots, when some stick-up boys ran up in the spot and laid the whole house down. Paul-Paul said everybody was cooperating when the niggas just got to pistol slinging up in that bitch. First, they blasted his man. Then, they tried to kill him and Sha'wayne. But Paul-Paul only ended up getting hit in the leg, fleeing out the back door with Sha'wayne.

The jail was on modified lockdown due to a murder that had taken place on the section. A dude named Brooks, from Westport, had come onto the tier one night on a handgun charge, and ended up getting stabbed to death before he could make bail. The night before he was butchered, he was up, late night, talking to another dude from around his neighborhood about something he had no business discussing. Let alone out the door for anybody to hear. However, it just seemed like it was something about being around niggas with murder charges that made dudes want to start talking about murders to fit in.

It was nice and quiet, maybe around 2 a.m., when Brooks began talking about how he and a few of his homeboys had jumped some dude on Patapsoo Road inside the Bushman Record Store. The problem was, anybody and everybody who was up that night could hear. And the jail never slept. So, as Dontae went on bragging about the incident, the dude's cousin sat at the grill listening, plotting, and planning to avenge his folks.

The next morning, when the cells opened for recreation, it was on, and the rest, as they say, remained a part of prison history. I was right there, though, when the dude's cousin got on Brooks' ass like an animal and put him down. I'd never witnessed no shit like that in my life, and I didn't waste no time locking the fuck in the cell.

There was no reason to stand around. After all, I wasn't dying to be a witness. And I damn sure wasn't dying to be a suspect.

After witnessing how Brooks had come over the jail and gotten devoured, I really wanted to get my hands on Hyme, Meat, or Fat Relly. But, I'd heard that they were all found guilty and shipped off into the system to serve their time. The jail was beginning to drain me. Honestly speaking, if it wasn't for Chanae and the family keeping me on my feet, I didn't know what I would've done.

After getting off the phone with my mother and joking around with Miss Glover, I headed for my cell to grab my shower gear as directed. On my way to the shower, I noticed niggas checking me out. *Hating ass niggas!* I thought, laughing to myself. I only wished Sha'wayne could see me now. I teased Miss Glover a little more, stole a quick kiss in the utility closet, and jumped in the shower before the next group of guys were let out.

I had just stepped underneath the shower head and began soaping my washcloth up when the shower door opened and about seven or eight dudes strolled in with their shower grip. I instantly noticed that Lil'Ray and his brother's rap buddy, Don, were holding knives in their hands, looking around anxiously. *Who the fuck they about to hit?* I wondered, trying to rinse off real quick as other niggas began turning around. Then, it hit me as they moved in my direction. I was their target.

"You know what it is, bitch," Lil'Ray began, bringing the knife up before I wacked him across the face with my soap-covered rag and sent him stumbling backward into the well.

"Shit, I can't see, yo!" Lil'Ray complained, desperately trying to get the soap out of his eyes as I turned my attention to Don.

"Chill, Don," I pleaded before he stabbed me twice. I tried to grab Don's arm, but he hit me again. "I ain't got no beef with you, yo," I exclaimed, trying to bluff my way out of the shower so I could get to my own joint. It didn't work, though, because Don swung the knife again. So, I knew he had his mind made up.

I finally got a hold of Don's arm, but with all the soap on my hand, it was hard to hold him or get the joint out of his hand. By this time, Lil'Ray had begun to recover also. So, shit was getting ugly quick. I hit Don with a two piece and started tussling with Lil'Ray. I was bleeding all over the place. But, Lil'Ray and Don weren't showing me no mercy.

I knocked Don into the shower wall and went down to one knee. Somehow, Lil'Ray got behind me and from that point on, I knew I didn't have any win. I fought them niggas with everything I had, though. Heart, guts, and pride, but it wasn't enough, because they tore my ass up. Lil'Ray and Don stabbed me in the head, face, and body, until I heard Miss Glover scream for help before I felt mace all in my eyes and lungs.

A few seconds later, there were correctional officers rushing into the shower to pull us apart. But, I never even heard Miss Glover call the code for assistance.

When I got to medical, I found out that I'd been hit fourteen times and needed to be transferred to an outside hospital for treatment.

Delmont Player

Chapter 11

Sick Ass Gangster Like Me

I was placed on administrative lockup the moment I got back over the jail. Don and Lil'Ray were sitting on lockup, waiting for me to make a statement. Of course, I refused to cooperate with the investigation. Even in the joint, I always kept it street.

At first, I was getting mad when the CO's tried to get me to give up Lil'Ray and Don. But, after seeing how so many other so-called men and gangsters had given statements about the incident, I stopped taking it personal. On my first visit after getting stabbed up, Detauwn went off, Chanae cried, and Jamaine just stared at me with hurt and rage in his eyes. "Look, they got me, they caught me slipping," I admitted. "But, I'ma fucking gangster! So, you know I'ma get mine," I spat with a half-smile.

I understood Jamaine's pain and frustration. Especially when it came out that Don was Dana's little brother. But still, he had to understand that the jungle was still the jungle, be it in the streets or on the section.

"Man, I'ma crush everybody that even deal with them niggas," Jamaine fired.

"Nah man, I got a better idea," I whispered, leaning forward. I knew now that most prison beefs were conditional. You stab me, I stab you. If I catch your brother, I hit him, and so on. What I wanted to do was show Don and Lil'Ray that I wasn't most niggas. I wanted to teach them to look before they leaped. "Listen, Lil'Ray got a brother named Kenny Bean. He was just on the news with Don behind that Westside Shopping Center shit."

"Yeah, I seen that." Detauwn shook his head. "Real pie-faced type nigga, Kenneth Williams, I think his name was."

"Yeah, that's him," I admitted.

"I wonder if he's from down that way?" Detauwn questioned. "I'ma call Black's son's mother, Nikki to see if she knows these niggas. You know she's from Catherine."

"Nah, Detauwn, man, chill. Let Jamaine handle that shit," I directed. I knew that my brother had put a few dicks in the dirt, but killing wasn't his game. Detauwn was a hustler first and this wasn't about getting money. If it was, Detauwn would've been the first motherfucker I called. Because if my brothers didn't know anything else, them niggas knew how to get money. But again, this was a different part of the game. The part where gun play was involved. So, Jamaine was the best man for the job.

"Jamaine, you sure you got it?" Detauwn questioned, ready come out of retirement for his little brother.

"Yeah." Jamaine smiled. "You can sit this one out, oldhead."

I hated talking in front of Chanae, but there was no other way around it. Plus, I knew from the shit with her brother that she could hold water. At least when it was something serious.

"Maine, get with Nikki and find out if she knows this nigga, Kenny Bean," I instructed, ready to show Lil'Ray and Don that I could hit them from the bricks.

"I'm all over that shit," Jamaine assured, and for once, I believed him. I mean, honestly, over the last couple of months, Jamaine had proven to be a real piece of shit. Loyal only to himself. But, he could still be trusted to carry out a mission. After all, it was about him and his ego.

"Holler at Monique, and see if he can get anything on Don," I suggested, looking at Chanae. I could tell that she was still brokenhearted by the stitches and bandages on my face and head, even after I'd finally gotten her to calm down. "Hey, beautiful." I directed my attention to Chanae, but she wouldn't really face me. "Chanae! Chanae! Look at me!" I ordered, and continued when she complied, "You know I'ma soldier, right?"

"Of course." Chanae blushed slightly. "I wouldn't love you if you weren't."

"Then, you know that I can handle myself," I professed, needing her to be strong. If there was one thing that I truly despised, it was a weak woman, because weak women couldn't be trusted. Venus had taught me that.

"Yes," Chanae admitted. "That's why it scared me so much seeing you like this," Chanae confessed, almost as if she didn't remember that I was human.

"I'm your Superman, baby." I smiled.

"Yeah." Chanae smiled back, and I knew that she would he okay. "That's why I love you so damn much, boy."

"Don't worry, I'll be back better than ever in a couple weeks," I assured.

After my visit was over, I went back to the section and sent Willie Bates a kite. I needed him to look into if anybody else had something to do with me getting hit on K-section. I also informed him that I needed a makeshift handcuff key and knife, so when I went up for the ticket with Don and Lil'Ray, I could slip the cuffs and chop their asses up. Then, I put my headphones on and fell back.

***

Lil'Ray and Don had a horseshoe. Because the very next morning, Don, Lil'Ray, and I were called up for the write-ups before Willie Bates could get back to me. In the hearing room, I told the hearing officer that I was certain that Don Pully and Raymond Williams hadn't stabbed me. In fact, I explained how they'd attempted to help me. They beat the assault, but got found guilty for the weapons. There was nothing that I could do about that because of the way Glover had written the tickets.

"This shit ain't over, bitch," I mumbled under my breath to Lil'Ray as I waited to be escorted out of the hearing room. "I did that because I'ma fucking gangster, nigga!" I added, wishing the lockup worker had gotten back to me before the hearing. "And what I'm 'bout to do next, I'ma do because I'm sick."

Chapter 12

Young Gangsters on the Rise

"Ayo, you're not going to believe who I just stumbled up on," Paul-Paul exclaimed, climbing into the car with Jamaine.

"Who?" Jamaine inquired curiously before checking the rear-view mirror and pulling off.

"The dude, Kenny Bean, Dak was talking about," Paul-Paul revealed with an evil grin.

"The Westside Shopping Center nigga from the news?" Jamaine wanted to be sure.

"Yep." Paul-Paul shook his head. "Caught yo coming up out of the basement at this bitch house over in East Baltimore I be fucking," Paul-Paul informed. "Nigga scared the shit out of me too. I almost bust his dumb ass."

"Oh yeah." Jamaine paused for a moment. "What, that's shorty peoples or something?"

"I don't know," Paul-Paul admitted. "I asked her who yo was, but she said he was her twin sister's friend."

Jamaine fell silent again, as if pondering his next move. "You think he's laying low over there?"

"I don't know, he could be just passing through. I know that nigga had bedroom slippers on, though," Paul-Paul explained.

"Then he's probably staying there," Jamaine declared. "You say he fuck with your girl's twin sister?"

"Yeah, that's what Raquel said," Paul-Paul revealed. "So, how you wanna carry it?"

"Nigga, how do you want to carry it? That's your girl's spot," Jamaine retorted, coming to a complete stop at the end of the tree-lined block.

"You know I'm down for whatever. Dak my nigga!" Paul-Paul replied. "And Raquel ain't my girl, nigga, that's my gangster bitch!"

"Say no more." Jamaine turned left and stepped on the gas. "Call her up and tell her that you're coming through tonight then,"

Jamaine instructed, ready to really put Paul-Paul's loyalty to the test.

"You ain't said nothing but a word, nigga, pull over at the next pay phone," Paul-Paul replied, accepting the challenged.

Jamaine stopped at the next phone booth and waited as Paul-Paul jumped out to make the call. He wondered what Kenny Bean was doing at the moment. "Goofy nigga, probably in the basement playing PlayStation, watching TV or something, thinking shit sweet. Never even suspecting that his number about to be called," Jamaine said to himself.

"Yo, what, are you in this bitch talking to yourself?" Paul-Paul questioned, climbing back into the passenger's seat.

"Just thinking out loud," Jamaine confessed. "Wondering if this nigga know that his girl's twin sister about to open the door for the Grim Reaper."

"That's why I always say that you got to choose your women like you choose your guns. Very carefully." Paul-Paul smiled at the thought of Raquel's pretty, fine ass. "You definitely can't have that bitch jamming up or letting you down when you need her the most."

"There's a crack in every relationship. That's how nigga's like me get in." Jamaine laughed. "I'm like ammunition."

"Nigga, you're like an opportunist," Paul-Paul corrected.

"Opportunist, bullets, whatever you want to call it, nigga. When that bitch start acting up, I'm the one who oils that ass up."

"Bitches are cruddy and disloyal. That's why niggas always end up in a fucked up situations fucking with them."

"Nigga, as long as that pussy get wet, I don't give a fuck if she's loyal, cruddy, or straight up retarded! I'm trying to go," Jamaine assured.

"That's probably why you stay in some shit." Paul-Paul stared at Jamaine for moment. He knew that a man with any weakness could never be completely trusted. It didn't matter if he was weak mentally or morally, weakness was weakness. "So, how you want to do this though?"

Jamaine pulled out into traffic again before answering. "First, we need to drive over there, so that I can scope out the scene. Then, we can come up with a plan," Jamaine replied, and Paul-Paul didn't need to hear nothing else.

***

Jamaine parked the stolen cab at the end of the twins' alleyway and made his way to Raquel's back yard to wait for the signal as planned. Since Paul-Paul knew that Raquel's bedroom didn't have any windows, he decided to use the bathroom light to alert Jamaine when the coast was clear.

Jamaine hopped the twins' gate and squatted down beside a trash can before looking up and down the alley to make sure he hadn't drawn any unwanted attention. It was dark outside and he was wearing all black. But still, it was better to be safe than sorry. Especially since he didn't need no murder coming back to haunt him. There was an upstairs light on across the alleyway and some old school rap music leaking from a cracked window a few houses down. But beyond that, everything else appeared pretty normal. There were no curtains moving, no unexpected backdoors opening, and no strange noises, as if someone was trying to be sneaky. Jamaine slowly eased his gun out and remained completely still. He knew that what he was about to do went against everything that he'd been taught, everything that Dak and Frank stood for. But, a man couldn't continue to uphold the golden rules when he was at war with opponents who weren't playing fair.

Jamaine saw the bathroom light flash a few times through the upstairs curtain and knew that Paul-Paul had gotten Raquel out of the way. Taking one more look around, Jamaine slowly stood up and moved toward the backdoor. The backdoor was unlocked as ex-pected, so after slowly turning the doorknob, Jamaine carefully eased the door open just enough to slip inside. After gently securing the backdoor, Jamaine paused to listen and heard nothing. Paul-Paul had told him that Kenny Bean would most likely be in the basement with Raquel's twin sister, Rachel. So, Jamaine tip-toed across the kitchen toward the basement door. Placing his ear up against the door, Jamaine listened again. He knew that his escape had to be sweeter than the execution, because once he killed a female, the entire city would turn against him.

Again, hearing nothing, Jamaine took a deep breath and pushed the basement door open. There was no sense in procrastinating. What had to be done, had to be done. Niggas had stabbed Dak up over the jail and Kenny Bean was about to answer for it. Anybody who was present was going on GP.

"That you, baby?" Kenny Bean called out as Jamaine began to descend the squeaky basement stairs. "Please tell me that you grabbed some blunts." When Jamaine first emerged from the shadows of the stairs and spotted Kenny Bean sitting on a waterbed, barefooted, in a pair of small ass silk boxers with marijuana plants on them, he had an odd but curious look on his face. "Who the fuck are you, homeboy?" Kenny Bean questioned, placing the TV remote on the bed. He hadn't noticed the weapon yet. "If you're looking for Rachel, I'm sorry to tell you, but she's already got company," Kenny Bean spat sarcastically.

"Well, it's a good thing that I'm looking for you then." Jamaine smiled.

"Nigga, if you're looking for me, you must be looking for trouble." Kenny Bean stood up, looking Jamaine up and down.

"Is that right?" Jamaine folded his arms in front of him so that Kenny Bean would notice the gun.

"Whoa yo, hold up!" Kenny Bean tried to take a step back and ended up almost tripping over the bed. "Slow your roll, I was playing with you, nigga!" Kenny Bean kept his eyes on the murder weapon and played the submissive role.

"Nah, nigga, keep talking that shit! You say your name trouble, right?" Jamaine taunted, waving the gun around. "Bring your stupid ass here and lay on the floor." Jamaine gestured toward the ground with the gun. Jamaine was so happy that Paul-Paul's girl's twin sister, Rachel, wasn't present. Because he honestly didn't know if he had the stomach to kill a bitch, even if she was just collateral damage. He loved pussy too much. "I'm not going to ask you again, nigga!" Jamaine fired, knowing that time was of the essence.

Kenny Bean kept his hands where Jamaine could see them. "What's this all about, yo?" Kenny Bean inquired softly. "Rachel your sister or something?"

"Nigga, if you don't get your ass over here. I'ma split your motherfucking wig right now!" Jamaine threatened through clenched teeth, aiming the gun. Kenny Bean hadn't budged.

Kenny Bean took one more step and then dove backward over the side of the bed, going for his weapon. Jamaine immediately stepped forward and opened fire. Bullets ripped through the water mattress, bed sheets, and thick wooden bed frame as Jamaine continued to pull the trigger.

Jamaine stepped up and peeped over the waterbed to see Kenny Bean lying face down, clutching a big ass chrome Desert Eagle in his hand. "Fuck!" Jamaine shouted, looking toward the stairs. Jamaine thought for a second. There was water squirting and running everywhere. Jamaine hurried over to Kenny Bean's body and removed the DE before shooting him twice in the head to be sure the deed was done. Then, he ran out of the house, hopped the back gate, sprinted up the alley, jumped into the stolen car, and fled the scene.

Chapter 13

Same Gangster, Different Gangstaration

I was laid across the bunk, on administrative lockup, staring up at the ceiling, talking to my neighbor, an old head named Rico, who was back over the jail on appeal, about some of the dumb shit I'd done in life, as we waited for our showers. Things like teaching Chanae how to load and shoot a gun, tricking my god-brother into eating a glaze-covered donut after I had covered it in roll-on deodorant, and getting put out of all city public schools.

"That's the one thing that I'll always regret about my Booker T days," I admitted, referring to the incident that had gotten me expelled from Booker T. Washington Middle School.

"What? Fighting the teacher?" My neighbor sounded surprised.

"Nah, putting my hands on Janet," I confessed honestly. "I don't be hitting no women. That's sucker shit! Plus, I used to like Janet's pretty ass too. I was just so mad that she pushed that dirty cookie in my mouth and wouldn't apologize. Then, everybody was laughing and shit. I lost it. That's why when the teacher said something to me, I went straight at 'em."

"So, you never saw her again?"

"Nope," I replied, immediately realizing my mistake. "Nah, my bad, I did see Janet again. I ran into her downtown last summer. My rap buddy was pressing up on her homegirl and she called me out." I smiled at the memory. "I didn't even recognize her at first, because I was so busy checking her out. She had on this royal blue bodysuit, killing it," I explained, remembering the incident like it was yesterday. "Once I realized who she was, though, I instantly cracked for the number."

"Hold up, slim, you tried to holler at that girl?" My neighbor began laughing. "What she say?"

"I wasn't trying to holler at her like that," I corrected. "I mean, don't get me wrong, she was still bad as shit! But, I just wanted to make up for putting my hands on her. I didn't want her to think that I was a woman beater and all that weak shit. I asked if I could take her out to lunch or something and explain what happened. I told you, Janet and I used to be cool. She used to help me with my classwork and stuff. I was on her. But, I don't know if she was on me or not."

"So what happened?" My neighbor appeared interested.

"She gave me a phony number," I confessed, smiling again. "I dialed that number four, five times thinking she was playing. I'm still fucked up about that. Because she probably really think a nigga be beating on women."

"And I thought I did some wild shit in my day. But, your little ass takes the cake, slim."

"That ain't nothing," I assured. "One time, my stupid ass had been dumb enough to break into a well-known neighborhood hustler's house and steal all his clothes and jewelry. Then, I started wearing the shit right back around the way. I can still remember the look on that nigga's face, when he caught me coming out of Yellow Bowl with his chain and sweatsuit on. He yoked me straight up. But, like I said, damn near my whole family gangsters. So, he knew not to put his hands on me. My brother, Detauwn, was still livid though. And went around C.C. Jackson...."

My neighbor and I continued to kick it until my grill popped open for a shower. "I'll holler at you when I get back," I said, grabbing the recent letter I'd gotten from Paul-Paul along with my shower grip before making my way down the tier toward the showers. Since everybody on the section was either on lockup or under some form of investigation, we all showered alone.

"Don't ever say that I didn't do nothing for you." I stopped outside Lil'Ray's cell and tossed Paul-Paul's letter inside.

"Oh, your bitch ass ain't get enough of getting chopped up yet, huh?" Lil'Ray untangled the mummy-like blanket and got up out of the bed to pick the letter up off the floor.

"Nigga, I'm doing you a favor." I put my hands up in surrender and took a few steps back. "I heard you hollering over to Don about your brother. So, I just wanted you to know what happened."

"What, nigga?" Lil'Ray unfolded the letter, mumbling something underneath his breath.

I stood there and watched Lil'Ray's facial expression change from curiosity to rage as he read Paul-Paul's letter. I could tell exactly when he got to the part where Paul-Paul explained how someone had caught Kenny Bean barefooted with his pants down over a broad's house in East Baltimore. "You wild, bitch ass nigga." Lil'Ray looked up with bloodshot red eyes, balling the letter up. "You a dead—"

I hawk-spit straight in Lil'Ray's mouth before he could finish.

"Happy birthday, bitch!" I smiled as Lil'Ray ran to the sink, spitting repeatedly, and began rinsing his mouth out. "Tell that nigga Don, his folks next."

"Shorty, I'ma fucking murder everything you love!" Lil'Ray threatened before reaching between the bars to try and grab me. "I swear to God, nigga! When I catch your bitch ass...."

I shook my dick at Lil'Ray and headed on to the showers as he continued to stand at the grill and go off, making a scene. But, I didn't give a fuck. I didn't have no sympathy for that nigga. They'd tried to kill me. So, it was all fair in love and war. Besides, a man's actions bring him certain consequences and certain rewards. So, unless he no longer desired to be a man, he had to accept the consequences just like he accepted the rewards.

I took my fifteen-minute shower like everybody else. All I kept thinking about was the look on Lil'Ray's face when he realized that I was responsible for his brother's death. I didn't know who the fuck he thought he was beefing with. But, he knew now that he had his hands full fucking with me. I quickly dried off and made my way back toward my cell.

"Lil'Rayyyyyy," I taunted, approaching his cell. "Don't be mad at me, nigga, you drew first blood," I reminded, walking over the grill to taunt him as he sat on the bed. "What, are you crying, nigga? You know—" Lil'Ray's hand flew up out of his lap with lightning speed before I knew what was happening. I felt something slimy hit me in the face. "Bitch!" I stumbled backward, dropping my shower grip. "Yo, what the fuck was that?" I began trying to wipe my face off as the strong, undeniable smell of piss, sour milk, and shit began to penetrate my nostrils.

"Yeah, nigga, that's that freak-ass!" Lil'Ray confirmed, laughing, as I used my shirt to wipe feces off my face. "That should hold your bitch ass until I can put that knife in you again."

"You got that, bitch!" I took off my shirt and threw it at Lil'Ray as he stood there laughing and making jokes. "You got that." I shook my head as my mouth began to taste funny. Then, I picked up my shower grip and ran back down the tier to jump into the shower before the CO could say anything.

***

"Ahhhhh!!!" I came up out of my sleep simultaneously screaming and rolling off the bunk, knocking something off the side of my face. "What the fuck?" I saw what appeared to be a big ass cockroach sprinting across the floor and tried to stomp it before it disappeared into the dark corner of the cell.

"You good over there, Dak?" my neighbor called out, concerned.

"Yeah, I'm good," I replied, shaking my sheets and blanket out to make sure there weren't any more cockroaches hiding inside. "A big ass cockroach was in my bed."

"You over there crying about a cockroach, killer?" Rico teased.

"Man, that shit was on my face," I defended. "And that motherfucker was like the size of a baby rat," I added.

"That's 'cause you ain't seen the baby rats yet." He laughed, and I immediately got on the bed and pulled my feet up. "They're the size of kittens."

"Ayo, I don't play about no rats!" I assured, looking around.

"All that gangster shit you talk and you're scared of rats?" Rico paused for a second as if he thought maybe I would answer. "Well, since we're up now, you might as well grab these pictures."

"My bad, yo," I apologized, knowing that I'd probably awakened half the tier.

"Nah, I was already up anyway," Rico revealed. "I told you I had to dig the flicks out."

It had been about thirty days since the incident with Lil'Ray. By now, he'd been moved over to the other side of the section with Don. Though not before I paid a zapout named Lunchmeat from Washington Boulevard to boil some shit and throw it into his cell. I'd never seen nor did I ever want to smell anything like that again in my life. That shit had the entire section reeking for like two weeks. It smelled like something had crawled up inside the walls and died.

"Oh, you a night owl over there now, huh?" I questioned.

"If I wasn't, I would be with you doing all that hooting and hollering over there," he joked. "Grab these flicks real quick though."

I double checked the floor. Then, I slung the *Fast Track* urban book I was reading under the bed to make sure the coast was clear. I couldn't handle no more surprises. "Where you at, yo?" I got off the bunk and walked over to the grill.

"Right here," Rico replied, sticking his arm out the grill to pass me an old beat-up envelope. "These the joints I was telling you about earlier."

"The ones you wanted me to see?"

"Yeah," Rico confirmed as I accepted the raggedy envelope. "Don't worry about the niggas you see with their faces scratched out. Them niggas rats."

I clicked the light on, sat down on the bed, and removed the photos from the holey envelope to see what Rico had going on back in his heyday. "I see you, smooth." The very first photograph was of Rico inside a nightclub, surrounded by a gang of fine ass women. "You got the gators and everything on, player. Who the two pretty chicks up underneath your arms with the minks on?"

"First of all, slim, them there are Stacy Adams, baby," Rico corrected. "Don't ever confuse them for gators," Rico continued. "Now, them dime pieces you see under my wings, that there's Kim-Girl and Terry Hill. They're from up your neck of the woods. Cold-blooded gangsters too. I used to sic them on niggas all over the city," Rico bragged. "A lot of major players came up missing fucking with Kim-Girl and Terry Hill."

"Okay." I shook my head respectfully. Pretty women had always been a nigga's downfall. "Where you at on here?" I wondered curiously, not really recognizing the backdrop.

"Shortstop," Rico confessed. "It's a little lounge in South Baltimore, near Carroll Park."

I continued to look through the old photos of Rico shining back in the late eighties, early nineties. I could tell that he was getting some money too. "I see you all out Vegas!" I commented as I came up on a picture of Rico inside a casino with a large amount of dollar bills in both hands.

"Yeah, we almost broke the bank that weekend, slim," Rico exclaimed, and I could hear the excitement in his voice. "I bullshit you not. We hit them white boys for three hundred large," Rico added. "They offered us everything from ringside tickets at the Tyson fight to a Caesar's Palace penthouse suite with all the baddest showgirls Las Vegas had to offer, trying to convince us to stay."

"I know you took them up on it too."

"Nah, I had Babygirl and Terry with me," Rico admitted. "They don't get no badder than that. Plus, I wasn't about to let them crackers stroke me to sleep. I took my winnings and got the hell out of town."

I stopped when I got to a picture with about fifteen men and women on it. "This the crew, huh?" I said, analyzing the photograph. "Y'all definitely look like y'all doing it big boy style," I admitted. "What's up with all the x's across niggas faces?"

"Oh, damn, I forgot all about that. Them the niggas that left me for dead," Rico explained. "For real, though, the only niggas on any of them photos I still fuck with are Sam and Little Randy from Pigtown, and my man, Lil'Ant, from out Lakeland," Rico clarified. "The rest of them niggas ain't worth shit! But check out the two dudes hugged up on the white girl."

"Who the niggas in the matching Coogies?" I strained to get a good look. "They jive look familiar," I confessed, trying to place the faces.

"They should," Rico advised. "Especially since your peoples be hanging out with one of them."

"Who peoples?" I took another look. *It can't be*, I thought, trying to remove the ink off the photograph with my thumb. "One of their name's not Sha'wayne, is it?" I stood and walked over to hold the photo up near the light.

"Yep," Rico revealed, throwing me for a loop. "And that's your man Strong standing beside him."

"What?" I stared at the photo, confused. I didn't get it. *How the fuck does Rico know about my situation with Strong?* I wondered, unable to gather my thoughts. Better yet, how in the fuck did Sha'wayne know Strong? Had that nigga been playing me all along? "I don't understand, I'm lost, yo," I admitted.

"Come on, Dak, what, you want me to spell it out for you? You can't read between the lines, slim?" Rico challenged as I tried to figure out his angle. "Sha'wayne is Strong's cousin," Rico continued after I remained silent. The truth was, I couldn't talk. I couldn't find the right words.

"Where you know Sha'wayne from?" I finally managed, trying not to sound too anxious.

"South Baltimore, Bayard Street. We practically grew up together. See, Strong and them used to run back and forth between Bayard and Cross Street, up top. But, Sha'wayne was like me. Down bottom nigga for life," Rico disclosed, and that was all I needed to hear.

"Why are you telling all this?" I was sure I would've never known.

"I told you them niggas crossed me, slim," Rico reminded.

"Sha'wayne reached out to me a few weeks ago about you. I didn't put two and two together until I heard you and that kid, Little Ray, going back and forth," Rico explained. "But, like I said, I don't fool with niggas who only show up when they need you."

"So, what now?" I wanted to know. "I owe you or something?"

"Nah, slim, we're square. You don't owe me nothing. Do whatever you want with the information. That's why I gave it to you."

"Good looking out, yo." I really appreciated the heads-up, because Sha'wayne had rocked me completely to sleep.

"Don't mention it," Rico said. "I learned the hard way to never go against the future for the past."

"Aye, I'ma fall back real quick and write my peoples," I admitted honestly, my mind on Sha'wayne and the damage he could cause uptown. "We'll finish chopping it up later."

"That's a bet," Rico agreed. "I got to finish going over this legal shit for court anyway."

Grabbing a pen and some paper, I immediately sat down to write Jamaine and put him on point about Sha'wayne. *Fuck!* I thought again. I'd brought this nigga right into the house. How the fuck had I missed all the signs? The shit with Paul-Paul? The shit with Lil'Ray and Don? The picture of him standing on Cross Street that I had forgotten to question him about. Everything seemed crystal clear now. I had to tip my hat to Sha'wayne, though. The boy had outsmarted me from the very beginning. But all good things had to come to an end. Just not always the end we expected. I explained everything to Jamaine in the letter. Nothing else needed to be said. He knew Sha'wayne had to go. It wasn't how you started, but rather how you finished that counted. *You should've finished the job when you had the chance, nigga*, I thought about Sha'wayne as I sealed Jamaine's letter inside the stamped envelope and began to write out the address. I knew that mail didn't run until Monday morning. But, I would be ready the moment the tier officer came around to collect it.

Chapter 14

A Game for Gangsters

"Ayo, you feel like taking a ride with me real quick?" Jamaine questioned Sha'wayne as they exited one of the Sandtown stash houses after checking his beeper.

"It depends on where you're going, because I have to pick up my little sister later on," Sha'wayne, replied rubbing his hands together as the early morning chill hit him.

"Oh, it's not going to take long," Jamaine assured. "I just got to grab this weight for my man, Hook, so he can stop getting on my nerves."

"A'ight," Sha'wayne agreed, following Jamaine to the car. "You talk to Dak?" Sha'wayne questioned, climbing inside the car.

"Nah, you know he can only get on the phone like twice a week on that admin shit," Jamaine explained honestly. "I did get a letter from him though."

"I'm trying to go see that nigga," Sha'wayne informed, slipping into his seat-belt as Jamaine started the car.

"Man, you know Chanae got that nigga visits on lock," Jamaine declared. "You gonna have go down there with her."

"I tried to hook that up, but you know better than me how Dak is when it comes to shorty. That nigga told me that he would just get at me when he came home," Sha'wayne said, laughing.

"Don't feel bad, you're not special. That's how Dak rolls when it comes to Chanae and his mother," Jamaine revealed, knowing that Dak didn't trust practically nobody when it came to any of the women he loved. "He keeps them completely separated from his street friends. I remember that nigga ate an armed robbery change to keep his mother from getting locked up." The latest 2Pac began pumping from the speakers as soon as Jamaine started the car up. "This that shit right here." Jamaine stated, pulling out of the parking space in route to his house.

"That's money over bitches 'cause they breed envy. Now rule two is a hard one, watch for phonies. Keep your enemies close, nigga, watch your homies. It seemed a little unimportant, when he told me I smiled. Picture jewels being handed to an innocence child. I never…" Jamaine sang along to "Blasphemy" as he pulled up in front of the little spot he'd gotten in his aunt's name and parked. "I fucks with this joint right here. This shit like my life story!" Jamaine fired over the music, rocking his head to the beat. "Listen, listen, getting high than a motherfucker, bless me please. This thug-life will be the death of me. Come on, yea, and I remember what my poppa told me. Remember what my pops told me, blasphemy!"

Jamaine made Sha'wayne listen to the entire song before they climbed out of the car and headed for the house. "I gotta keep Dak's pit bulls over here, so don't get to acting all scared," Jamaine warned, sticking his key into the door, looking back at Sha'wayne.

"Do they bite?" Sha'wayne paused as Jamaine opened the door.

"Of course, they bite, they're dogs." Jamaine smiled at Sha'wayne. "But, they're harmless. They won't just attack you or nothing," Jamaine confessed. "I'm only keeping 'em because Chanae didn't want them in the house after Dak got locked up."

As soon as Jamaine and Sha'wayne entered the house, the two pit bulls came flying down the stairs. "Oh, Dak got a boy and a girl?" Sha'wayne stated, squatting down to pet the dogs on their large heads as they sniffed him out.

"Yeah, Balls and Knuckles," Jamaine replied, tossing his jacket across the back of the couch in the front room.

"Balls and Knuckles, huh?" Sha'wayne repeated. "I like that."

"Yeah, Balls got his name because he'll fight anything. And it's obvious how Knuckles got hers."

Sha'wayne noticed that Knuckles was all red with white paws. "I bet she the meanest too." Sha'wayne rubbed Knuckles' head again. "Hey girl, hey girl." Sha'wayne gently scratched Knuckles' ear. "Do he be mating them?"

"Man, I don't know what the fuck Dak be doing with them dogs," Jamaine confessed. "All I do is feed and clean up after them bitches. Which reminds me, I need to feed them anyway." Jamaine headed toward the kitchen.

"Fuck Dak got you feeding these motherfuckers?" Sha'wayne wondered, following behind Jamaine. "They're big as shit."

"Raw meat and gun powder."

After feeding Balls and Knuckles, Jamaine left Sha'wayne in the kitchen and went upstairs to grab what he needed to grab so he could take care of business. He had just pulled out a half for Hook and was in the process of getting three-quarters together for this wild Eastern Shore dude named Biz he'd just started fronting weight, when a gut feeling made him look up over his shoulder. "What the fuck is you doing, yo? I told you to wait downstairs." Jamaine closed the safe and went to stand up.

"Nah nigga." Sha'wayne quickly stepped forward and pressed his forty-five to Jamaine's head. "Open that shit back up!"

"Ayo, don't even play like that, nigga!" Jamaine snapped, thinking Sha'wayne had to be crazy for pointing a gun at him.

"Do I look like I'm playing to you, bitch?" Sha'wayne spat before cracking Jamaine upside the head with the forty-five. "Open the fucking safe, nigga!" Sha'wayne ordered again. "Fuck y'all niggas thought, that y'all wasn't going to pay for murking my peoples?"

"Hold up, Sha'wayne, yo." Jamaine held his head with both hands as blood began to run. "I don't even know what the fuck you're talking about."

"Just shut up and open the safe!" Sha'wayne demanded. "It's time to pay the piper, nigga!"

After making Jamaine empty the floor safe, Sha'wayne whacked him two more times and then began to drag him across the floor toward the closet so he could tie him up. By now, Jamaine was bleeding all over the place. "Come on, yo, you got what you want," Jamaine pleaded, still kind of dizzy, hoping that Sha'wayne would just take the money and coke and go.

"Nah, bitch." Sha'wayne's eyes continued to scour the room. "What, do I look like I'm stupid?"

"I'm telling you, yo. You don't have to go through all the trouble." Jamaine cleared his throat as Sha'wayne snatched one of his dresser drawers open and began shoving things around, looking for something to shut Jamaine up with.

"I don't want no trouble!" Jamaine put more emphasis on the word 'trouble' as Sha'wayne stuffed a pair of Polo socks into his back pocket, because 'trouble' was the code word Dak had trained Balls and Knuckle to attack on.

"Nigga, you already know what's next." Sha'wayne kicked the nightstand over next to the bed and yanked the extension cord from the wall.

"So you went through all this *trouble* to kill one nigga?" Jamaine laid on the word trouble again.

"What?" Sha'wayne asked, gathering the extension cord the moment he heard the quickly approaching sounds of dogs' paws and realized his mistake. Sha'wayne had just dropped the extension cord and began to aim the gun in Jamaine's direction, when Balls and Knuckles came charging into the room. Sha'wayne fired awkwardly as Jamaine scrabbled for cover. Sha'wayne missed Jamaine and tried to swing the gun in Balls's direction, but it was too late. Balls leaped into Sha'wayne, knocking him down to the floor. Sha'wayne grabbed Balls's thick neck and shot him twice in the body. But again, it was too late, because by now, Knuckles had enough time to get a lock on Sha'wayne's leg and began to shake.

"Ahhhh!!!" Sha'wayne screamed at the top of his lungs and shot Knuckles three or four times in the head. But, Knuckles was a tough bitch. She took the three slugs to the head and continued to attack. Shaking Sha'wayne's legs like she wanted to rip that motherfucker off. When Balls finally forced his way past Sha'wayne's arm and locked on the side of his neck and shoulder, it was over. Balls and Knuckles tore his ass apart, shaking him every which way his body would go.

Jamaine ran from the room as Sha'wayne unconsciously began firing wildly. Once the gunfire stopped, Jamaine dashed back into the room , grabbed a pillowcase and began clearing the safe of all money and drugs. Balls and Knuckles had Sha'wayne over in the corner, still ripping him apart. But, it was clear that he was deed. Jamaine ran down the stairs, knowing that he would've had to answer for what had happened one way or another. For the moment, however, he had to get the fuck out of dodge before the police arrived.

Jamaine wiped the blood out of his eye and exited the house as his neighbors watched from their doorways and windows. His mind was all over the place. Jamaine needed to figure out exactly what he was going to do and quick. He climbed behind the wheel of his car, tossed the pillowcase on the passenger's seat, and burnt rubber all the way down the block.

Jamaine didn't know if he was more upset with himself or Dak for allowing Sha'wayne to catch him slipping. Jamaine saw the police fly by and slowed down some before wiping his face again. Then, he tried to figure out exactly what he was going to do.

Before Jamaine realized it, he was pulling up in front of his cousin Tierre's house. After looking around, Jamaine grabbed the pillowcase, hopped out of the car, and banged on the front door. He had a plan, but he needed to get rid of the money and drugs first.

"Who is it?" Tierre sounded irritated.

"Jamaine!" he revealed and instantly heard the locks clicking.

"Boy, why you banging on the damn door like that?" Tierre fired, snatching the door open.

Ignoring her, Jamaine rushed inside. "Where Gwenny at?" Jamaine looked around for his aunt.

"Upstairs asleep." Tierre stared at Jamaine like he was crazy. "Why is your head bleeding?"

"I got hit by something," Jamaine lied, because he didn't need Tierre's gossiping ass telling all his business. "I'm about to go to the hospital right now," he added. "But listen, I need you to hold something for me and I'ma lookout for you."

"What?" Tierre looked at Jamaine questionably.

"Some drugs," Jamaine disclosed, watching her closely. He didn't want to tell her about the money also. "It's only for a few hours. I'ma try to have somebody come pick it up."

"You know Gwenny going to go crazy if she find some drugs in this house Jamaine, and I don't be touching that stuff. Plus...." Jamaine went into his pocket and pulled out a knot of bills as Tierre continued to act like he didn't know that her hot in the pants ass be holding pills and shit for them older niggas around North Avenue. "How much money that is?" Tierre stopped ranting long enough to ask.

"About six hundred," Jamaine replied. "You want it or not?" Jamaine asked. "Hold up!" Jamaine pulled his hand back when Tierre tried to grab the money.

"Why you playing?" Tierre rolled her eyes.

"I ain't playing," Jamaine retorted, handing her the money. "But listen, yo, you can't say nothing about this shit to nobody."

"I'm not." Tierre smiled, stuffing the money inside her bra, already thinking about calling Margaret.

"I'm serious, Tierre," Jamaine warned. "If you ever mention this shit to anybody, and I mean anybody, I'm done fucking with you."

"Okay boy, I got it, damn," Tierre assured.

"Thanks yo, I owe you one." Jamaine hugged Tierre.

"Boy please, we're family. And family always comes first," Tierre said.

"I heard that." Jamaine broke the embrace. "I love you."

"I love you too," Tierre echoed. "Now take your ass to the hospital before you bleed to death."

Chapter 15

Gangsters as Usual

I was finally released from administrative lockup and placed on N-section. The first thing I did was get Monique to drag Jamaine down to the jail to see me. I couldn't wait to see this dumb ass nigga so I could curse him out. I had sent him a detailed letter about Sha'wayne and he had the nerve to be telling niggas that it was my fault that he and his aunt had gotten taken in for questioning.

"What's up, nigga?" Jamaine asked with a fake smile, sitting down in front of me as if he hadn't been running around talking shit behind my back.

"Ain't shit," I fired nonchalantly, before turning my attention to Monique. "What's up, big bruh?"

"Look man, I didn't come down here to play no games with y'all little niggas," Monique argued. "Y'all going to talk or what?"

At first, nobody said anything. So, Monique began looking back and forth between Jamaine and me, as if waiting for one of us to be the bigger man and speak up. But, neither one of us did. "A'ight, since both of y'all niggas acting like little girls right now, I'll start." Monique shook his head. "Jamaine, did Dak write you about the dude, Sha'wayne?"

"Yeah, but—" Jamaine began.

"No buts," Monique cut him off and turned to me. "It's on you, Dak."

I knew it was now or possibly never, because as soon as Chanae found out that I was off of administrative lockup, she'd lock my weekly visits down again. "If you got my letter, yo, why is you running around acting like I'm the reason you got caught down bad?"

"'Cause, nigga, that shit would've never happened if you didn't introduce me to that nigga!" Jamaine retorted stubbornly.

"Nigga, it wouldn't have happened if you had read my letter like you were supposed to," I argued, about to get frustrated.

"How the fuck I'm supposed to know you had all that shit in the letter?" Jamaine challenged. "That you're on lockup, next door to some old nigga who Sha'wayne crossed back in the day?"

"Come on now, you know better than that, Jamaine," Monique chimed in. "How many times I done personally told you about always answering Dak's calls and reading his mail? It may be the call or letter that saves your life or keeps you out of jail."

"I meant to read it, I just sat it down and forgot," Jamaine admitted, lowering his tone. "Then, when I read that shit, I just got mad."

"Aunt Gwenny a'ight?" I questioned out of genuine concern.

"Yeah, the police just keep harassing her about the safe. But, she told them that the deed to her house and some old family photos had been the only thing inside."

"What about you?"

"You already know I'm straight. I basically told them bitches the truth. They made me open the safe, took everything, and began to tie me up when the dogs attacked! That's how—"

"Hold up," I interjected, surprised. "Sha'wayne wasn't by himself?"

"Nah, that's what I was trying to tell you on the phone," Jamaine exclaimed. "It was two of them niggas."

"So how the hell you get away with the money and shit?" I questioned. This was all news to me. I had just assumed that Sha'wayne was alone.

"How I get away with all the money and shit?" Jamaine repeated, like I said something wrong. "I didn't get away with shit! Sha'wayne's man left with the bread and work first. That's when Sha'wayne gets to looking for something to tie me up with, talking about killing me."

"Why the fuck would you take some nigga you don't even know to your spot?" I snapped before lowering my voice.

"I wanted to know the same thing when I found out," Monique spoke up.

"Fuck I look like I'm stupid, nigga?" Jamaine challenged, staring me down. "Sha'wayne must've had that nigga following us. He had to have let him in once I went upstairs."

"What they say about Balls and Knuckles?" I inquired about my pit bulls because I didn't even want to hear what Jamaine had to say no more. *This nigga has to be the dumbest nigga alive*, I thought, staring at him.

"They put them down," Jamaine confessed.

"They put them down?" I spat. "You let them bitches kill my dogs, yo?" I swear I wanted to punch Jamaine right in his fucking mouth.

"What the fuck was I supposed to do, nigga? They were both laying in the room, bleeding to death, chewing on Sha'wayne when animal control got there."

"You know what gets on my nerves more than unforeseen obstacles?" Monique interrupted, probably feeling the tension. "The way niggas respond."

"What?" Jamaine and I replied in unison, looking at Monique like he was crazy.

"Unforeseen obstacles, you know, like when a cat runs out in front of your car," Monique explained. "You have two choices. You can either hit it and keep going, or swerve and crash. Meaning, are y'all going to let this shit stop y'all or do y'all keep going?"

Losing damn near a hundred in cash and more than a half a bird wasn't as easy for me to swallow as it was for Monique. "I feel you, but man," I paused to take a deep breath. "That's going to put a dent in a nigga's pocket."

"Shid, that's not it," Jamaine warned. "You know the dude, Earny-Perny, we were using to make the runs and cook up the work?" Jamaine waited for me to nod. "Yeah, well, his spot got hit too."

"Come on, Maine, yo." I threw my hands up in defeat. "What, you just took Sha'wayne to all our spots?"

"First of all, nigga, the police hit Earny-Perny's shit!" Jamaine retorted, checking me. "Secondly, that was the first time I ever took that nigga to any spot!"

"Fuck!" I fired. We were just losing all the way around the board.

"Man, I got to get home," I proclaimed, knowing that only I could make shit right.

"Well, that shouldn't be too long. Elizabeth told me that you got a trial date," Monique mentioned my lawyer.

"Yeah, May twenty-first," I mumbled, instantly calming down. The state wouldn't be able to protect their rat forever. Eventually, it would have to come out of its dark hole, and that's when it would walk right into a rat trap.

Chapter 16

The Gangsters Are Watching

"I'm just trying to understand why niggas doing all this mumbling about my business?" Jamaine questioned as Monique pulled up in front of the Crazy John's Pizza Shop on Baltimore Street. Over the last few weeks, things had gotten crazy and questions were being asked. First, Monique wanted to know where Jamaine had gotten the bread to bust out with a brand-new Lincoln Navigator. Now, Dak was questioning why his name was ringing over the jail.

"Pump your breaks, Champ," Monique cautioned, looking over at Jamaine before shutting the car off. Jamaine remained silent, so he continued. "Like I was saying, dudes all over the jail saying that you're moving major work. And that's not good, because we all know what happens when the streets start talking, Champ."

"Niggas need to mind their fucking business!" Jamaine fired, wishing he knew who was talking.

"Did you ever find out who the boy Sha'wayne was running with?" Monique watched Jamaine closely. He still didn't believe Jamaine's entire story. Something just didn't add up. "Who may have been in on that lick?"

"Nah." Jamaine shook his head. "I been looking though. Plus, I put the word out."

"You know, some of them little Sandtown niggas been whispering to Dak. They're saying you might have set the whole thing up," Monique revealed, trying to read Jamaine.

"Who?" Jamaine inquired, ready to shut niggas up.

"I don't know who exactly, but niggas definitely saying that's how you came up all of a sudden."

"Niggas don't know what the fuck they're talking about!" Jamaine argued. "I been had some bread put up! That's how I paid for Frank's lawyer and shit."

"Don't kill the messenger, Champ." Monique tapped the horn as a fine ass red bone strolled by. "I'm just putting you on point that niggas are getting in Dak's ear, that's all."

"Thanks." Jamaine give Monique his fake smile. *Dak could come home and play crazy if he wanted to*, Jamaine thought. He wasn't Quincy.

"Come on, let's go grab something to eat," Monique requested, opening the car door. "I'm hungry as shit."

Jamaine climbed out of the car thinking about Paul-Paul. He was the only person putting that bullshit in Dak's head. So, Jamaine had something for his ass. He wasn't worried about nobody else. They were loyal to whoever was feeding them.

The instant Jamaine came around the car and stepped foot up on the sidewalk, police came from everywhere with their weapons drawn.

"Freeze! Baltimore City Police! Get on the ground!" And before Jamaine and Monique realized what was happening, they were body slammed to the ground.

"Stop resisting!" one of the officers ordered for absolutely no reason, smashing Jamaine's face into the cold concrete as he was placed in handcuffs. Before long, both Jamaine and Monique were handcuffed, picked up off the sidewalk, and sat down on the curb. Then, a body warrant was produced for Monique.

"Sebastian Monique, you have the right to remain silent. Anything you say can and..." One officer began reading Monique his *Miranda* rights as another officer uncuffed Jamaine.

"Ayo, what you want me to do?" Jamaine asked, concerned.

"Go to my sister's house and let her know what happened!" Monique yelled over his shoulder as the cops threw him up on the hood of his car and began searching him. "Make sure you tell her where my car at too!"

Jamaine stood there in a daze until Monique was stuffed into the back of a police cruiser and driven away. Then, he flagged a yellow cab down and got the hell from downtown.

***

I'd just heard about the shit with Monique when the tier officer informed me that I had an attorney visit. I wasn't really tripping though. I knew that Monique was too sharp to get caught slipping. So it was probably some bullshit. They probably just wanted him for questioning.

It took me a minute to finally make it to the bullpen to see my lawyer because I had skated all the way down K-section, trying to lay eyes on Miss Glover's pretty ass. When I finally walked into the bullpen, though, there were two clowns squaring off, practically on the verge of coming to blows.

"You a straight-up bitch, nigga!" the larger one of the two spat, pressing his forehead against the other dude's.

"Nah, nigga, you the bitch!" the smaller one retorted, pushing the big guy back out of his face.

"Boy!" The big guy cocked his fist back as if he was about to strike.

"Yeah, nigga, I wish you would," the little dude dared. "Come on, and see if your bitch ass don't end up with another charge!" the little dude threatened. "Do it, nigga! I dare you! Your bitch ass already going to jail!"

"Nah, nigga, you the one going to jail." The big guy lowered his fist and backed off. "Don't forget who pulled the trigger, baby. And I know all about them drugs at your mother's house too." *What the fuck I just stumble into?* I thought, keeping my distance as I made my way across the bullpen. I'd now seen it all.

"Them niggas rap buddies." An oldhead appeared to read my mind as I took a seat in the far corner.

"Hey!" the guard who had opened the grill for me called out. "If y'all going to fight, then go ahead and fight. Otherwise, have a seat and shut the fuck up!" he spat, securing the grill. "It's always you fucking punks acting like...." He began to mumble to himself as he walked away.

When the guard popped back up and called me for my attorney visit, I hauled ass out of that bullpen, hoping that whatever it was that them old negros had, wasn't contagious, because I knew there wasn't a cure.

My face lit up the moment the guard locked me inside the visiting booth and I laid eyes on Elizabeth Franzoso. For an older white chick, she was still a jazzy motherfucker. Plus, she had the sweetest personality. "Hey Lizzy the Lion," I teased, making her blush.

"Hey Dakaron," Ms. Franzoso greeted in her high-pitched, country-girl voice, smiling. "How's everything going?"

"Fine, especially now that my lion in a skirt is here with good news." I laughed, checking Ms. Franzoso out before taking my seat. She was sitting there a crème-colored business suit with a brown blouse and matching heals.

"I don't know about good news, but I did get a call from the state's attorney office Thursday. It appears they want to schedule a meeting." Ms. Franzoso reached down and began removing folders from her leather briefcase.

"What kind of meeting?" I questioned as she placed a folder on the table.

"Depends," Ms. Franzoso replied. "It could be anything from a plea offer to disclosure. I'll reach out to co-counsel once I get back to my office to see if he's heard anything."

"I told you, I ain't taking no deal," I reminded.

"I know, you're ready to rumble, as you say." Ms. Franzoso smiled softly. "I just had to tell you what it could be," she added. "Okay, let's go over everything from the top." Ms. Franzoso was so high spirited and cool that if a nigga didn't know any better, he could easily convince himself that she was flirting with him. Ms. Franzoso and I sat there and went over trial strategy for about an hour. She still wasn't able to get her hands on the sole witness name and it was starting to scare me. "They're going to have to give up something soon." Ms. Franzoso sounded frustrated herself.

"Did you hear from Monique?" I questioned out the blue.

"Concerning?" Ms. Franzoso asked.

"Him being arrested," I disclosed.

"Monique was arrested?" Ms. Franzoso appeared surprised. "When did you hear this?"

"I was on the phone with my brother and they told me I had an attorney visit. He was with Monique when he was arrested," I explained. "He said it was a body attachment."

Ms. Franzoso immediately cut the visit short. "I'll look into this meeting and try to figure out exactly what's going on with this only witness. I'm beginning to wonder if the state's bluffing and this witness doesn't even exist," Ms. Franzoso explained, quickly gathering her things.

"That would be nice." I smiled.

"It surely would." Ms. Franzoso got up. "'Cause I could sue the entire police department," she added. "But, we're going to get to the bottom of it. I'll be back down to see you next week also, okay? Take care!" With that, Ms. Franzoso was gone.

I watched her exit the visiting room and then got up to knock on the booth door and notify the guard that I was finished. When I got back to the bullpen, I was glad to see that 'Hot and Hotter' were gone, but I wasn't trying to stick around too long. So, when the guard said that I could go, I didn't waste no time getting out of there.

As soon as I got out in the corridor near post fourteen, my mind instantly went right back to my baby. I strolled down to the post that led over to the other side of jail, since one of my K-section male groupies had informed me that Miss Glover had been working over on T-section lately and noticed that the fat, lazy ass guard was still asleep. *Look at this fat nigga! I bet if I bust a Snickers open he'll wake up!* I thought, shaking my head. He was out like a light with an open, half-empty tray sitting firmly up on his big ass belly.

"Hey," I whispered. "Officer Fat Ass!" I laughed and strolled on by. I wanted to see my baby and let her know that I was off. And I damn sure wasn't about to let no 'Mall Cop' stop me.

Chapter 17

Gangster Him, Gangster Me

"Damn." I shook my head as Paul-Paul continued to update me on the latest with Monique. "So, they're still holding him over the bookings?"

"From what I understand, yeah," Paul-Paul replied. "Earny-Perny said they were up on the unit together, sleeping in rubber tubs because of bed space before they shipped him over. So, I don't know why they holding Monique."

"Where Earny-Perny at now?"

"I think he said he's in the dorm." Paul-Paul paused. "I know his ass out all day because he been burning my phone up, crying like a motherfucker. My bill going to be high as Fat Charles ass, watch."

"He's probably on P and Q. That's the only dorms actually in the jail," I said, but honestly, my mind was on Monique. "What else he say about Monique though? Was he good over there?"

"Hell yeah," Paul-Paul fired without hesitation. "He said everybody was looking out for that nigga. Even the guards. Especially the females." I smiled at the thought of everybody catering to Monique. Gangsters always got what their hand called for.

"That nigga still think he's a boss," I said, satisfied. "Did he say anything about what they got him for exactly?"

"Nah, not really, but you know how Monique is. Yo old school. So, he's going to keep his cards close to his chest."

I had to agree. Monique was cut from a different fabric. He'd come up in another era, like my brother, Detauwn, and them niggas just moved differently. Everything they did was strategic, calculated. "You're right. Plus, he don't really know Earny-Perny like that anyway."

Paul-Paul and I talked until the operator ended the call. Then, I went on into the dayroom to play some spades with Murdock. I had been fucking with Murdock since me and one of his East Baltimore homeboys ended up getting into it when I was on the hopper tier fighting the gun charge. Things had damn near gotten ugly after I fucked up his homeboy over in the square and began to stomp him out, because Murdock wasn't having it. From that point on, I respected him and the feeling appeared to be mutual. Because when I first hit the section, Murdock was the only nigga to pull me up and offer me what he liked to call, 'an equalizer.'

"Don't trust none of these old niggas, yo," Murdock had warned when I first hit the tier. "They play a lot of dope-fiend games over here. I had to tear the fur off one of 'em right after my second mistrial for trying me."

"I'm on point, believe that!" I had assured with a smile. The situation with Lil'Ray and Don had taught me to read things that weren't there.

"I got three bodies and an attempt," I revealed to Murdock, laying my hand face down on the table.

"Let me see, I got ummmm…" Murdock paused to pick through his cards. I watched closely as he scratched the top of his head and twisted his face up like he was in deep thought. "Four, I'm not going to count the possible. It's head shots or nothing with me."

"You wanna go eight?" I looked to Murdock for approval, but he only hunched his shoulders, as if to say, it was on me. "A'ight, give us eight," I ordered, banking on my king of heart to slip through, since I only had two hearts in my entire hand.

"We're talking a board." The to my left oldhead quickly scribbled the numbers four and eight on the piece of paper laying in front of him as I played the first card to get the hand going.

"Ayo! Who last name Truesdale?" A chubby brownskin dude with some little twisters and a very noticeable bald spot on the top of his head strolled into the dayroom as everybody played on my ten of heart.

"Me." I held my hand up to get his attention before collecting our first book. "What's up?"

"The CO said they want you down medical," he explained as Murdock followed up with a seven of heart after winning with the ace.

"Shit!" I fired, playing the king of heart. I knew we were about to bust these old niggas' asses. Murdock had already picked up on the hearts play too. "Tell her let me finish this hand," I instructed, never taking my eyes off the table.

"I think she about to go on break," he informed, making me second guess. I definitely didn't want to miss the move. I was trying to meet up with my rap buddy. Which was why I'd put the sick-call slips in to begin with.

"Ayo," I called out to a dude watching the game. "Finish this hand for me," I requested, playing a spade as I stood up from the table.

"Nah, young blood seen my hand!" the oldhead complained.

"Man, Unc, yo ain't see your hand," I retorted, knowing that he was gaming because we were gambling. "He was sitting all the way over there." I pointed to the other side of the dayroom.

"Like I said, he saw my hand, young blood." The old nigga's aggression made me smile because I knew that he wasn't strapped.

"Books made then," Murdock declared, tossing his cards up on the table. "Your deal, Unc." I tossed my cards on the table too. Then, I waited to see what Unc would do next. Because if he got to punt faking in any way, we were going to tear his old ass up in that dayroom. "Come on, Unc, deal! You know y'all couldn't stop that shit!" Murdock added, piling all the cards together before sliding them across the table in front of Unc.

"Don't forget we're gambling, young blood," Unc warned, picking up the cards to shuffle like he had an attitude. But, I suspected he knew like mostly everybody else who had ears knew, that Murdock didn't have no gripes about slinging that knife. He was a hopper-tier legend when it came to putting in work.

Once the tension died, I slipped out of the dayroom and headed up to the cell to put my knife up and grab some sweat pants real quick. *That was fast as shit!* I thought, sliding into some dark-gray Maurice Malone sweat pants. *I just put them sick calls in the box last night.* When I got to medical and saw Miss Glover on post, I forgot all about Frank. I was so happy to see my baby that the sick-call slips I'd submitted in me and Frank's names the night before disappeared from my mind. Shid, I could always send him a kite. I hopped in the sick-call line with the quickness.

"How you doing, Miss Glover?" I was all smiles as I laid my pass down on the desk like everyone else.

"Are you here for sick call or dental?" Miss Glover picked up my pass, looking at me over the rim of her glasses.

"Huh?" I looked around, lost. "The officer up on the section said somebody called for me," I fired, wondering if Miss Glover was trying to play me like a little boy or something. *It must be the new glasses*, I thought.

"Oh, you're Mister Truesdale," Miss Glover said my name almost as if she didn't know it. Like she hadn't just called it a hundred times the other day as she was chasing me off T-section, after I had managed to skate over there and let her know that I was off admin. "The nurse is already waiting for you," Miss Glover informed, leaning over to see around me. "Go through that door right there." She pointed. "Make a left and go down the hall until you see a door marked x-ray. It's at the end of the hall. You can't miss it," she instructed before turning her attention to the guy in line behind me. "Name and pass, sir...."

Oh, she on some bullshit! I thought, stepping off after she basically dismissed me. I followed Miss Glover's directions to a tee and ended up in what appeared to be an old x-ray room with a bunch of broken equipment. I waited and waited and waited and waited. But, nobody ever showed up. Then, I heard voices and movement just outside the door but still, nobody came. I was just about to say fuck it when the door busted open and Miss Glover came rushing in.

"We don't have long," Miss Glover informed, locking the door. "The new girl I switched with gave me twenty minutes." Miss Glover turned around and was in my arms before I could even get a good look at her. She smelled so good that I wanted to rip her uniform off and tear her to shreds right there. But, I knew that we were on a strict time limit. "I missed you so much," Miss Glover confessed in between kisses. "You just don't know."

Her lips were softer than I remembered and her tongue was so slippery that it almost slipped down my throat. "I missed you too, baby." I inhaled her fragrance and slid my hands down her back until I found her ass cheeks. Then, I palmed that healthy mother-fucker and shook it. "Just like I remembered," I whispered in her ear, shaking her ass cheeks again as she giggled like a little school-girl. Miss Glover knew how much I loved squeezing and feeling the weight of her thick ass cheeks.

"Pull your sweats down and sit over there," Miss Glover di-rected, gesturing toward an old x-ray table, and I immediately com-plied.

I couldn't lie, I was feeling the wire-rim glasses she was sport-ing. They made her look even more innocent and sexy. *Damn!* I thought, biting my bottom lip as I dusted the cushion off and hopped up on the examination table. I could not wait to feel her soft, tight, wet pussy sliding up and down my dick again as she rode me. But, it was obvious that Miss Glover had other plans, because once I pushed my sweats down around my ankles and slid to the edge of the table with my dick standing seven inches tall, Miss Glover grabbed a cardboard box and placed it on the floor in front of me before kneeling down in front of me.

"I was mad as hell I didn't ever suck this dick before all that stuff happened." Miss Glover pushed my legs open, took me into the soft palm of her hand, and slowly began stroking my dick. "That's all I kept thinking about. Like, what if I never get to taste it?" she added, moving around until she was comfortable between my legs. It was almost like she was talking to herself.

I sat there on the edge of that table with both my legs and my mouth wide open. I had been having dreams about Miss Glover sucking my dick with those cute little pouty lips since the very first time she spoke to me.

Miss Glover never broke eye contact as she leaned forward and kissed the head of my dick. Chills went through my body and pre-cum instantly appeared on the tip of my dick and began rolling down the side of my length. When Miss Glover placed her tongue flat against the side and slowly licked up the cum. I almost lost it. "You like that, don't you?" she teased, and I swear to God her wire-rim glasses were driving me crazy. I felt like I was going to cum right then and there.

"I love it!" I admitted, watching Miss Glover like a hawk as she leaned in again.

However, this time, Miss Glover surprised me by very slowly taking the head of my dick into her warm mouth. I tried to keep my breathing under control. Especially when she began to slowly take me into her mouth. It was almost like I could feel everything. The way my dick glided across her slimy tongue. The way the head paused at the back of her mouth before easing down her throat. The way her neck muscles massaged and caressed me. But more importantly, I felt the heat.

"Ohhhhhh," I grunted, grabbing the back of Miss Glover's neck. My eyes almost rolled out of their sockets as Miss Glover went to work. Her slow neck felt like some good pussy. I watched as she slowly worked her way down to my nuts and began teasing my balls with the tip of her   tongue, before she made her way back up to the head of my dick and began flicking the underside of it with her tongue. Then, without warning, she suddenly lunged forward and deep-throated me until her nose disappeared into my pubic hair. I closed my eyes and let my head unconsciously tilt back. I was in heaven. When all the electricity finally finished shooting through my body and I looked down again, Miss Glover's head was slowly bobbing in my lap as her hands encircled my dick, stroking it as she sucked. "Ohhhhh," I grunted again, gripping the sides of the examination table.

Miss Glover slowly came up for air, spit on the tip of my dick, and carefully swallowed me down to the balls again, applying just enough suction to make my toes curl. *It was always the shy ones*, I thought.

"You didn't think I could take the whole thing, did you?" Miss Glover smiled devilishly, stroking my saliva-coated dick. But, all I could do was shake my head 'no' and cup the back of her neck again to force feed her. Her dick-sucking techniques were amazing.

Miss Glover smiled at me proudly and went back to work. She held my dick up like it was a large ice cream cone on a hot summer day and began slowly licking, sucking, and nibbling on the head as if it was about to spill over. I warned her that she would make me cum doing that, but she only intensified her attack. When the first blast hit the back of Miss Glover's mouth, I thought that she would back off. But she kept sucking until she satisfied her sweet tooth for cum. By the time Miss Glover finished draining and squeezing the last drop of nut out of my dick, I was hard again. "Come on, boy! We gotta go." Miss Glover slapped my thigh, getting up off her knees, wiping her mouth. "Come on!" she repeated as I continued to sit there, slouched back on the table.

"Hold up," I pleaded with a gentle smile. My mind needed a moment to catch up with my body. It wasn't every day that a young nigga had a bad, sophisticated, older chick down on her knees giving him brains.

"Give me a second," I exhaled, grabbing a hold of my dick. "Plus, I want some pussy anyway."

"Ungh-ungh." Miss Glover shook her head. "I told you the new girl I switched with will be back to relieve me soon."

"So what, are you over this side permanently now?" I questioned, concerned.

"Yeah, I got T-section now," Miss Glover disclosed, and it felt like somebody had just rammed a stake through my heart.

"I'm moving then!" I declared with an attitude. I wasn't feeling that at all. "You got any beds open?"

"You ain't got to worry about that. The new girl and I got something worked out." Miss Glover blushed.

"What new girl?" I was now curious.

"Don't worry about it," Miss Glover replied.

"I ain't trying to hear that! She know about me and my business!" I fired, ready to challenged Miss Glover if she bucked. "Who is this new girl and what y'all got worked out?"

"Her name is Hopkins," Miss Glover revealed. "She got a dude down on my section. So, she asked me if I would be okay switching post with her off the books from time to time," Miss Glover explained. "Now she knows what's up, just like I know what's up."

I was familiar with Hopkins. A pretty little brownskin rookie that everybody was chasing. I'd seen her around once or twice. She was definitely bad. She just wasn't my speed, too friendly. My father had told me a long time ago that women who were too friendly could never be trusted. Still, I knew all the hype was mostly because Hopkins was fresh meat. So, the minute she let a coworker or two hit, her stock would go down and she'd become a part of the never-ending 'city jail' soap opera. "What about that bitch ass Trinidad nigga?" I questioned, knowing I was still going to punch that whore ass nigga's number the first chance I got.

"He's the one that got me moved before you came off," Miss Glover admitted. "Once he found out you were coming back on that side of the jail, he got the captain to relocate me. But, what he doesn't know won't hurt him," she added, raising her eyebrows sneakily.

"Yo a real lame." I hopped off the table. I definitely wanted some of that pussy now. I had to re-mark my territory. "Pull them pants down and put your hands up on the wall right there," I demanded. "You know how I like it!"

"Dakaron," Miss Glover complained but still followed my commands. I stood there and watched her wiggle them uniform pants over her ass cheeks before pushing them down to her mid-thigh. Then, she stumbled over to the wall to do as she was told. "You got three minutes."

Miss Glover looked back over her shoulder all seductively after checking her waist watch.

"Shid, all I need is two!" I assured, closing the gap between us. Watching all that honey-roasted ass spill out of those uniform pants like a tub of Pillsbury Doughboy biscuit had me ready to nut.

I stepped right up behind Miss Glover and slapped her on that big ol' ass. I knew there wasn't enough time for me to enjoy that phat, pretty little, hairy pussy the way I really wanted to. But, I had to do something. So, I squatted down just long enough to stick my face in between Miss Glover's ass cheeks and slowly lick her from her clitoris to her asshole a few times. Her pussy still tasted good, like fresh, juicy peaches.

"Sssssss, boyyyy!!!!!" Miss Glover whined, going up on the balls of her feet as her back arched. "You're going to get us in trouble. You can eat it next time." She pushed her ass back into my face so I could dip my tongue in and out of that honey jar one more time. "Come on, your two minutes started."

I straightened up, got right up behind Miss Glover, and rubbed the head of my dick back and forth between her wet pussy lips. Then, I slowly slid in, stretching that hot, tight pussy open as she cried out. "Oh-my-god! That motherfucker thick!" She slapped the wall with the palm of her hand and looked back at me angrily as she readjusted to my size.

After a few long, deep strokes to get that pussy nice and loose, I started knocking the bottom out. *What he don't know won't hurt my ass!* I thought, intentionally going balls deep, making Miss Glover run. "Stop running!" I slapped her across the butt again as her pussy began to talk to me and cum all over me.

I didn't know if it was the new glasses, Miss Glover's good ass pussy, her broken cries, the fact that I had all that ass in front of me again, or just a total combination of everything. But, I felt my nuts tightening up and knew it was all she wrote.

Chapter 18

Gangster Carpet

The bitter cold that poured through the broken-out city jail windows, wasn't the only thing niggas had to ward off up on N-section, during the winter months over courtside. In fact, some would argue that there wasn't anything as cold over the jail as a predator. Especially, the ones who prayed on anybody and wanted a piece of everything. I had personally witnessed myself how treacherous the jail could be. I'd seen dudes get robbed for everything from their welfare bags to their state- issued blankets. I had even saw one guy get roughed off for his manhood—— I guess your welcoming party determined the price you had to pay for being a bitch.

City Jail was off the chain and niggas really got what their hands called for. It didn't matter if you were a one-man-army or your entire neighborhood was on the tier. If you were a bitch. You got treated like a bitch. You did all the hard labor and was the easiest target. What made it worst though, was the fact that there was no help available. I mean, the system was actually designed to where whenever an individual was arrested for murder, robbery or rape. N-section was one of the few sections you were bound to end up on. And the administration didn't give a fuck if you were frequent flyer or if it was your first flight. To them, you were just another passenger on their criminal airline. It had been that way for decades. To be honest, I couldn't count the times I'd heard weak niggas and correctional officers alike, grumble about the system and how unfair it was--niggas who prayed on society at that. But, none of them really wanted to pay the necessary price for going on record to upset it. Surely, not the suckers and damn sure not the guards who tried to play cool. It would make their stay and or job a hell of a lot harder. Especially when you consider the fact that, the current system made it easier for a predator to eat and placed a gangster in a better position to turn a guard for profit or pussy.

"I don't even see how they can both try me for the same crime!" Monique proclaimed, moving his lady-rook to the center of the chessboard for absolutely no reason.

"What Miss Franzoso say?" I questioned studying the board before I moved. Monique and I were sitting in the dayroom at one of the tables, discussing his case over a game of chest. Or more like rather, he was teaching me how to play as we discussed how both the federal government and state district attorney wanted a pound of flesh.

"She's only representing me on the state level." Monique replied as I captured his free rook with one of my knights. "As it turns out, the state only grabbed me because they got wind that the feds where about to close in."

"If it's free! It's for me baby!" I teased sitting the rook next to the chessboard with the other three pawns and knight I'd already taken.

By now, both Earny-Perny and Monique were on the section. Monique due to his charges and Earny-Perny due to a favor. I had gotten Willie Bates to pull some strings to have Earny-Perny moved over on the strength because he kept sending my kites. The benefits of having a homeboy on the inmate counsel board.

"Free's not always free." Monique brought his bishop out of the corner to take my pawn. "Remember to always pay attention where your opponent's pieces are," Monique reminded. When he had first hit the jail, everybody started flocking to him, dick-riding like crazy. Even the tier officer, he just straight up took the tier-rep spot and gave it to Monique and niggas laid down like it wasn't an issue. "Don't sleep."

"Why your lawyer can't represent you with the feds if you paid her?" Earny-Perny inquired, making me cut my eye at him. No wonder why Monique didn't like his little chimpanzee-looking ass. He was too fucking nosey.

"She hit me with some conflict of interest shit," Monique explained, keeping his cool. But, I could tell that he was a little irritated by Earny-Perny's presence. When it was Monique's move again. He brought the queen completely across the board and sat it directly in front of my king. "Check!" He declared. "Mate in three." He warned.

"Mate in three?" I repeated analyzing the board with a smile. I didn't know what Monique thought he saw, but he was wrong. "I'd like to see that," I challenged. I mean, I knew that I was just learning, but I wasn't that sweet. Monique was slipping. He was probably blinded by his frustration. Especially since, the feds and state were tag-teaming his ass. Hitting him with all types of charges. Shit I had never even heard of, like security fraud. It almost seemed like every week somebody from one agency or the other was paying him a visit, contacting Ms. Franzoso or just simply bringing him up on new charges. Whatever the case, if Monique thought that he had me cornered, he had another thing   coming. "You're good, but not that good." I blocked the check with a knight.

"Don't forget who taught you how to play, Dak," Earny-Perny added his two cents but I waved him off. I was trying to concentrate on winning.

"You know what your problem is Champ?" Monique pushed his man- bishop-pawn to bishop six.

"Why don't you tell me." I countered by snatching his bishop-pawn off the board with another pawn.

"You can't see the bigger picture," Monique slide his other bishop out. "You're so focus on what you don't want to lose, that you have forgotten about what you can."

"Yeah, I know. But checkmate in one," I stood up and pumped my fist up in the air, smiling. "The student has become the teacher!" I taunted, knowing that it was over. Monique had fucked around and slept on me. He talked all that chess master shit and got his ass whipped. I thought as he sat there staring at the board trying to figure out what had happened.

"You know the difference between those who succeed and those who fail isn't what they have--it's what they choose to do with their resources," Monique slowly picked up his other knight with the tips of his thumb and index-Finger and held it in the air, above the board before continuing. "You see Champ, when a king knows how to use his pawns, he always comes out on top. Even when it may appear he's on the verge of defeat," with that being said, Monique swung the knight around in an 'L' shape and sat it down on the board. "Checkmate!"

"Hell no!" I fired staring at the board in disbelief. I had been so sure I had him. "How the fuck I slip that?"

"What we believe to be true, becomes what's true," Monique schooled me. "I tell you all the time Champ, you're too nearsighted. You got to learn how to see the whole picture. The start as well as the finish. That's the only way you're ever going to win at this game we call life."

"Man, we're moving in together!" I exclaimed excitedly soaking up all the game Monique was giving me. "I'ma master this chess shit!"

"I hear you," Monique smiled. "If you can master chess, you can master life. Because it teaches you how to always make the better move for the king."

"I was tripping you didn't see that coming," Earny-Perny interjected. "I peeped the move as soon as he castled."

"Nigga, you didn't peep shit!" I retorted, and even Monique couldn't help but to laugh.

Chapter 19

A Gangster and a Gentleman

Getting back over the jail. I hopped in the shower and then went to jump on the phone after telling Monique what had happened in court and getting the run down on Murdock's situation. "What's up baby?" were the first words out of Chanae's mouth after she pressed one to accept the collect cell.

"Nothing really, ready to get this shit over with," I admitted frustrated. "These bitches keep playing the postponement game."

"I know," Chanae agreed supportively. "I love you, Dakaron."

"I love you too, baby," I replied. I knew Chanae was just trying to encourage me to stay strong and really didn't know what to say. "Why Shawn and Ebony didn't come to court today?" I questioned knowing I needed all the support I could get up in that courthouse.

"I don't know," Chanae confessed. "But, I'ma call and find out because I told everybody you went to court today."

Chanae and I sat on the phone in silence for a moment. And I thought about Frank's warning before I decided to go ahead and address my issue. "The next time you send me a letter of lies, we're going to become unbenefit," I threatened, referring to the letter Chanae had mailed in response to my letter accusing her of hanging out with some clown. I wasn't trying to hear all that shit Frank was talking about, not jeopardizing an accomplice for an ally. I didn't even know the difference. And the whole explanation about one only supporting you for so long and the other riding to the bitter end didn't change that.

"Dakaron, don't start with me, okay?" Chanae warned.

"You heard what I said," I retorted. "You ain't got to lie to me. If you want to get your pussy wet, go ahead."

"You know what, Dakaron, whatever." Chanae sucked her teeth and exhaled all dramatically.

"Yeah, whatever then," I snapped. Chanae knew how much I hated liars. Especially now that I was constantly surrounded by them in jail all day. Any person who would lie when they could just as easily tell the truth was weak in my eyes.

"Like I said in my letter, people kill me, they didn't even know what they're talking about. Eugene just cool. He know what it's like," Chanae defended, and I couldn't help but to laugh sarcastically.

"Look, they're about to lock us in for an emergency count," I needed to get off the phone with Chanae before we got into it because I knew all about the 'just cool' category. A lot of dudes over the jail with me girls had told them the same thing. Next thing they knew, the same 'just cool' guy became a major factor. "I'll try to call you back if we make it back out."

"Okay. I love you, Dakaron, and I'm here," Chanae said before I hung up the phone.

"You went out there and said something stupid to that girl anyway, didn't you?" Monique questioned the moment I stepped back in the cell with my face all ballad up. "I told you to leave that shit alone, Champ. You got to pick your battles in the joint. And that's not one you want to fight as long as she's taking care of business."

That was easy for Monique to say because he didn't give a fuck about women. To him they were all a means to an end. Nothing more, nothing less. "She lied to me yo," I shook my head in anger.

"What do you think that's the first time she lied to you?" Monique smiled at me in wonder.

"Yeah," I admitted, lying was equal to cross. "I mean, she may have lied about some bull shit," I corrected. "But, she ain't lie about nothing that matters, because she knows how I feel about that." I thought back to some of the conversation Chanae and I had about lying.

"She knows I'll never look at her the same again because it only takes one lie to destroy the trust. I even confessed when I burnt her because I'd rather tell her the truth and hurt her. Then, to have her find out on her own."

"Yeah well, trust me when I tell you. All woman lie. Especially to niggas locked up," Monique disclosed harshly. "This just the first time you caught her Champ."

"Man, I don't even want to talk about that shit no more," I mumbled walking over to the bunk. My head was hurting. "I'ma bout to lay down."

"You got a lot to learn about women, Champ," Monique said exiting the call. "A whole lot."

Chapter 20

Gangster When Nobody Else Is

"What, you about to go call wifey?" Monique inquired as I stood at the sink, brushing my teeth.

"Nah, we're still beefing," I replied, spitting toothpaste into the toilet. "I got to run up this gym real quick," I added before rinsing my mouth out with water. "I told you Willie Bates sent me a kite last night."

"You want me to talk to Earny-Perny for you?"

"Man, fuck Earny-Perny," I barked over my shoulder. "I said all I had to say to that nigga last night. He talking all that, 'I'm not hurting his feelings shit!' But, he better not pull me up about none of these niggas no more," I spat seriously. I was already mad at Chanae too.

"Cool, you know I don't like his little ass anyway. He complain too much." Monique sat up and slipped his feet into his slippers, yawning. "You better get that girl before sport-coat really lock that thang down," Monique joked.

"Let me finish getting myself together before they hit these doors." I ignored Monique and turned back around to continue washing my face and stuff.

I usually didn't play the early morning gym. Especially on Saturdays, because I was too busy getting shaped up or trying to figure out exactly what it was that I was going to wear down on the dance floor to see Chanae for my weekly visit. But, since we were beefing and I didn't even know if Chanae was coming, I decided to go fuck with Willie Bates and see what was on his mind. When the cell doors came open for gym, I grabbed my knife, left Monique at the sink brushing his hair, and strolled off the tier with everybody else in route to the gym to see Willie Bates. I walked into the gym focused. Slowly checking out the scene to see if anything was off as I made my way over to the bleachers. The situations with Fat Relly and Sha'wayne had woke me up and I would never sleep on niggas ever again.

"Up here, little Dakaron!" Willie Bates leaned out of the Inmate Counsel Office waving before I could get comfortable on the bleachers. I walked across the gym, hopped up on the stage and made my way over to Willie Bates. "What's up, yo?" I gave him some love.

"Ain't too much, jack," Willie Bates broke the embrace. "Come on in the office, so I can holler at you real quick."

I followed Willie Bates into the Inmate Counsel Office and sat down in the corner, watching the door. It wasn't that I didn't trust Willie Bates. That was my nigga. It was the motherfuckers on the other side of the door that I wanted to keep my eyes out for. "So what's up Chill?" I questioned ready to get straight to whatever it was that had him getting me out of the rack at eight o'clock in the morning.

"You know you my little man right, jack?" Willie Bates sat on the edge of the table. "And you know that I'd never bring you no bullshit?"

I immediately started shaking my head because I already knew what it was about. *These bitch ass niggas ain't stop acting like broads yet!* I thought. "Listen, Chill, before you even try to get me to bust a move, I'm telling you straight up yo, I don't got no horse." I declared honestly. The truth was Monique was the one with the horse. But, I was beginning to learn that there were more whores over the jail then, there was on Pennsylvania Avenue. I mean, these girlie niggas, would say or do anything to get some money. Even spread false rumors about me because I be going down to medical a few times a week.

"Nah jack, I don't wanna holler at you about no horse. That's your business," Willie Bates clarified. "I need to holler at you about your man, Monique."

"What about Monique?" I perked up, he had my attention now.

"Niggas, saying he snitching jack," Willie Bates stared at me.

"What!" I shot to my feet. "Who?" I wanted to know so that I could make a nigga stand on that shit. "Nigga don't know what the fucking they're talking about!" I fired defensively. "Who said it, one of these niggas in the gym?" I moved toward the door ready to put that knife in whoever behind Monique. "Who he telling on? He don't even have any rap buddies!"

"Come on jack, chill out," Willie Bates walked over to close the office door. "Look jack, you know I respect you. And you know that I would not come to you without doing my homework first," Willie Bates explained, and I couldn't do nothing but nod my head, because I knew that Willie Bates had never been the type to just run with something he heard. "That's why I'm pulling your coat-tail about it now. I know how much you fuck with Monique."

I took a deep breath and exhaled, trying to calm myself down. "So you investigated it?" I questioned, and Willie Bates nodded. "So, who is he supposed to be telling on?" I had to know.

"A dude named Little Ache from Murphy Holmes that's on the tier with me. And then, Big Head, our man down the 'Cut' doing life, confirmed it."

I couldn't help but to smile. "I know Lil'Ache, that's my brother's man," I revealed, knowing that shit would be cleared up in no time because Lil'Ache's word was good. "And you said, niggas saying Lil'Ache pushing that?" I wanted to be certain before I sent Lil'Ache a kite.

"Yeah, I talked to shorty personally," Willie Bates confirmed. "He even told me that Monique got Efrem and another cat named Hollywood put to sleep to keep the truth from coming out."

Willie Bates knocked the wind out of me when he said Hollywood's and Efrem's names. I sat back down and began to replay the incidents with Efrem and Hollywood over in my head. *Nah*, I thought, staring at Willie Bates with a blank expression. Monique had handed me Efrem as a birthday gift. And the nigga Hollywood was hot. Monique even thought he was the reason the feds got on my brother.

"You're too young to remember Efrem, his pretty-boy ass was before your time. He would've fucked with you though." Willie Bates brought me out of my daze. "Anyway, though, Efrem was robbing everything! He put that bite on Monique's ass a couple of times too. But see, Big Head put a stop to that shit because Monique was getting him. But, once it came out that Monique was a rat, Big

Head washed his hands with him and wolves came out. So, Monique...."

Willie Bates was blowing my mind. Could Monique actually be a rat? The same type of creature he claimed to despise. The same type of nigga he always preached to me about. I listened to Willie Bates until my head began to hurt. Then, I slowly walked back to the section lost. My mind was on all the things we talked about in the cell. All the secrets I'd revealed about myself and others. I started thinking about when Monique told me about how the game was so fucked up. How men and rats looked and acted so much alike that you couldn't even tell them apart at times. But, I knew what Willie Bates was saying could not be true.

Lil'Ache had to be hating on Monique or something. There had to be some bad blood. Maybe Monique had taken him off for the weed and blow he sent over. *What about Efrem and Hollywood though?* I thought, wondering how Monique would explain that. *What if this nigga really told?* I questioned, honestly, considering for the first time if Monique was fucked up. After all, Willie Bates was solid and his word was golden. I wanted to just forget about it until I got this allege paperwork from Lil'Ache, but my conscious wouldn't allow it, no matter how much I trusted and believed in Monique. The naive little pulp, who just automatically rejected anything bad against people he loved or respected was gone. He'd died and went down the drain along with my blood in that K-section shower when I almost died.

I hit the tier and shot straight up to the cell after checking the dayroom. I had to get to the bottom of this snitching shit immediately, because as they say, 'it was better to be safe than sorry.' "Ayo, you seen my cell buddy?" I asked my neighbor noticing that Monique wasn't in the cell.

"He went on a visit about ten minutes ago," My neighbor informed going back to whatever it was that he was doing.

I looked at my watch, 9:13 a.m. I had forgotten all about visits. But, I knew if Chanae was coming, she wouldn't be down until around twelve thirty, one. I walked back into the cell. I didn't know what to do with myself. I wanted to talk to somebody. But, Earny-

Perny and I weren't getting along too good because his goofy ass, kept trying to act like my father every time I had to lean on a nigga, and Murdock was on lockup for chopping a nigga up over a Baltimore Ravens game.

Before I realized what I was doing, I had flipped Monique's bed back and started going through his mail, looking for clues. I found a couple of letters from his sister and decided to see what she had to say. Shid, if he was talking to anybody about telling. It would be his sister. I opened the first letter and began to read before I realized that the letter had to be from somebody else, because it was talking about sucking dick, eating pussy and stuff. It kind of threw me off. But, when I opened the next the envelope and saw the butt-naked pictures of Monique's sister, I was fucked up. *This nigga got naked flicks of his own sister?* I thought staring at her for a while. I couldn't help myself. Monique's sister had always been a bad motherfucker. Every time I was around her, I'd be lusting. So, now that I knew that the body was banging too. It was over. She had her pussy hair trimmed nice and low, so I could really see the inside of her pretty pink pussy.

After lusting off Monique's sister for a few minutes, I decided to actually read one of her letters now. I wasn't two lines into the letter when I discovered that she wasn't actually Monique's sister. In fact, he was fucking her. Which I didn't understand. Why lie to me about it though? I stuffed the photos back inside the envelope and went under the bunk to go through Monique's legal work. I pulled the bag out, untied it and sat down on the bed to see exactly what was going on with my nigga.

The papers fell from my hands when I stumbled across confirmation that Monique was indeed a rat. A paid informant. A cold-blooded snitch. I felt a tear roll slowly down my cheek. I was crushed, confused. How the fuck could Monique be a rat? There had to be a good explanation for it. Maybe he was playing. Maybe he had just said he would knowing that he wouldn't. I wiped away my tears and picked up some more papers. This time I came across a statement in which Monique was giving up all the goods on some Nigerians. And then, I saw it, my victim's name. The detective had threatened to arrest Monique during an early interview, and his response was, he'd already given them the shooters on the Darryl Diggs murder. *This bitch ass nigga!* I flung the papers across the cell. He had been talking for years.

I had read enough. I began going through all Monique's shit. Taking my pictures back and everything. I took all the butt-naked pictures of his sister. Then, I found some naked joints of a few bad bitches from around North Avenue and Longwood and took those also. *All this time, this nigga was a fucking rat!* I thought tossing his shit all around the cell. *I'm taking all this nigga shit!* I began looking around for a plastic bag.

I went through Monique's shit and took everything I wanted. I cuffed all the work and continued to tear his shit up until I found the cash he kept hidden in case he needed to make a move. I even went back and took all his so-called sister's nasty letters. I was so zoned out that I didn't even realize that so much time had passed until I heard Monique's voice on the tier and looked up.

"Man, what the fuck happen, Champ?" Monique surveyed the cell stepping inside. "Them bitches shook us down?" he questioned. "I keep telling you these niggas be talking." I stood up with the statements in my hand and handed them to Monique.

"What's that, yo?" I managed to ask as I began to shake.

"Ayo, what, you been going through my shit, Champ?" Monique tossed the papers on the bed and eyed me as if what I wanted to know meant nothing to him. "Is you fucking crazy, shorty?"

I reached over and snatched the papers off his bed. "Explain this to me, Monique," I pleaded, holding out the papers again. "This shit say ninety-two!"

"Nigga, fuck all that." Monique slapped the papers out of my hand. "Who told you to go in my shit?"

"Are you a rat, yo?" I finally managed to question. I had to hear the words come out of his mouth, even though I'd already read it in black and white. "Niggas are running around saying you're a rat!"

The Birth of a Gangster 2

"So! Fuck them niggas! Which one of them niggas going to do something about it, huh?" Monique challenged. "None of 'em. All them niggas going to do is keep whispering behind my back like suckers! 'Cause they know if they get out there, I'ma tear their asses out."

"But, you're telling, yo." I didn't know what else to say. I couldn't understand how he could be so cool being a rat.

"Yeah, I'm getting money too though," Monique declared. "And I'm 'bout to be back in the streets fucking these niggas' hoes while they're locked up."

"Yo, you lied on me and Frank though." I looked around on the floor until I spotted the other statements. Then, I picked them up and threw them in Monique's face. "You blamed some shit on us that you know we didn't have nothing to do with."

"Nah, you was tripping then. And that little nigga Frank was uncontrollable," Monique explained. "But, I'ma straighten that shit out. I just needed you out of the way for a second, so you could slow down. Champ, you know damn well that I wasn't going to let you go to jail. You're my little brother. It's us against the world..."

I honestly can't say that I remember whipping the knife out. But when I slammed it into Monique's chest all I saw was red. "Bitch!" I drew back and hit Monique again before he could grab my arm. Then again, and again, and again. Monique pushed me up off of him and ran out of the cell. But not before I could stab him one more time in the side of his neck and rush out behind him.

Monique took about three steps and collapsed on the tier. I was on his ass with the quickness. I started butchering his ass again and probably would've chopped his whole head off, had it not been for my neighbor screaming out something about, 'me killing him.' When I snapped out of it and looked up. There was blood all over the tier. Monique was unconscious, so I ran back inside the cell and flushed the knife down the toilet. Then, I quickly began stripping. I had blood all over me. My face, my hands, everywhere. I stepped back out of the cell and saw my neighbor still standing in exactly same spot, shellshocked, and told him that I needed him to go and get Earny-Perny for me.

"Move, nigga!" I ordered, knowing it would only be a matter of time before the dayroom closed or the tier officer made her rounds. And then, I was fucked. When Earny-Perny showed up and saw Monique stretched out on the tier, he instantly reached for his knife until I told him that Monique was a rat and explained that I was the one who'd punished him. At that point, Earny-Perny stomped Monique in the head and asked me what I wanted to do. I said I needed to get to the shower and clean up while somebody alerted the tier officer that Monique was hit.

Once the plan was hatched, I gave Earny-Perny some love and went to jump in the shower as he went back down to the dayroom to send somebody up to his cell to get some food.

I wasn't in the shower a good five minutes when a bunch of correctional officers swarmed the section and started locking everybody in the showers and dayroom. "What's going on?" I questioned no one in particular, trying to get a lookout on the tier.

"I think somebody got stabbed to death," one of the nosey niggas exclaimed over his shoulder, making me hurry back under the shower water. I had to get all the evidence off of my body.

Once all the blood and stuff was cleaned up and we were locked in, I hid all the weed and cash because I knew that it was only going to be so long before somebody gave me up. I mean, after all, the 'rat' was out of the bag now. When they started pulling dudes out for questioning. I was kind of surprised that they actually got to me before somebody snitched.

***

"So, you're telling me that your cellmate gets stabbed and you don't know nothing?" The intel-officer questioned and again, I explained that I'd went to the gym to play some basketball and when I returned, Monique was gone on a visit so I jumped in the shower. "I don't believe that."

"Yeah well, I don't know what else to tell you." I leaned back in the chair.

"Do you think somebody tried to rob him?" He questioned as the captain came through the door. "They say he was the big man over here."

"Man, I don't know nothing about that stuff. I minds my business."

"That's the cellmate?" I heard the captain question the tier-officer.

"Yeah, Truesdale." The tier officer nodded.

"A'ight, lock him up!" The captain commanded without hesitation.

"Lock me up for what?" I bucked.

"First of all, because you and Monique requested to be moved in together. So, that tells me that, if you didn't do it. Then, you definitely know who did." The captain stated matter of factly. "Either way you're going on admin." He added. "I can't have you around here retaliating."

"That's some bullshit!" I shouted as the tier officer walked over. "I didn't do nothing!"

"Stand up and put your hands behind your back." The tier officer cuffed me up and marched me back up to the cell to get my stuff.

"What's up yo?" Earny-Perny asked, concerned, as I was escorted past his cell in handcuffs.

"They're putting me on admin," I revealed before telling him to call Paul-Paul and let him know what was up.

After all my stuff was packed up, I was led to the dayroom to wait for transportation. "Oh, if it ain't my main man." Miss Glover's sucker ass, Trinidad boy toy showed up with another CO to walk me over to administrative lockup. "You love that room service, don't you?"

I ignored his chump ass because I couldn't control what may slip out of my mouth. "Did y'all check his property?"

"He's going on admin for a stabbing. I don't think he's dumb enough to have a weapon in his property," the tier officer declared.

"Y'all don't know my man. He keeps that knife with him. Ain't that right, Truesdale?" the chump taunted me. "Don't worry about it. I'll go through his shit once I get him downstairs," he warned, getting on his radio to inform traffic that, he was transporting one to M-section.

I just looked at him and smiled. He wanted to be a real police officer so bad that I'd not be surprised if he did find the bills and weed I'd taken from Monique and put up in my property. "You know, if you put that much energy into taking care of home, your girl wouldn't always need a plumber," I leaned over and whispered with a grin. I couldn't help myself. I had to say something. I wanted his clown ass to know that I was still blowing Tiphani's back out.

"Let's go!" he ordered in his little fake-gangster, Trinidad accent, jacking me up by the arm aggressively, before marching me out of the dayroom as the other CO picked my bags. "You think you're funny, huh?" He tried to twist my arm. "Let's see how funny you are when we get on these back stairs."

"Ayo, I swear to God." I looked over at him with murder in my eyes. "If you put your hands on me, when I come off, I'ma chop your bitch ass up, like I just chopped my cell buddy up. Think I'm playing," I threatened, and for some reason, I could tell that he knew I wasn't just talking. Especially after he eased up on my arm. I smiled inside because I had been known that up underneath his uniform, he was just another coldblooded chump using his little fake authority to get some get-back against men for real.

Chapter 21

The Word Gangster Will Never Be the Same Again

"So, even after all that shit, Dak still doesn't know for sure who's telling on him and Frank?" Jamaine questioned.

"Nah, the papers Dak sent me don't really go into all that," Paul-Paul explained. "Monique just told the detectives that he gave them the shooters."

"That shit is crazy, yo," Jamaine exclaimed. "I ain't never heard of no shit like that in my life. And Monique's hot ass still in the hospital?"

"Yeah, that's what Dak said. He's definitely not back in the jail. Earny-Perny been waiting on him. He said they're still holding his bed."

Jamaine thought for a second. Dakaron was scheduled to start trial in two weeks. "Yo, there got to be more than one witness." Jamaine just wasn't buying what Dakaron and Frank were saying. Them niggas knew something. There was no way that Monique could put that shit on them if they didn't know or something.

"The lawyer keep saying it's one witness," Paul-Paul said. "You talk to Frank yet?"

"I keep missing his call," Jamaine lied. The truth was he didn't really want to talk to Frank. Because he didn't really want to hear the truth about himself. "But, I'ma try to catch him before trial starts though. I definitely want them niggas to know that I'm here for them, you know?"

"Yeah," Paul-Paul mumbled nonchalantly, looking at Jamaine strangely, thinking he had to be kidding. "Besides that, how you looking on the re-up? I mean, I know the shit with Monique jive threw a monkey-wrench in your shit."

"Why you say that?"

"'Causa that nigga hot!" Paul-Paul fired. "And Dak put that knife in his ass."

"Yeah, but that ain't got nothing to do with me getting this money," Jamaine retorted. "I still got a business to run."

"So, hold up, yo, let me get this straight. You're still going to fuck with that nigga Monique after niggas found out that he's an informant?" Paul-Paul stared and Jamaine and waited for his answer.

"Fuck no, fuck that nigga!" Jamaine exclaimed. "I'ma still fuck with the niggas he had me hollering at though."

"I wouldn't fuck with them niggas either. You don't know how Monique into those niggas," Paul-Paul warned, but he could tell by the look on Jamaine's face that he didn't give a fuck.

"Man, I ain't worrying about none of that," Jamaine assured. "I'm just trying to get this weight."

Paul-Paul looked at Jamaine, hoping that he was about to say that he was joking. But, he never did. "I heard that," Paul-Paul said, falling back into his own thoughts. "Gangsters aren't supposed to make statements," Paul-Paul added, knowing that after today, he had to watch Jamaine. Because any nigga who would knowingly deal with an enemy of his friend, better yet, his so-called brother, was a nigga that could never be trusted.

"So, you still need to cop?" Jamaine changed the subject.

"Nah, I'm good," Paul-Paul lied. "I'ma chill for a minute anyway. Especially since all that shit with Monique just happened. Ain't no telling what that nigga was up to. I'm just glad I ain't never start really fucking with that nigga like that."

"If them bitches want me, they're going to have to come and get me. 'Cause ain't nothing going to stop me from getting this money."

Jamaine pulled out a knot of cash and waved it in Paul-Paul's face.

"You're crazy."

"I'd rather be crazy than in jail." Paul-Paul opened the car door. "I'll catch up with you later."

"Bet." Jamaine started the car and drove off. There was no way that one rat was going to deter him from getting money.

Chapter 22

Gangster Time

I stepped off the court van Wednesday morning, squinting my eyes, wishing I could raise my hand up to block the early morning sun light from blinding me. It was go time. Frank and I had finished picking our jury yesterday evening and we were ready for war. We still hadn't gotten the name of the state's sole eye witness, but the judge had assured the attorneys at our motions hearing that they'd have it before the witness took the stand. Being that I was still on administrative lockup. I didn't get to roll on the bluebird like Frank. Thank God Miss Glover's sucker ass boyfriend hadn't found the drugs and cash I had hidden, because I couldn't stand to be without the phone while I was in trial. When I got to the courtroom, the family was in full force. I saw my mother and smiled. *Old faithful*, I thought knowing that I couldn't allow her to attend my trial. There was no woman in the world equal to my mother. Which was why I planned to keep her out of the courtroom.

"What's up nigga?" I spoke to Frank after I was led over to the defense table.

"Shid nigga, waiting on you. Same crime different trial, trying to picture what you said," Frank joked.

"Yeah a'ight." I shot him an elbow. "Yo, it's thick up in this bitch." I leaned over and whispered.

"I know, everybody up in this joint." Frank replied as our attorney's entered the courtroom and made their way to the table. "Friends *and* foes."

"All rise!" the bailiff called while Frank and I were in the middle of asking our attorneys a few last-minute questions. "The Honorable Judge Priscilla Carter, residing." The bailiff paused as the judge took her seat. "You may be seated." The bailiff continued.

"I understand that there's another motion from the defense." Judge Carter stated after a moment of silence.

"Yes, Your Honor," Ms. Franzoso shot to her feet.

"Your Honor, if I may." Ms. Shakir got to her feet. "I was under the impression that we dealt with all motions yesterday."

"Well, it's not so much another motion, Your Honor." Ms. Franzoso corrected. "I would just like to go on record to make a continuing motion to dismiss for the same reasons I stated yesterday."

"Dually noted," Judge Carter acknowledged with a nod. "Anything else before I bring the jury in?"

"Yes, Your Honor." Frank's attorney, Chip Johnson, slowly stood up.

"After going over the statement of facts again at my office last night, I feel like the state overcharged. And I believe the state would agree that, if you really look at the circumstances in which the alleged crime unfolded, Mister Lace should've been charged with accessory after the fact. Maybe manslaughter at the most—"

"Let me stop you right there, Mister Johnson," Judge Carter interrupted Frank's lawyer. "Your job is to convey that to the jury. Motion denied," Judge Carter stated dismissively. "The case will proceed under the first-degree indictment until you prove otherwise. Bailiff, would you please bring the jurors out, Sir?"

After stating the case number, charges and representation. Judge Carter instructed the jury and then it was opening arguments. The jury consisted of seven men and five women. All the alternates were women.

"Ladies and gentleman," State Attorney Jacqueline Shakir began as the jury looked on. "Listen closely as you lean the story of two young men who chose the streets over school, bad over good and eventually, murder over morality. Watch as witness after witness tells a tale that ends in coldblooded murder. A tale that...." _ witness after witness? I wondered who the fuck Ms. Shakir was referring to as she paced the courtroom floor in front of the jury box, putting on a show. It's only one witness.

"...Franklin Lace and Dakaron Truesdale are not your average young men. And I intend to prove to you through the testimony of my eye- witness, that the victim, Mister Darryl Diggs and the defendants, Franklin Lace and Dakaron Truesdale, were what they like to call in the streets, friends turned foes...."

I peeped over at Frank and wondered if he was thinking the same thing I was thinking. We didn't even know this nigga. It was crazy how a motherfucker could just lie on you without consequence. I watched the jury closely, trying to see if they were buying what Ms. Shakir was selling. One juror seemed to be on the edge of his seat. I didn't know if he was eating up everything Ms. Shakir was feeding him because she was so pretty or he just honestly believed that shit. It took everything I had not to scream out that we didn't even know Darryl Diggs. But, I held my tongue and kept my eyes on this one younger chick, who appeared to be clocking Frank, and felt like if all else failed, she'd be the one who came through for us.

"...all I ask is that you listen very closely to the facts and return a verdict of guilty. Thank you." Ms. Shakir walked back over to the prosecution table and took her seat.

Frank's lawyer, Chip Johnson, went next. "Ladies and gentlemen of the jury, we are not here because someone was murdered. That much we know. Ms. Shakir wants you to believe that my client, Franklin Lace was a member of this imaginary gang she's cooked up. It's a waste of the tax payer's money..." Chip Johnson got busy and I was honestly surprised. Now, I understood why Frank decided to keep him. He was young, but smooth. Conscious yet calculated. By the time he finished, he made Frank look like Carlton from the '*Fresh Prince of Belair*' and had the jury eating out the palm of his hand. They were laughing and everything.

Elizabeth Franzoso was a pit bull in a skirt. She ate the case alive and it hadn't even started yet. She talked about the ambitious detectives and how they'd been after me since I was a kid. She talked about how I'd been shot several times and only survived by the grace of God. She educated the jury on reasonable doubt and the presumption of innocence. "....and again, just as they did when Dakaron was a child. Instead of going out to look for the shooter. They chose to charge Dakaron with a crime they know that he didn't comment. Dakaron is not an angel, but he shouldn't be punished for it.

In the end, all this case will come down to is common sense. And I trust that you will return with a verdict of not guilty. Thank you."

"Call your first witness," Judge Carter instructed and Ms. Shakir called the ME.

"Please state your full name for the record." Ms. Shakir requested after the medical examiner was sworn in under oath.

"Michelle Brown," the ME replied.

"And how long have you been a medical examiner, Ms. Brown?" Ms. Shakir asked.

"Fifteen years, give or take."

"And would you explain to the jury exactly what it is that you do."

"Sure," Ms. Brown shifted in her seat. "It is my job to determine the cause of death and prepare a report...." She began to go into great detail.

"Okay, do you remember preparing a report for case number 1982261012-14?"

"Yes, ma'am, I sure do. It was the case in which I was called to a crime scene only to be told that I would not be needed. Only to turn around and be needed," she explained.

"Do you have that report?"

"Let me check my files," Ms. Brown replied like she and Ms. Shakir didn't play this game every month. They probably attended the same Church. I sat there listening to Ms. Brown describing how she'd arrived to find frenzied paramedics working on Darryl Diggs in the rear of the ambulance. Somehow, her DOA had become stable. "So I am standing outside the back of the ambulance trying to figure out what's going on. Because usually when I am called to the scene of a crime. I am met with a body."

"Okay, so after the victim had succumb to his wounds and you got him downtown on your table. Did you ever determine the cause of death."

Ms. Shakir walked over to pick up a large manilla folder off the table. "And if so, could you explain to the jury what it was."

"Yes, of course," Ms. Brown nodded. "The cause of death was actually from the shot that Mister Diggs sustained to the center mass of his chest. The bullet actually went through his heart and...."

Ms. Brown continue to explain what everybody in the court-room already knew. That Darryl Diggs was shot to death. Ms. Franzoso said the ME didn't hurt or help us and past on the opportunity to cross-examine her. And Frank's attorney only asked Ms. Brown a few questions.

After that she was excused. The state called the first uniformed-officer to the scene next. His testimony seemed to confirm what the ME--Ms. Brown said. That Darryl Diggs was initially called in as a DOA before mysteriously finding life again only to turn around and die as the paramedics worked on him.

"The calls began to come in at approximately three twenty, during the wee hours of July seventh, nineteen ninety-eight. One caller, an elderly, black female, met me at the scene and lead me to the alley. At which point, I found the body of a black male, faced down near a pile of garbage. I immediately checked for a pulse and called in a ten-seven out of service. Commonly known as a DOA. Or dead on arrival.

"After that I secured the assumed crime scene by setting up a ninety degree perimeter. Then, I waited for back-up to arrive, so that I could canvass the area for potential witnesses."

"And did you by chance locate any additional witnesses?" Ms. Shakir questioned.

"Not at that time, no," the uniform officer admitted. "When the ME arrived, I was actually standing on the ambo's rear running board as the victim writhed on the scratcher, moaning with his legs buckling back and forth in slow motion. I thought he would survive. In fact, I turned to the ME and gave her the thumbs up. Especially once they put those pressure pants on him."

"Excuse me," Ms. Shakir interjected. "They put what on him?"

"Pressure pants," he repeated. "They are these pants that goes around a victims legs before being fully inflated with air. The device greatly constricts blood flow to the lower extremities. Thereby, maintaining blood in the head and torso. Most—"

"Objection, Your Honor!" Ms. Franzoso shot to her feet. "The officer's testifying to something that is clearly outside his scoop of expertise."

"Sustained." Judge Carter said. "Tread lightly, Ms. Shakir," Judge Carter cautioned, and the show continued.

The state paraded witness after witness into the courtroom. But, they were all police, lab technicians and dispatch. The only thing they seemed to confirm was what everybody already knew. That on July 21st 1995, at approximately 3:20 in the morning, somebody drug a screaming and kicking, Darryl Diggs into a west Baltimore alley and shot him to death. There was no gun recovered. No fingerprints lifted and no DNA left. Which really looked good for Frank and me. Ms. Shakir did, however, put this one sucker named Kevin Pressco from Edmondson Village on the witness stand. But, he only testified to hearing shots and seeing two guys who looked like me and Frank running from the alley to jump into a car. The crazy part was this clown ass nigga was trying to get a lesser sentence on a city jail knife charge.

Before the state called Detective Stanback to the stand, the judge ordered a quick recess and bench meeting. "Your Honor, I would like to know exactly when Ms. Shakir plans to disclose her alleged eye-witness statement?" Ms. Franzoso went off the minute the courtroom was cleared and we were at the bench.

"Ms. Shakir." Judge Carter looked to the prosecutor.

"Well, Your Honor, I planned on providing both Ms. Franzoso and Mister Johnson with a copy twenty-four hours before my witness takes the stand as state law requires."

"You don't have to educate me on the law, Ms. Shakir. I know it very well, in fact." Judge Carter appeared to take issue with Ms. Shakir's statement, and I smiled inside. "When do you plan on putting this witness on the stand? Because all I've seen thus far is a band of state officials, and I don't want to waste this jury's time."

"The witness will be testifying after Detective Stanback and possibly one other witness, Your Honor," Ms. Shakir disclosed.

"That's not what I asked you, Ms. Shakir," Judge Carter proclaimed.

"Friday afternoon, Monday at the latest," Ms. Shakir revealed after a slight hesitation.

"Well, for the sake of time, why don't you give the defense your witness's statement today," Judge Carter instructed.

"If you insist, Your Honor." Ms. Shakir looked over at Ms. Franzoso, and you could just tell that she was steaming.

"I do," Judge Carter assured.

"I'll have to run over to the office," Ms. Shakir informed.

"I'll go with you," Chip Johnson volunteered, and I suspected that his young ass might be sweet on Ms. Shakir. "That way you don't have to come back all this way."

"Why thank you, that would be nice." Ms. Shakir smiled for the first time as Frank and I cut our eyes at each other curiously.

Once everything was iron out. Ms. Franzoso assured me that as soon as the witnesses name and statement was in her hand. She'd bring it down to the bullpen. I told the family what was up before being lead from the courtroom. The escort officer was cool as shit. He let me slide into the general population bullpen with Frank, so that we could talk.

"Looks like you'll going to beat it to me. They ain't put a witness on the stand that said you'll did nothing yet." The escort officer said as he locked the grill.

"Thanks," I nodded and followed Frank over to the bench so that we could kick it.

***

"I told you to leave it alone, but if it was me. I'd cut her ass off." Frank spat as we seat in the bullpen talking about the situation between Chanae and I, waiting for the lawyers to show up with the key-witnesses names.

"Why?" I questioned really wanting to know.

"Because it's not the first time she's lied to you." Frank snapped.

"How are you going to say something like that?" I twisted my face up because he sounded like Monique now.

"Man.... that ain't the first time she lied yo. It's just the first time you can prove that shit." Frank explained as Ms. Franzoso and Chip came through the door calling us.

Frank and I got up with the quickness and rushed over to the grill, both dying to see who it was that the police had convinced to lie on us. "Did you get the name?" I spoke first.

Ms. Franzoso didn't response. She just gave me a look that I didn't understand and handed me the papers. "We have a serious problem Dakaron."

I accepted the pages as Frank's lawyer handed him his own copy. I immediately flipped past all the detectives, police officers, medical personal and lab techs. I wanted to get straight to the source of my problem. When I saw the name, my heart sank. It was almost like Frank and I looked up at each other at the same time. I would always told my brothers that if I ever took a headshot, it would be one of my friends who pulled the trigger. Someone I'd let my guards down with. An enemy could never get that close. So, I knew that I'd go out fleeing for my life or guns blazing in a hail of bullets. But, I never even considered the possibility of being murdered in the courtroom by the words of my own mentor.

"That bitch Monique," Frank spat, ice grilling me. I didn't know what to say. I didn't know what I could say. I mean, I'd been so nearsighted. Never seeing the bigger picture, just as Monique said. I was so focused on what Monique was showing that I had forgotten about the things that he hadn't. "That bitch Monique, Dak," Frank repeated as if I hadn't heard him the first time.

"So, what all is he saying in his statement?" I questioned Ms. Franzoso, ignoring Frank for the moment.

Ms. Franzoso took a deep breath before responding. "It's bad, Dakaron," she admitted. "He's saying he took you and Franklin to talk to Darryl, but didn't know that you were planning to kill him until you were getting out of the car."

"That nigga's lying, man," I lashed out in frustration, wishing I had killed Monique back on the section.

"Yeah, I know. But, he's cut a deal with the prosecutor. He's also cooperating with the federal government. Which is where our problem comes in," Ms. Franzoso explained. "The state's going to move to have me recused from the case because I am representing Monique at the federal level. He's also the one who paid your retainer. However, since your brother's name is on the check, there's no way for him to prove it."

"So, what are you saying? We can't finish trial?" I questioned, seriously concerned. We were already in it now.

"No, I will be representing you, Dakaron. I am just warning you of the state's tactics," Ms. Franzoso confessed. "I already informed Ms. Shakir of my intentions to drop Monique as a client. One thing I can't stand is a person who flips on their friends when trouble comes."

Everybody hates snakes, I thought, staring at Ms. Franzoso. "You and me both."

"Well look, why don't you keep that copy and go over it with Franklin. While Mr. Johnson and I go upstairs to see how we can prepare for Monique's testimony." with that Ms. Franzoso and Chip Johnson were gone.

I stood there for a moment lost. Even after reading what Monique had said to the police and putting that knife in him. I still found it hard to believe that he was telling. I thought about all the shit he'd confessed to me. *How the fuck is this nigga a rat?* "A yo, it should be illegal for some of these niggas to tell." I turned around to face to Frank.

"Man, I knew something wasn't right about that nigga!" Frank spat and I could tell by the look on his face that he secretly blamed me for our current circumstances. "But, every time something happen, you go running to that bitch ass nigga! Now, look what the fuck we done got caught up in."

"Yo, how the fuck was I supposed to know that nigga was an informant?" I challenged, staring at Frank.

"You seem to know everything else, nigga," Frank retorted.

"So, what are you trying to say, nigga?" I stepped into Frank's personal space.

"Read between the lines, nigga," Frank replied through clenched teeth.

"Come on, nephew, y'all chill with that shit." The oldhead who'd spoken to Frank when we first got in the bullpen walked over and stepped in between us. "Don't let no weak nigga divide y'all soldier." He turned his attention to me. "They been telling since our people got here. Since snitching was called, 'meritorious manumission.' They told to stop their own advancement. So, you know they're going to tell to stop yours." What the oldhead was saying made all the sense in the world. We couldn't allow what Monique was doing to draw a line between us.

"You're right, Unc," I admitted, stretching my hand out. "My bad, yo, you're right. I should've peeped that nigga's moves a long time ago."

"Nah, yo, I didn't mean it like that," Frank corrected, but I knew that the truth usually came out in the heat of passion. "I'm just saying that nigga was sneaky as hell."

Frank and I slid into the bathroom to keep niggas out of our business as we went over Monique's statement, hoping to be able to punch holes in it. Reading Monique's words brought tears to my eyes. I mean, I was really hurt. Because I was so loyal that I'd have gladly given my life or freedom to protect his. That was just how I was cut.

***

Back in the courtroom Ms. Shakir revealed Monique's identity and did exactly what Ms. Franzoso said she would do—tried to have her recused from the case. But, Ms. Franzoso went to work explaining to the judge that she'd already recused herself from Monique's case and had never actually represented him in open court, though she had been retained by him for several years. When it was all said and done, and Judge Carter finished speaking in what seemed like a language I didn't understand, I 'knowingly and intelligently' waived my rights for an appeal if the issue should ever come up and Ms. Franzoso was able to represent me at trial. Ms. Shakir called Detective Stanback to the stand and it was on. She spoke about how Monique had come to be the star witness.

Apparently, they were investigating him for a series of homicides and finally found a break. However, before they could close in, Monique voluntarily walked into the Homicide Unit and declared that he had information concerning an open case. As it turns out, Monique claimed to know who pulled the trigger on a West Baltimore murder for hire and was willing to hand them over in exchange for a lighter sentence. Detective Stanback explained how against the idea Detective John David was. He felt like when you did the crime you should do the time. But, it wasn't his call. So, in the end, Monique was able to stay out of prison and avoid jail time. Especially once he began cooperating with the FBI, DEA and ATF in several ongoing investigations.

"One last question." Ms. Shakir stopped in her tracks on her way back to her table and turned around, almost as if she'd forgotten something of importance. "Are the men who you say Mr. Monique identified from the photo line-up as the shooters present in the courtroom today?"

"Yes ma'am." Det. Stanback leaned forward to speak clearly into the microphone.

"Would you be so kind as to point them out for members of the jury?" Ms. Shakir egged Det. Stanback on and sure enough, this bitch pointed straight at me and Frank. "Let the record reflect that Detective Cassandra Stanback has positively identified both Franklin Lace and Dakaron Truesdale." Ms. Shakir spun around on her heels and continued to her table. "No further questions, Your Honor."

"Your witness, Mister Johnson," Judge Carter informed, and Chip Johnson jumped on Detective Stanback's back and rode her ass off into the sunset. He basically made her admit that she and her dickhead ass partner, Det. John David, had been after me since I was a little snotty-nose kid running the streets of West Baltimore. By the time Ms. Franzoso got a hold of her, Ms. Shakir was informing Judge Carter that she did in fact now intend to call Detective John David on the stand. Judge Carter called a recess for the day, and everybody went back to their respective corners to get ready for when the bell rang again.

Chapter 23

2 B Gangster Is 2 B Cursed

The moment court was in session Ms. Shakir went in for the kill. She used Detective John David to make Frank and I look like baby faced killers. Especially after she put Darryl Diggs's headshots up on the large television screen next to the jury box and left it there. I saw one jury crying and knew it was all over. Chip Johnson and Ms. Franzoso hopped on Detective John David with both hands, but he was trained to go. He bobbed one question and weaved the other all while making it look good. when Detective John David got off the stand I wanted to slide down in my seat and hide under the table as the jury eyed me. I was so happy when the judge decided to release the jury for the evening so that we could go over our witness list and time needed to present our defense.

"....it shouldn't take me more then another day and a half, maybe two before I rest, Your Honor," Ms. Shakir explained as Judge Carter took note.

"And what about the defense?" Judge Carter turned her attention to Chip Johnson and Ms. Franzoso. "How long will it take to present your case?"

"Well, Mister Lace does plan to present an alibi defense. But, I'll only be calling his mother and sister," Chip Johnson spoke up first.

"Ah, yes, Your Honor. Mister Truesdale will be presenting a few witnesses," Ms. Franzoso informed as I looked back at Chanae, knowing that my next move would probably destroy our relationship. But shid, at the end of the day, my life was on the line.

"Does either defendant plan to testify?" Judge Carter inquired, and Ms. Franzoso looked over at me. I shook my head no with the quickness.

"No, Your Honor. Mr. Truesdale does not wish to take the stand," Ms. Franzoso replied.

Chip Johnson explained that he and Frank had discussed the possibility of Frank taking the witness stand and he, too, had expressed his wishes to leave it in the hands of the jury.

"So, what are we looking at? Three, maybe four days total?" Judge Carter inquired.

"Five tops," Ms. Franzoso interjected.

After it was determined that we would probably be resting our case around the following Thursday, Judge Carter said that she wanted to be able to hand it over to the jury no later than the coming Monday.

Ms. Franzoso and Chip Johnson disclosed our defense witnesses names and Chanae got up and walked out of the courtroom. But like I'd told Frank when we first discussed the situation in the bullpen. I loved Chanae with all my heart and I never wanted to hurt her. But, when it came down to hurting her or going to prison, she had to get hurt. Shid, after all, I could still make it up to her if I was free.

***

On our way back to the jail, Frank and I rapped about what everybody would say when they got on the witness stand. I told Frank I'd thought about calling Tinika as an alibi witness. But, I felt like calling Venus would kill Chanae enough. When we hit the jail, Frank and I gave each other some love as best we could in the shackles, handcuffs and waist-chains and went on about our business. I was allowed a court call once I got up on the section. So, I called SweetPea because I knew that Chanae wouldn't answer my calls at the moment anyway. I explained the situation to SweetPea and told her exactly what I needed her to do.

"Look, you don't got to explain that shit to me. This about your mother fucker freedom!" SweetPea snapped always down to ride. "Bitches be killing me, acting like they're not out here getting their pussies stretched out regularly. Like—"

"A'ight, SweetPea," I said before she could really get started. If my daughter's mother wasn't nothing else. She was a gangster through and through and she didn't bite her tongue for nobody.

"I'm just saying, that phony shit gets on my nerves," She continued. "Anyway, whatever you need I got you. I always got you."

I gave SweetPea Venus's number to call on the three-way after we went back and forth about why I hadn't called or used her as my alibi- witness.

"Hello," A female voice answered the phone after the third ring.

"Can I speak to Venus please?" I requested.

"Who should I say is calling?" the female voice I recognized as Venus's asked.

"Dakaron," I revealed.

Click. The phone went dead. "Hello! Hello!" I repeated when I heard the dial tone.

"I know that bitch didn't hang up on us," SweetPea spat, ready to fight.

"Call that hooker back," I demanded, ready to handle Venus myself.

"And let me handle it, SweetPea," I ordered, knowing I had to come correct because my freedom was on the line.

"Mmm hmm," SweetPea mumbled before clicking over to dial Venus's number again.

"Hello!!!" Venus answered with attitude this time.

"Can you at least hear me out? It wasn't always bad,." I stated, hearing SweetPea suck her teeth in the background of the phone line.

"What do you want, Dakaron?" Venus asked.

"Look, I got you down as a witness in my case," I admitted truthfully, allowing my statement time to take its toll. "I need you."

"I am listening," Venus retorted.

I laid my situation out for Venus and gave her Ms. Franzoso's information. "All you got to do is tell the truth. Speak whatever's on your heart. I don't care. Just tell the truth."

"Is Chanae going to be in court?" Venus questioned curiously, and I admitted that she would be. "Then, I'll be there," Venus assured before SweetPea clicked her off.

"I love you, SweetPea," I said, shaking my head.

"Yeah nigga, whatever," she fired back. "Any more dummies you were out here fucking you want me to call?"

I made a few more three-way calls. Then, I stayed on the phone joking with my daughter's mother until the phone cut off. After that, I headed on to the cell to think about what Venus's crazy ass might come up in that courtroom and say. I tried to act like the shit with Monique didn't affect me, but it did. It hurt like hell. I mean, after all, I looked up to this nigga. His weak ass was like family to me.

Chapter 24

A Gangster and His Girlfriend

The next morning, around 10:00, they called me for a visit and I knew it was Chanae. On my way to the visiting room, I dropped a sick-call slip in the sick-call box, hoping to see Miss Glover whenever I was called up to medical. I bumped into my man, Flake and the escort officer let us rap for a minute. I put him down with Monique and he put me up on a buster name Leo from South Baltimore who was telling on him.

I just shook my head, gave him some love, and went on to face my fears. It just seemed like everybody was starting to tell now.

"Hey baby," I spoke as Chanae took her seat.

"Hey," Chanae replied nonchalantly. "What does Venus have to do with your case, Dakaron?"

Here we go, I thought. "It's a long story."

"We got a whole hour," Chanae retorted, staring at me.

"I mean, where you want me to start?" I questioned, trying to stall for time.

"With the truth!" Chanae fold her arms. "You always talking this shit about lying. So, I want to know everything." Chanae fell silent, and I could tell that she was upset. "I'm waiting!" Chanae's eyes beamed at me, and I knew that she'd probably been up all night filling in her own blanks. But, I honestly wasn't sure if she was ready to hear what I had to say.

For the next forty-five minutes, I told Chanae everything. Hell, everything that I knew would probably come out during trial. By the time I finished explaining myself, Chanae was in tears. "How could you do that to me?" Chanae asked as tears rolled down her face.

"I fucked up," I admitted. "You know there's nothing in this world that means more to me than what we share."

"I can't tell. You threw it all away for some pussy," Chanae snapped. "I hope it was good."

It was definitely good. I couldn't lie about that. Just not that good. "I'm sorry. I'm sorry, baby. I slipped up, that's all I can say."

"You know what, Dakaron? You are sorry. You're a sorry ass excuse for a man," Chanae spat. "After all the years I gave you, this is how you repay me." Tears were rushing from Chanae's eyes. "You talk all that shit about loyalty. All that shit about honor. But, you don't know what honor is and you're not loyal to nobody except yourself. You talk about Jamaine being a snake. Nigga, you the biggest snake of them all!

"I been here for your black ass when everybody else started faking on you. I was there to answer your call when you couldn't get none of them phony ass, so-called friends of yours on the phone. But, no more, nigga! No fucking more!"

"Chanae, don't say that, baby," I pleaded. "You know I would never intentionally hurt you."

"Nigga, please!" Chanae barked. "Your words don't mean shit to me! And stop calling me baby."

"Hold up, don't act like you haven't done your dirt," I fired defensively, immediately regretting it.

"You know what? This was a waste of my time." Chanae pushed her chair back and stood up on the other side of the glass.

"Nah, I didn't mean it like that," I tried to explain. "Sit back down, Chanae, so we can get through this. You know I love you."

"Fuck you, nigga! You love yourself, that's who you love," Chanae screamed and turned her back to leave.

"Please don't walk out on me like this, Chanae," I begged, not knowing if I could ever forgive her. "Let's talk. Whatever we decide, I'm cool with that. Just don't leave me guessing about our future."

Chanae paused, but never turned around. "As far as I'm concerned, we don't have no future." I saw her wipe away tears. "And for the record, just so you'll know, I did fuck ol' boy, and he's not that only one," Chanae spat and walked out.

I felt too numb to speak. So, I just stood there and watched as the love of my life walked out of the visiting room crying. I prayed that it would not be the last time I saw Chanae. But, I was having doubts. The shit with Venus seemed to hit her a lot worse than any of the dumb shit I'd done in the past.

***

Back in the cell, all I could think about was how bad I had fucked up. I loved Chanae with all my heart and soul. But shit! I loved my freedom too. Venus might be my ticket home. I had to use my secrets as a weapon. Nothing could hurt me physically. But to see the women I loved the most hurt was more painful mentally than any physical pain. I didn't know what to do. I screamed and punched the wall. Which didn't do anything except fuck up my hand.

For the first time in a long time I just cried. I sat down on the bed and cried. I cried for all the pain I'd ever cause those I loved and cared about. I cried for my daughter. I cried for my mother. I even cried for Tybo. More importantly though, I cried for myself until I cried myself asleep. when I woke up, it was around dinner time. I'd slept through lunch. I felt relieved. Refreshed. I felt at peace. I knew I was doing the right thing. I put my headphones on, slipped 'The Miseducation Of Lauryn Hill' tape into the tape-deck and began writing my mother. If there was anyone in the world who understood me. It was my mother.

Delmont Player

Chapter 25

Toy Gangsters

Monday morning, back in court, the state threw everybody a curve ball and popped up with a surprise witness. Some young, skinny, jailhouse snitch nigga who claim that I'd told him that I'd shot Darryl Diggs to collect on a drug debt. After a bunch of legal mumbo-jumbo, the jailhouse snitch was permitted to testify over the objections of both Ms. Franzoso and Chip Johnson.

The little, fuck-boy, jailhouse snitch nigga testimony was so good that I started to wonder if I'd actually had a conversation with his ass before. Even though he was young, I could definitely tell that he would have had some serious practice. But, he fucked up when he said that I'd told him all of this when we were over on L-section. Because I'd never made it to the hopper-section on this charge. I was still in the hospital after being shot. There was no reason for Chip Johnson to cross-examine him. His statement didn't hurt Frank one way or the other. But, Ms. Franzoso tore his ass to shreds on that witness stand like a true pit bull in a skirt. 'Snitch nigga, bitch nigga. Tuck your tail,' I mouthed as he walked past to exit the courtroom after getting off the witness stand, so that only he could read my lips. Then, it was time for the main event. Ms. Shakir called Monique to ride the state's wooden dick. And this sucker ass nigga had the nerve to stroll into the courtroom with his cane, mugging me like I was the one playing for the wrong side.

"Please state your full name for the record," Ms. Shakir requested after the bailiff helped Monique get comfortable up on the witness stand.

Monique adjusted the microphone and cleared his throat before he responded, "Sebastian Monique."

"And how old are you, Mister Monique?"

"I'll be forty-seven in November." Monique looked around the courtroom. Everybody was present. Even his older homeboys. They'd all come out to see if Monique was really going to try and put the final nail in my coffin.

"Okay, Mister Monique. Now, would you like to tell the jury in your own words, exactly what took place on the night of July 21st of last year." Ms. Shakir took a step back so that the jury could clearly see Monique.

After all the swearing to tell the truth and nothing but the truth, Monique's whore ass sat on that stand and started lying. "Yeah well, I met up with Frank and ummmm, Dak around two because I had owed them some bread. We—"

"Sorry to interrupt you, Mister Monique, but could you please explain to the members of the jury what you mean when you say bread?" Ms. Shakir appealed.

"Oh yeah, my bad. Bread is money." This wild bitch Monique had the nerve to smile.

"And please refrain from calling either of the defendants by their nicknames, Mister Monique," Judge Carter warned. "Either call them Franklin and Dakaron or Mister Lace or Mister Truesdale."

"Yes ma'am." Monique nodded. "No problem."

"Okay, Mister Monique, please continue." Ms. Shakir instructed.

"So yeah, I owed Dak, I mean Dakaron, fifteen hundred for two ounces of coke...."

Lying ass bitch, I thought, wanting to blow Monique's brains out.

"....so when I pull up, Franklin's all jumpy about some dude who been owing up for about two months across town, but keeps playing the ducking game," Monique continued.

"The ducking game?" Ms. Shakir inquired.

"Yeah, basically hiding from them because he doesn't have the money he owes and everybody knows how Franklin and Dakaron gets about their bread when it's time to pay up," Monique explained.

I sat there staring at this lying nigga pitifully. I mean, I now felt sorry for his ass. Because it had to be a shameful feeling to know that you were a coward at heart. To know that you couldn't stand up like a man when it was time to face the fire.

"...One time, Dakaron made this Edmondson Avenue and Carey Street dude's baby mother suck his dick to foot the bill. Excuse my language." Monique paused for a moment.

"Objection, Your Honor," Ms. Franzoso shouted, coming to her feet.

"My client's character is not on trial here!"

"Sustained," Judge Carter agreed. "The jury will disregard that final remark," Judge Carter directed. "You may continue, Mister Monique. But, please do us all a favor and keep Mister Truesdale's personal affairs to yourself, Sir."

Monique sat up on that witness stand and continued to tell lie after lie. I could tell that he was just making shit up as he went along. I really couldn't believe this whore ass nigga was trying to bury Frank and me. He was talking about how Frank and I was talking about killing Darryl Diggs before we even got there and everything.

"This nigga is lying, man!" I snapped, pounding the table. I couldn't take it no more. "Your bitch ass know we didn't do that shit!"

"We'll see who the bitch is when you drop that soap, nigga!" Monique held up his middle finger at me.

"Your Honor," Ms. Shakir cried out. She was losing control and needed the judge to intervene.

"Order!" Judge Carter banged her gavel as the courtroom exploded into loud whispers. "Order in this court!" Judge Carter banged her gavel until the entire courtroom fell silent. "I will not tolerate those kinds of outburst in my courtroom from either the state or the defense. Is that clear?" Judge Carter ordered the testimony to continue once she was sure all the parties involved had gotten the point.

I was mad as shit as Ms. Shakir continued to question a lying ass Monique. Ms. Franzoso and Chip Johnson must have felt it because they kept whispering to me not to speak out. But that shit was hard. I mean, having to sit there and watch a nigga play games with your life. So, I just leaned over and told Ms. Franzoso she had to trip that nigga up on cross-examination.

"Sebastian, is it?" Chip Johnson stood slowly, buttoning up his suit jacket as he walked toward the witness stand, ready to have the first crack at Monique. "Is that how you pronounce it?"

"Yeah, that's it," Monique replied, kind of stand-offish.

"But, you actually go by your last name on the streets also, is that correct?" Chip Johnson asked.

"Yeah, so." Monique seemed frustrated.

Chip Johnson appeared to ignore Monique's response. "Mister Monique, I heard you say that you owed Franklin and Dakaron money. Is that correct?"

"Yep." Monique nodded.

"Would it be accurate to say, money in which you never gave them?"

"I don't understand what you mean." Monique looked toward Ms. Shakir, but she couldn't help him.

"You said you owed both Mister Lace and Mister Truesdale, correct?" Chip Johnson waited for Monique to nod before he continued. "Yet, you never said you actually paid them."

"Ummm, excuse me a moment, counselor," Judge Carter intervened. "But, Mister Monique, you're going to have to give a verbal answer, Sir."

"I said yeah," Monique fired, frustrated. "How long is this going to take? I already been up here like three hours." Monique added, making a few jurors snicker.

"I don't know, Sir," Judge Carter informed. "But, I can assure that you have not been on the stand three hours."

"Mister Monique," sensing Monique's frustration, Chip Johnson pounced right back on him. "Whatever happened to the money you owed Franklin and Dakaron, Mister Monique?"

"I gave it to them," Monique spat.

Walking back to the table, Chip Johnson grabbed some papers and approached the witness stand. "Would you care to read this, Mister Monique?" Chip Johnson handed Monique the papers. "Read this line right here." He pointed.

I didn't know what the hell Frank's lawyer was up to, but the look on Monique's face told me that he was on the right path. "Care to change your statement, Mister Monique?" Chip Johnson inquired, and I couldn't help but to smile.

"Yeah, I mean, well, not really. I just forgot that," Monique stuttered.

"Have you ever heard the term, 'to be a good liar, you have to have an excellent memory?'" Chip Johnson spun and headed back over to the table with a tender smirk on his face, as if he had gotten exactly what he wanted.

"Objection!" Ms. Shakir was on her feet.

"Sustain, the jury will disregard that." Judge Carter focused on Chip Johnson. "Don't test me, counselor."

"Sorry, Your Honor." Chip Johnson took his seat. "I have no further questions."

Ms. Franzoso was up next, and she seemed to pick up right where Chip Johnson left off. She produced photos of Monique's lavish lifestyle. The expensive clothes, countless women, cars, trips, etc. You name it, and Ms. Franzoso brought it out. She even had photographs of one of the homes Monique shared with his so-called sister out in Temple Hills.

"So, again, Mister Monique, I ask you. How is it that you have all these things and my client, Mister Truesdale, has nothing. Yet, you say you owe him money that you want this jury to believe that you were barely able to come up with?" Ms. Franzoso questioned.

"I don't want the jury to believe nothing!" Monique defended. "I'm just telling you what happened." After Ms. Franzoso finished handing Monique's ass to him, Ms. Shakir rested the state's case. The judge decided to recess for the day so we could start fresh first thing in the morning. I looked around the courtroom, but saw no signs of Chanae. Maybe it was for the best. She didn't need to hear how I'd betrayed her anyway.

After the jury was gone, the bailiff let me hug and kiss my daughter before escorting Frank and me back down to the holding area where we ran into Earny-Perny's bluffing ass. He had just copped out to a 'probation before judgment' plea because as it turned out, the police didn't even have probable cause when they hit his spot. I hipped Earny-Perny to the shit Monique was pulling, and he just shook his head and said that 'we should've killed him up on the N-section' when we had the opportunity.

The oldhead, Jim Bean's partner, Montray Muhammad, was in the bullpen also. I kicked it with him for a moment and told him how trial was coming along. I still felt like it was a 50/50 chance. He said 'Allah Knows Best' and told me not to judge the brother—Monique—because the enemy had a way of turning us against one another for a false sense of freedom. But, I wasn't trying to hear none of that shit! Monique wasn't no brother of mine. He was a sworn enemy. When we got back to the jail I called to check on moms. Detauwn made sure she and my father knew what was going on in court. Because like I said before, only a fool would allow his parents to attend his murder trial not really knowing how a victim's family was thinking or may react.

***

"Sick call, Truesdale." The tier officer strolled up to the cell just before shift change. I was sitting on the bed going over some court notes. "You going?"

"Give me five minutes," I requested, instantly getting up to brush my teeth. After putting the gun, bka the toothbrush, in my mouth, I got Polo fresh and threw on some brand-new, crispy butter Timberlands, hoping to lay eyes on Miss Glover's fine ass. I bounced up in medical dope-boy fresh and spotted Ms. Hopkins sitting behind the desk. "I got one for sick call," the escort officer informed as we approached the desk.

"How you doing, Ms. Hopkins?" I spoke, trying to get a look down on T-section.

"Look, it's two fifty, I don't even know why they called him." Ms. Hopkins rolled her eyes, ignoring me.

"Nah, they called for him earlier but he was out for court," the escort officer justified.

"Yeah well, you can put him in one of those lockup cages and let the next shift deal with him," Ms. Hopkins instructed like she had an attitude. *Who the fuck got this bitch thong in a bunch?* I thought as the escort officer led me over to the cage. The instant he was gone, I tried to holler at Ms. Hopkins. But again, she ignored me and stepped off. Not even five minutes later, though, my baby showed up looking good as always.

"Hey, bright eyes," I called Miss Glover by the pet name I'd given her, smiling. "I was hoping to see you."

"Look, I only came up here to tell you to your face that you're a fucking clown!" Miss Glover snapped.

"What?" I questioned, a little taken aback.

"You talk too fucking much! Your clown ass got me under investigation..." Miss Glover went in on me for what seemed like forever as I stood there in the cage with my mouth hanging open. "So, please lose my number and forget my name!" she finished, turned around, and stormed out before I could even begin to defend myself. I stood there feeling like a straight lame by the way she had carried me. And to be honest, I didn't know if Monique or the chump ass Haitian nigga had given us up. Either way, it was my fault. I had put Miss Glover under the gun, and now she looked at me just like another cornball. *Fuck!* I thought, squeezing the bars of the cage.

Delmont Player

Chapter 26

Gangster in the Mirror

When the transportation officer woke me up for court Tuesday morning. I was still mentally exhausted because I'd just dozed off. The situation with Miss Glover had me fucked up. All I keep thinking about was how I'd messed up my chances of getting her alone uptown, so that I could really take advantage of all that ass. If that wasn't enough to keep a nigga up all night though. I gets a letter from my brother, Antauwn in the feds. Confirming what I'd already figured out. That the dude Hollywood I had murked for Monique was solid. Antauwn said that, Hollywood was the reason why they couldn't stick him with the 'Rico Act.'

When we got to the courthouse, it was showtime. Didn't nobody seem to care that I would kill a good nigga and lose some of the best pussy I'd ever had. The state still wanted my life and Darryl Diggs's family still wanted my head. Frank's sister and mother took the stand on his behalf. Ms. Shakir went at them hard, but they did good. Which I knew they would, because they were actually telling the truth. *Damn, Aunt Evon a gangster!* I thought as Ms. Shakir challenged her credibility with an old murder conviction. After Frank's mother finished holding her ground, Judge Carter called for a short recess before I could present my case, because one of the jurors had an emergency that could not be ignored.

Even though, at the last minute, Frank and I had decided not to put on a big defense, I still put two character witnesses on the witness stand. Because I felt like sometimes, the truth did in fact need a little support. When Ms. Franzoso called Venus to the witness stand, it seemed like the air went out of the courtroom as my greatest chance for survival strutted into the courtroom wearing a white, form-fitting bodysuit and some black, leather, knee-high come-fuck-me boots.

This bitch just got to show off, I thought, eyeing Venus as she made her way to the witness stand looking sexier than ever. If Venus wasn't nothing else, she was a bad motherfucker. I suddenly bit the tip of my ink pen to keep from licking my lips, knowing that Chanae, who was seated on the front row today, was probably watching me like a hawk.

"Please state your full name for the record," Ms. Franzoso instructed after all the normal formalities.

"Venus Danielle Coleman," Venus disclosed.

"Okay, Miss Coleman, and what is your relationship with the defendants, Mister Truesdale and Mister Lace?" Ms. Franzoso asked, and I held my breath.

"To be honest, I can't stand either one of their asses," Venus fired.

"Excuse me." Ms. Franzoso looked to me, surprised, as the color drained from her face. I knew that Venus' statement had probably caught her off guard.

"I said, I. Can't. Stand. Either. One. Of. Them. Niggas," Venus repeated very slowly so there weren't any misunderstandings, and I saw the jury perk up. "As far as I'm concerned, their asses should be under the jail. But not for something that they didn't do."

"How do you know that they didn't do it?" Ms. Franzoso moved closer to the witness stand.

Venus went on to tell the jury how she'd fallen in love with me. She talked about how we met and snuck around. And she appeared to stare at Chanae when she spoke about how much sex we used to have. Venus lied about my feelings for her, but I wasn't tripping. The damage was already done. When Ms. Franzoso began to question her about my street life, Venus began talking about what she called my infatuation with Monique. Venus said Monique was like a god to me. She explained how I worked for him and would do anything he said. Then, she revealed that she was fucking Monique behind my back. She explained how it started out. She said that Monique was just a shoulder to lean on at first. That she would vent to him about me not leaving Chanae and wanting to have my cake and eat it too. Then one night, they kissed. At first, Venus said she thought it only happened because they were both tipsy. But, Monique showed up at her place and they ended up sleeping together.

"....after that, it just became a regular thing," Venus confessed.

"Monique would come get me whenever I was mad at Dakaron, and we'd fuck. The more I was with Monique, the more he began to confide in me. Now, I don't know if it was because he was falling for me and I still wanted Dakaron, but he would say things like, 'you chasing that little nigga and he works for me,'" Venus explained, fucking my head up.

"But Dakaron's not the type to stay underneath nobody's thumb forever. And I expressed that to Monique. But, he always assured me that Dakaron would never get the power he had. I would laugh and tell him that they had something in common then. Because he could never have my heart or pussy the way Dakaron did. Monique would get mad, sniff some dope, and fuck me for hours...."

After Venus finished testifying, I felt like a straight idiot for being so loyal to Monique. I was blinded by his bullshit. I'd shot my childhood friend for that nigga and everything, and in the end, he just turned out to be another weak nigga with a strong word game.

Ms. Shakir tried to shake Venus by going at her full force. Asking her all kinds of inappropriate questions. Things like, 'if she'd ever slept with me and Monique on the same day?' 'Did she ever receive money from either of us for sex?' But, she quickly changed her approach when she realized that instead of making Venus uncomfortable, she was, in fact, affording her an opportunity to express how much she loved sex. When Venus left the witness stand, Ms. Shakir put Monique back on the stand for re-direct and tried to clear a few things up. But, it was hard to unring a bell.

"We'll recess for today and begin closing arguments first thing in the morning," Judge Carter explained. "That way we can go over the verdict sheet and rest...."

Delmont Player

Chapter 27

Can't Knock My Gangster

Wednesday rolled around so fast that I almost thought that I was tripping. Closing argument was a lot about who said what. Ms. Franzoso brought up Venus's testimony. Chip Johnson spoke about Frank's alibi, and Ms. Shakir harped on Monique's own words about how gangster's weren't supposed to testify. She keep repeated how brave he was for coming forward. Then, Judge Carter instructed the jury on the laws of reasonable doubt, alibi, conspiracy, etc., and their duty as a jury and gave them the case.

After that, the jury returned to the jury room to deliberate and decide our fate.

"That shit crazy, Cuz," Frank began the moment we were alone in the bullpen. "Them bitches trying to take a nigga's life." He shook his head.

"Yo, don't start that shit," I warned, knowing how Frank was every time he started hitting me with that 'Cuz' shit. "All is well," I assured, hoping he didn't get to losing sleep and shit again. "We're going to beat these bitches. Get back uptown, kill that whore Monique and get some money." I was at my best when my back was up against the wall.

"I hear you." Frank didn't sound too confident. "But, this shit ain't over yet."

I wanted to tell him that whether we were guilty or not, all this shit was a part of the game. You had to take the bitter with the sweet. Instead, I said, "No matter what happens, I'm going out the same way I came in. On my fucking feet, standing tall!" I pounded my chest with my fist.

"You know, I'm ten toes regardless," Frank assured. "I might complain and shit, but I always stand the tallest."

"Nigga, I'm so stand up, that they're going to have to put my closet in the ground straight up when they bury me."

"You're stupid as shit, yo." Frank smiled. "But yo, the game ain't shit no more. Mostly everybody is snitching. All the suckers got the money and power."

"You're not lying about that," I agreed. "It's like men that bit the bullet and took both sides of the game serious don't mean shit. It's niggas on my tier who stood up getting carried like they did something wrong. Niggas can't even get a fuck you letter." I added wondering what part of the game was that? "You know shit is bad though, when the rat who's telling on you got more murders."

"That shit crazy yo," Frank shook his head and I could see tears in his eyes. "That bitch ass nigga, Monique, man."

I could tell Monique's actions had truly fucked Frank up. "Yeah, it's hard to win with them caliber of niggas in the game. They'll kill you in the streets or the courtroom."

"That's why, win, lose or draw, yo, I'm done." Frank used his shirt to wipe his eyes. "These niggas aren't turning snitch overnight. That shit already in them. It just take the right pressure to bring it out."

"They got to live with that cowardice forever. They got to wake up every day and know that they're a rat," I reminded. "Now, they have the same honor and respect they used to have for standing up the game. But, there's still absolutely no love for a rat."

"Shid, man, these niggas love these rats!" Frank replied. "Especially when they're eating off of them."

"True," I admitted. Frank was right. The game was watered down and a lot of niggas were doing and accepting anything for a dollar. "But, what you always say at the end of your letters?"

"It only takes balls to be a male. But, it take honor and integrity to be a man!" We said in unison.

"You better fucking know it!" Frank continued standing up.

"And what else?" I stood up.

"A man *is* what a mother fucking man *does*, and I am a man!" Frank laughed giving me a pound and warm brotherly hug. "To the death nigga!"

"To the death." I repeated sincerely breaking the embrace. Come what may, Frank would always be my nigga. Frank and I sat in the bullpen until the judge decided to release the jury for the day. They had held out and couldn't reach a verdict.

Delmont Player

Chapter 28

It's Still 'G' Season

Sandtown was pumping as usual. Jamaine had brought Hook in since Paul-Paul started acting funny. "Ain't nobody seen that nigga Monique yet, huh?" Hook questioned, passing Jamaine a blunt.

"Nah, not that I know of." Jamaine accepted the blunt. "I don't think that nigga home yet though. I think they're waiting for Dak's verdict."

"I'ma crush that nigga, watch." Hook was slouched back in the passenger seat of Jamaine's smoke-filled car. "That nigga know he can't come through Longwood. I'ma barbecue that old nigga."

"How you going to barbecue something I done already fired, nigga?" Jamaine joked a second before somebody knocked on the car window and scared the hell out of both Hook and Jamaine. "Ayo, you just scared the shit out of me, K.C.," Jamaine confessed, rolling the window down.

"Bitch, you blew my high," Hook spat as thick weed smoke escaped out of the cracked window into K.C.'s face.

"Fuck you, Hook!" K.C. snapped, but Jamaine knew that they were fucking on the down-low. K.C. loved them young thug niggas.

"What's up, K.C.? Don't pay this nigga no mind." Jamaine waved Hook off, hoping that K.C. had the cash she owed him and wasn't trying to get into the cipher for free.

"Paul-Paul's around my house buck naked with his dick swinging all over the place," K.C. exclaimed.

Jamaine started choking on the weed. "Damn, I don't need to know all that!" Jamaine fired before having another coughing fit. "What you do in your house is your business."

"Jamaine, please, Paul-Paul is not even my type. You know I like them young, dumb, and full of cum." K.C. smiled, and Jamaine just shook his head. K.C. was bad and she knew it. And her gangster attitude only added to her sex appeal. "N-e-way, I think he got robbed."

"What?" Jamaine quickly put the blunt out. "Fuck you mean, you think he got robbed?"

"That nigga probably drunk," Hook suggested nonchalantly.

"I know when somebody's drunk." K.C. rolled her eyes at Hook. "He's not drunk, Jamaine. He came running to my house but he won't tell me what happened. He better be lucky my kids weren't home." K.C. threatened. "He wanted me to go around his sister house and get him some clothes, but I saw y'all sitting down here."

Jamaine and Hook jumped out of the car and ran around the corner to K.C.'s house to see what the fuck was going on. "Paul-Peul! Paul-Paul!" Jamaine burst through the front door first.

"How you know I was here?" Paul-Paul walked into the living room in a pair of socks and one of K.C.'s robes, and Jamaine and Hook fell out laughing.

"Yo, what fuck you got on?" Hook was laughing so hard that tears began to fall from his eyes.

"Man, fuck y'all niggas!" Paul-Paul walked over to peep out the window.

"Man, yo, niggas high, yo." Jamaine tried to hold his laugh in but couldn't. "Nah yo, seriously, what happened?"

Paul-Paul wasn't paying Jamaine nor Hook no attention. His mind was on murder. "Keep thinking shit funny until I get that biscuit in my hand," Paul-Paul warned.

"Seriously though, for real, yo. What happened?" Hook finally stopped laughing.

"Then Dome niggas brought me a move," Paul-Paul confessed.

"Who?" Jamaine wanted to know who had a death wish.

"I'm not sure," Paul-Paul said. "It was so many of 'em."

"Hook, go grab that bag out the trunk of the car," Jamaine instructed, tossing Hook his car keys before turning his attention back to Paul-Paul. "Call up some of them crazy Sandtown niggas."

"Maine, what the fuck is you up to, nigga?" Hook questioned, moving toward the door.

"We're about to show these niggas how Sandtown gets down."

Paul-Paul knew that he should deal with the situation himself. But, at the same time, his emotions were getting the best of him, so he said, 'Fuck it' and went to grab the telephone to call up Vinny, Slick-Wabb, Moe Capone, and the Archer Brothers.

After some more jokes. Jamaine armed a small army and rolled over to the Dome to represent for Paul-Paul. "We're not doing no talking when we get over here," Jamaine explained as the carload of niggas crossed Dru Hill Avenue. "These niggas robbed and banked Paul-Paul, so we're smashing these niggas!"

When Jamaine turned the corner and saw the crowd, he stopped the car, jumped out, and started cranking without hesitation. He wanted everybody to know that he would let his gun go off for his homeboy. Dome Boys scattered in every direction as everybody else climbed out of the car and started shooting. Paul-Paul went nuts. Moe Capone had brought him an extended clip Calico and he was spraying everything in sight.

There were bodies falling everywhere. Niggas were running into each other and all that. when all the shooting finally stopped and the gun smoke cleared.

Jamaine and them hopped back into the car and sped off into the night, never noticing the kid in the second-floor window watching the entire thing.

Back on their own turf, Jamaine and them got drunk and talked shit about who had put in the most work. For some reason, nobody ever even considered what the morning could bring. They just enjoyed the victory and before they knew it, the sun was coming up.

"Damn, time be flying." Hook broke the silence.

"What time is it?" Jamaine inquired.

"Six thirty, maybe seven," someone revealed, looking at their watch.

"Oh shit!" Jamaine came up out of his daze. "We gotta be at the courthouse by nine."

"Let's bounce then," Hook said, slowly getting up. Jamaine and Hook gave everybody some love and rolled out.

Chapter 29

Dear Gangster God, Can U Save Me?

Getting dressed for court this morning was hell. I was so tired of sitting in the bullpen all day. The verdict wasn't in yet and I was starting to wonder what was talking these people so long to find niggas not guilty. Especially after they wanted to know if they had to believe Monique's testimony.

"Man, I hope these bitches do something today," I confessed, listening to dudes talk about their cases. It seemed like everybody was innocent. Ms. Franzoso had already come down to check on Frank and me that morning.

"You and me both," Frank assured as we sat there and continued to listen to dudes trade war stories.

"Yeah, what's up?" I stood up and walked over to the grill when a guard called my name. "What's up?" I questioned. It had to be around three o'clock.

"They want you and Lace upstairs," the guard informed. "I think y'all's verdict came down."

"It's showtime," I said, turning around to face Frank. "The verdict's in."

"Good luck, brother," an older dude said as Frank jumped up.

"A nigga gonna need more than that," I assured, following Frank out of the bullpen. Walking into the courtroom felt funny, but I was ready to get this shit over with one way or the other. The spot was packed wall to wall with supporters. My cousin Iesha had even come down from the Big Apple to show some love. I winked at my brother and turned around to see what it was going to be.

"All rise! The Honorable Judge Priscilla Carter residing." The bailiff paused to let the judge enter the courtroom and take her seat on the bench before continuing. "You may be seated."

"I understand we have a verdict," Judge Carter spoke, getting comfortable. "Ladies and gentlemen, no matter what the outcome is there is going to be some disappointment. Because the verdict will effect both sides. But, under no circumstances will I tolerate any nonsense in my courtroom. I will hold you all in contempt if I have to. Okay, let's bring the jury in."

The bailiff went and tapped on the jury room door twice and a few seconds later. A silence I'd never heard before fall over the entire courtroom as the jury began spilling out one by one to fill in the jury box. "Madam forelady, has the jury reached a verdict?" Judge Carter inquired after every jury was seated in the jury box.

"Yes, Your Honor, we have." The forelady got to her feet.

"Bailiff would you please hand me the verdict," Judge Carter requested and the bailiff complied.

After reading the verdict, Judge Carter handed the verdict back to the bailiff telling the forelady to read the verdict into the record.

"As to count one, murder in the first degree. We the people for the State of Maryland in Baltimore City find the defendant, Dakaron Truesdale, guilty as charged," the forelady declared without even looking my way.

My heart sunk, but I continued to stand tall.

"As to count two, murder in the second degree," the forelady continued, "we find the defendant, Dakaron Truesdale, guilty as charged."

I looked at Ms. Franzoso. "How they find me guilty of first and second-degree murder for one body?"

Ms. Franzoso reached over and squeezed my hand and continued to take notes.

"As to count three, use of a handgun in the commission of a crime, we find the defendant, Dakaron Truesdale, guilty as charged." The forelady kept hammering nails into my coffin.

"Y'all some bitches," Jamaine shouted.

"Please remove that young man from this courtroom before he finds himself in contempt," Judge Carter directed, looking toward the bailiff.

"You may continue, Madam Forelady," Judge Carter said after Jamaine exited the courtroom.

"As to the defendant, Franklin Lace, we the jury find..."

I blanked out for a moment. The only thing I could hear was the sound of Chanae screaming and crying as the forelady continued to read the verdict. When I came out of my daze, Judge Carter was thanking and excusing the jury. I couldn't face Chanae. Especially not while she was hurting and I couldn't comfort her. It would break me and I refused to let motherfuckers see my weakness. So, I did the only thing I'd ever been taught. I controlled my emotions and stood tall.

Ms. Franzoso whispered something to me about a new trial motion as I watched Ms. Shakir hugging Darryl Diggs's mother, but I was out of it until we got back to the bullpen. Inside the bullpen, I broke down and cried. "I fucked up, yo," I confessed. "I fucked up big time," I added as the sounds of Chanae's broken cry echoed in my ears. I cherished the women in my life. When they hurt, I hurt. But with Chanae it was even worse, because she was my kryptonite.

"They're going to lay us down, aren't they, Cuz?" Frank wasn't paying me no mind. But, I didn't blame him. I had been so zoned out in the courtroom that I honestly didn't know what the fuck he'd been found guilty of.

"Probably so," I agreed, knowing that they were likely to hit us with the bench. I mean, there was no sense in sugar-coating shit now. We were all in, and life as we knew it was probably over.

Chapter 30

A Gangster and His Future

Over the next few weeks, Chanae and I really began working on our relationship. The first thing I wanted to know about was ol' boy. Of course, Chanae claimed to have only been trying to hurt me like I hurt her. *Yeah, a'ight!* I thought.

My mother took the verdict like a soldier. Which didn't surprise me, because there was no way that I'd have been able to stand up the way I did if I didn't have a strong mother. I had no fear of prison. I mean, I knew it was dangerous. But, I also knew that I could handle myself in hand-to-hand combat. I was not a gun gangster and I had never been a sucker. My brothers wouldn't allow it. I only feared losing that which I truly loved, Chanae. I knew that my family would be there regardless. That's just how we were cut. Truesdale over everything.

Despite my situation and the fact that Hook had gotten picked up for the Dome shooting—twelve accounts of attempted murder—Jamaine was still in it to win it. Paul-Paul was doing his own thing, and Monique was nowhere to be found. On the morning of sentencing, I gave all my stuff to my neighbor, a wild nigga from Harford Road, who loved putting that knife in dudes. I went for him because he reminded me so much of Murdock.

After all the normal proceedings, Judge Carter denied my motion for a new trial, which made me mad as fuck. Then, I had to sit there and listen to the Diggs family speak about who he was and how much was lost because of his death. All I kept thinking about was the fact that we really hadn't murked yo though. *Monique's bitch ass probably did that shit himself!* I thought as the judge began to address Frank and me.

"Now, I'll give each defendant a chance to address this court and or the family of Mister Diggs," Judge Carter explained. "Of course, neither of you have to speak. But, I must warn you that your words, or lack thereof, will play a major role in terms of how I may sentence you here today. So, with that being said, I'll start with you,

Mister Truesdale." Judge Carter locked on me. "Would you like to take this opportunity to address either this court or the family members of Mister Diggs, who are here today?"

"Yes, Your Honor." I slid my chair back, stood up, and looked around as I cleared my throat. The only people who were present were my brother, Detauwn, Paul-Paul, and my cousin Earl. Chanae had said that she couldn't make it. But, I knew that she just didn't want to hear what could possibly be the end for me. "Your Honor, I know this may sound harsh, but I'm innocent of these charges. I was straight-up railroaded! The state let that man come up in here and just lie on me and the police know that nigga was lying." I looked toward the family. "I'm sorry y'all had to go through all of this, but I didn't shoot Darryl. I didn't even know him."

"Well, you can just be seated Mr. Truesdale," Judge Carter demanded. "You know, you were found guilty, Mister Truesdale, and that says something. Now, you can stand there and play innocent all you want. But, the jury believed Mister Monique and I have...."

The judge went on to give me life for first degree and thirty for second degree, which she merged before giving me a consecutive twenty years for the handgun. In the end, I got life plus twenty years. Which I still didn't understand because there was only one body. How could a nigga be found guilty of two very different degrees of murder for one body? Judge Carter gave Frank life all suspended except thirty-five years for first-degree murder. Frank had beat the handgun and conspiracy charge. Which was another thing that I couldn't figure out. But, I guess in the judge's mind, the jury had found us guilty, so we had to be guilty. The fact that it only took the impression of guilt to convict an innocence man didn't matter.

Being that you couldn't have time walking around city jail, Frank was placed on administrative segregation pending transfer with me when we got back to the jail.

***

Frank and I sat over the jail for about three more days before we were shipped over to the DOC House on East Madison Street and given new identification numbers. Somehow they fucked the spelling of my name up, though. Once we got to see case management, we were informed of the exact prisons we would probably end up at due to the nature of our crimes. They still didn't correct my name, though. But, I said fuck it once the public defenders' office assured me that would not affect them filing a Notice of Appeal on my behalf. Frank and I got the captain to put us in the cell together on the seventh floor since we were rag buddies.

Frank was the first to go. There was no warning or nothing. One of the pretty ass female guards just came around after breaking, calling names, telling niggas to pack up. I gave my nigga some love, told him to hold it down until I got there, and watched him walk off the tier. I think that's when it hit me that shit was real.

Later on that day, I found out over the phone that Frank had been transferred to the Penitentiary-Annex in Maryland. I was like, damn! Because I'd heard that the Annex was a straight gladiator school. Niggas were flown up out of that motherfucker left and right. But, I knew that Frank would be good. He was quiet, but dangerous. So, if a motherfucker got out there, he was in trouble. Plus, I was coming right behind him.

I stayed over the DOC for a good three weeks before they shipped me out, because a body dropped in the Annex. I wasn't tripping, though. DOC had some of the baddest bitches working in the Division of Corrections. Especially on the seventh floor. I was on a couple of them too. Clinton, Green, Day, Brown, Romarez, and Ms. C's chocolate ass. Plus, I finally got to hug and kiss Chanae again, and it felt good after such a long time. I grabbed her butt and squeezed that chunky motherfucker. It was thicker than a Snicker and I loved it.

When the bus pulled up outside the Maryland House of Corrections, nicknamed *The Cut* for its representation, I was amazed at how large but castle-like the penitentiary was. I thought about all the rumors I'd heard about it being the worst penitentiary in the State of Maryland due to the high rate of stabbings, killings, and assaults. The oldheads used to say that if The Cut and the Annex were movies, the Annex would be Chucky because it was child's play when compared to the R-rated shit that went on in The Cut.

When we got inside, we were led to a place called Center Wall, where everybody in the prison could see us even though we couldn't see them. "They got us on display like fresh fish," said one of the guys I had gotten off the bus with. "I hope y'all ain't no enemies."

I was just taking everything in. Getting mentally prepared, because I knew I was going to have to earn my bones if I wanted niggas to know I wasn't going for absolutely nothing. I mean, I wasn't looking for no trouble, but at the same time, I wasn't on no "Friendly Fred" shit because I didn't need another rap buddy. Which was why my first order of business was to get my hands on a serious weapon.

"Dokoran *Truesdole*!" The CO mispronounced my name, and I just shook my head. I still didn't understand how they had fucked up all the a's in my name and then turned around and put it on my ID card even after I told them it was spelled wrong.

After being interviewed, I was told where I would be sleeping, handed a handbook, given directions to the property room, and sent on my way. As the black gate to my new world opened, I put on my game face. Because if city jail hadn't shown me nothing, it had shown me that you had to be an animal to survive in the jungle. You had to get it how you lived; eat or be eaten. I thought about the family and everything I was leaving behind. Yeah, I knew they loved me, but I didn't know how many of them would last.

Once the black gate closed, locking me inside, I instantly felt like a hostage because I knew some serious shit awaited me. I just didn't know exactly what it was.

Chapter 31

Gangsters R Us

I ended up on the west wing, on a tier called Temporary House, in cell thirty-one. The cells were tiny but single, so that in itself was a blessing. After missing afternoon yard to go to the property room again. I found out everything that I needed to know. I was in the small ass cell, cleaning up when an older, dark-skinned, baby-oiled-up cat with no mustache pulled up and started asking me a thousand questions. I told him everything I thought he wanted to hear and refused anything he offered as I sized his old ass up. I even gave him a phony address to a female cousin who didn't exist up Park Heights. My plan was to stall for time until I could figure out what his angle was. Which was why when dinner came around, I choose not to come out.

The next morning I was on my feet before the doors hit - penitentiary_ style, trying to find some kind of weapon. Shid, I didn't know who fucked with who and with all the shit my family had done over the years. Wasn't no telling who might be gunning for me. when the cells opened for breakfast I stepped out and made my way to the kitchen. The tiers were long as fuck and it seemed like it took me five minutes just to get off that motherfucker. The kitchen was kind of big too. There were tables and everything. I jumped into one of the two lines and scoped out the scene. Niggas had on the latest street clothes. Maurice Malone, Kenneth Cole, Polo, everything.

"Ayo, you think I can get a couple more pancakes and some of them eggs?" I asked the guy behind the kitchen counter, serving the food. Shid, I hadn't seen food like that since I'd left the streets.

"Yeah," he replied, laying a pile of smoking-hot pancakes up on my tray with a smile before covering them with butter-flavored syrup. "That's all you want?"

"What's up with them sausages?" I pointed and he immediately tossed a few of them on the tray.

"You can have all this shit, youngin'. It ain't about nothing!" He assured probably realizing I was new because of the DOC jeans and shirt.

"You ain't got nothing to drink?" I looked around behind the counter. _

"The milks at the end and the fountain over there," He pointed before continuing. "Just grab you a cup."

I nodded and stepped off. I picked up two milks, grabbed a cup and headed over to the juice machine. *Oh shit!* I thought looking around. *These motherfuckers got a real juice machine. I was fucked up.* I by passed the grape and coffee and went for the orange juice. I'm not even going to stand here and lie. I fucked that orange up too. I drunk that shit until the old nigga in line behind me said that it wasn't going nowhere and that I could refill as many times as I wanted.

I refilled my cup one more time and found an empty table toward the back of the dining hall as a means to watch my surrounds. The first bite of pancakes instantly fucked my stomach up. It had been so long since I had hot food that my stomach couldn't take it. I sat my spoon down and tried to let my stomach settle down some before I fucked around and threw-up in the kitchen.

My stomach was just beginning to feel better when I looked up and saw my cousin Little Phil strolling into the kitchen.

"Phil!" I shouted loud enough to get half of the kitchen's attention, but my cousin didn't even look my way. "Cuzzo!" I called again standing up. *What the fuck?* I began moving in the direction of the breakfast line with my eyes on Little Phil.

I stopped in my tracks when I saw Little Phil remove what look liked a sword from his hip. Then, I watched as he weaved through the feed-up line, grabbed a tall, slim, red nigga with long cornrows by his shoulder and spun him around.

"Rat bitch!" Little Phil yelled loud enough for everybody to hear, slamming the sword into the dude's chest.

Everybody started moving, nobody was trying to get hit by the murder weapon my cousin was swinging. Little Phil stabbed the dude in his head, neck and face repeatedly as I stood there with my mouth hanging out.

By the time the COs were finally able to peel Little Phil up off of the dude, the damage was done. Little Phil had chased him around until he collapsed behind the feed-up counter, and it didn't look like dude was going to make it.

I didn't snap out of my daze until a one-legged old head—I would later find out name was Bodie Barksdale— walked by in a Lexington Terrace t-shirt and said, "Welcome to the Cut." When I got back to temporary housing, I just knew that we were getting locked down. I mean, Little Phil had just butchered a nigga in the kitchen. But, sure as shit, about two and a half hours later, the cell doors came open for morning yard.

I hit the yard and headed straight for the phones, so I could call home and let the family know exactly where I was. I saw niggas sizing me up and figured that they could tell that I was fresh meat from the DOC pants and shirt I had on just like the dude in the kitchen.

The phones were located on the second floor of the gymnasium in what was referred to as the phone room. There were about twenty phone mounted to the wall. So, it didn't take me too long to get on.

"Ma," I wondered the moment somebody accepted my call.

"This Detauwn, yo," my brother revealed. "Mommy just stepped out. Where they got you at?"

"The Cut," I confessed, scanning the room. *Some of these niggas old as hell!* I thought.

"Be careful down there Dak. Them niggas in there don't need a reason," Detauwn warned.

"I'm focused."

"When y'all visits down there though?"

"I don't know," I admitted. "Hold on." I put my hand over the mouthpiece and looked around until I saw a dude who didn't appear to be on the phone. "Excuse me, big man."

"What's up, soldier?" He looked at me curiously.

"Do you know the visiting days down here?" I asked, remembering the handbook that I'd been issued, but never read.

"Yeah, every day except Tuesdays. You can have five visitors at a time, but no more than three kids," he explained. "Oh yeah, the visits are from one in the afternoon until eight. But, your folks got to be in by six forty-five."

"Thanks," I said, before conveying the information to Detauwn.

"I'll be down there tomorrow," Detauwn assured.

"Bet," I said. "Ayo, get a ink pen real quick," I ordered, and heard Detauwn fumbling around in the background.

"What's up?" Detauwn questioned, picking the phone back up.

"Write this down," I requested and gave my brother the 'Cut' address. Then, I went on to explain the package situation. Since I'd just arrived. I was allowed a clothing package from home. So, I told Detauwn that there was no reason to go out and buy a bunch of new shit because I still had clothes and tennis that I hadn't even worn yet.

"I got you, bro," Detauwn assured, and I knew that his word was good. "You run into Little Phil, John, or Stucksy down there yet?"

"Yeah, but I'll holler at you on the visit about that," I replied, not wanting to get into it over the phone for obvious reasons. The main one being that dude may not have survived. after realizing that the phones didn't cut off every thirty minutes like over Baltimore City Jail. I got Detauwn to use the three-way to call everybody for me. I talked until the CO showed up, saying 'last call' for showers. I gave Detauwn my love, hung up and went to hit the showers.

The shower room was tucked off, all the way upstairs on the west wing above all the tiers. When I stepped inside and saw naked niggas just walking around freely it fucked my head up. *Where the fuck these niggas think their at? A high school locker room?* I looked around. You had niggas hand-washing clothes in and outside of the shower, niggas holding a rap-battle, gambling and some more shit. There were even dudes on the phone up in that bitch. It was crazy.

I stepped in the shower and rotated my way up underneath one of the six shower heads with about twenty other men. I'd never seen no shit like that in my life. Then, some of them niggas had the nerve to be ass naked or in jockstraps. I did my shit city jail style like a young nigga -in my boxers and got up out of that mother fucker with the quickness. Fuck all that standing around, buck naked, talking about who lost the game and shit.

I needed some steel quick. Shid, it felt like something could jump off at any minute. I was already thinking about hitting my next door neighbor up for asking so many weird ass questions. The old ass nigga had me thinking that he was gump or a rat, and either one could get him fucked over in my book. I mean, to each his own, but I didn't play that pussy shit in no shape, form or fashion. So, if he was coming at me on some wild shit, all he was going to end up getting was several inches of steel. When I got back to temporary housing. I peeped down on the bottom flats and saw my cousin, Little Phil walking around in an orange jumpsuit with the letters MHC printed across the back. I guess some things never change. *That same jumpsuit must be worldwide!* I thought.

"Cuzzo!" I called down to the lower tier.

"Dakaron?" Little Phil looked up at me as if he wasn't sure.

"Yeah," I confirmed, happy as shit that I could finally talk to someone I actually knew.

"When the fuck you get down here?"

"Monday."

"Where you sleep at?" Little Phil asked.

"Cell thirty-one."

"Man, your little ass done got big as shit!" Little Phil smiled, rubbing his hands together. "Wait until John sees you."

After the CO locked me in the cell, Little Phil stood up on a table on the bottom tier right in front of the cell so we could rap. We rap about everything. Little Phil told me that John was up on the tier with me in the very last cell under investigation. He would be out for his one—hour walk later on.

Little Phil laughed when I told him where my mind was at without niggas being able to pick up on what I was saying. He explained that a few old heads were on ass. But, knew who to play with. He also informed me that my neighbor was cool. He actually knew the nigga and called him to the door and told him straight up what time it was with me. Then, he said, 'yo just didn't know when to shut up.' But, he still said he would make sure that I had some steel before the day was out.

After night yard ran, John came out for his recreation and hollered at me. I was still on idle status, so I wasn't allowed to go outside to the night yard. John brought me some food, smoke and steel. Little Phil had already sent me a few outfits so that I could get out of that DOC shit. John put me down with the whole kitchen situation concerning Little Phil and told me who was *who*.

"Whatever you do, stay away from that watered-down gang shit!" John cautioned after stressing it was a coward's paradise.

"Oh, you ain't got to worry about that," I assured thinking about how niggas had been misusing me my entire life. When I ran the tapes back in my head. I discovered that niggas just weren't cut like me. None of the jokers I ran with or looked up to was willing to give what I would've given. My blood, my honor, my loyalty, my liberty, even my life! Because that's how serious I took that gangster shit!

"My advice is never speak up for s sucker, never step out there for a rat. Never back down from a challenge, hide behind a religion or open your mouth under no circumstances," John lectured. "In a nutshell, mind your business and mind your manners."

John when on to explain that everything was fair game in prison. He told me if I got into anything, to smash whoever was involved. No picks. "And watch them clicked up niggas too. Even punks get heart when they're deep." John continued to school me about how a lot of niggas had come to prison and gotten tricked out of their lives. I didn't want that to be me, so I listened closer to what he was saying.

John said that the penitentiary was a world unto itself and if you weren't careful, you'd easily he tricked out of something. "The Cut ain't no place for the weak or the dumb Dakaron. Everybody has a story, but everybody's story ain't true. So, if you're not careful, you'll thinking you're working them but they'll really be working you." John continued to give me tools that would become very useful throughout my bid.

The Birth of a Gangster 2

***

I went on my visit about five o'clock and was surprised to see that Detauwn had brought Chanae along. They didn't usually get along too well. To make a long story short. They both felt that I put the other before them. We hung out and took some photos after I promised an old picture man with salt and pepper hair named Mr. Percy that I would pay him in commissary.

At the end of the visit, I ran my hands all over Chanae and kissed her like we were about to have sex. "Damn, I love how thick you done got." I teased before Chanae strutted out of the visiting room.

On my way out of the visiting room, a sexy ass, honey-roasted peanut-complexioned CO, who smelled good enough to eat, informed me that I needed to submit a complete visiting list as soon as possible. She said that she'd already added Detauwn and Chanae to the list. But, I had room for thirteen more people. She also told me that I could get seven visits a month total, nine if I moved in one of the honor dorms.

"What's your name?" I inquired, staring her pretty ass straight in the eyes. There weren't too many things more attractive than a fine ass big girl with confidence. Plus, they always had the tightest pussy.

"Officer Turner," she confessed with a gorgeous, pearly white smile.

"I'ma remember that," I assured, slowly backing up, biting my bottom lip. It was just something about older women that just always did it for me.

"You do that," Ofc. Turner said.

A few days later I was placed on the mandatory school list and moved into C-dormitory. After I got adjusted to school and the dorm, I started going out in the yard to fuck with John and Little Phil, and to work out with a couple old heads from Cherry Hill on a regular basis.

Delmont Player

Chapter 32

Gangster Rules in Full Effect

Six months passed fast as shit. I had all my property, radio, CDs, fan, clothes, etc. My cousin had gotten transferred to the Penitentiary-Annex and John had given me his TV before he was sent down the Baltimore City Supermax. My direct appeal had just been filed and word was that Monique was back in the streets getting to it. I even heard whispers that Jamaine was coping from him again. But, I wasn't sure if it was true or not. If it was, though, I honestly wouldn't be surprised. Monique had learned how to control Jamaine a long time ago by feeding his desires. Whatever the ease, I wasn't slowing down. I had to get that lawyer money, so I was hustling hard as shit. And just like in the streets, with hustling came drama. So, before long, I ended up having to put my hands on a couple dudes over dope bills.

There was this one nigga that I really wanted to make an example out of though. I mean, I wanted to stab this nigga up so bad that my dick got hard. The only reason I didn't was because of my man, Michael Sligh, from Washington DC, who worked down the infirmary. If I hadn't fucked with and respected Michael Sligh and his right-hand man, Joppy, so heavy, I would've made that nigga eat my knife.

It was a couple of days before Christmas when I rolled out into the yard strapped for war to meet up with my partners, L.A., Bugeye, and Pole. "What's up?" I walked up giving everybody some love. I'd been sitting in the dorm chilling, watching repeats of Martin when Pole sent word.

"Man, Pole gots to hit this nigga Doogy," Bugeye proclaimed.

"Hold up," I requested, knowing how impatient Bugeye could be when he thought somebody was trying him or one of his walking buddies. "What happened?" I questioned curiously. The last time I'd spoken to Pole he told me everything was good.

"This nigga keep playing money games. That's what happened," Bugeye retorted. "It's been over a month and this nigga ain't paid up yet."

I looked over at Pole to see what he had to say. "I keep telling Bugeye I got it," Pole confessed. "But, if niggas wanna go at him, you know I'm with it."

"Nah, if he's getting hit. You're doing it yourself." I argued knowing what such a move would bring. Doogy was a part of what was known around the Cut as *3-D*, which consisted of Doogy and his two rap buddies, Damon and Dodger. Two certified knife slingas who would surely retaliate if we touched Doogy up.

"You know I ain't got no problem putting in work." Pole scratched at his fresh cornrows.

"Nah Dak, fuck that!" L.A. spoke up. "Pole with us. So, his problem is our problem!"

I knew what L.A. said was right. If Doogy was trying Pole, he was trying us all because he knew we ran together. Which also meant, he knew that we hustled together. "A'ight, but look, Pole is going to put the work in. We're just to be there to back his play in case Doogy start getting out on him or something."

"I say we just hit all three of them niggas before the yard close," Bugeye suggested. "Because I'll bet any amount of money them niggas are in on it. They done did that same shit to mad dudes and they keep letting them get away with that shit!"

"Just let me holler at Red Burn and Outlaw real quick," I said, moving across the yard quickly to put my workout partners on point just in case shit got crazy. There were rules that were always in effect. Rules that governed the yard and letting those, everybody knew that you were close to know what was up, was one of them. Red Burn and Outlaw had done the same thing for me when they had to make a stand against the Muslims a few weeks earlier over a snitch trying to use the community for protection.

"Ayo, Lil' Dak, let me holler at you real quick." Dodger and Damon pulled up on me before I could even get to Red Burn and Outlaw.

"What's up, yo?" I looked back to make sure L.A. and them saw what was taking place. "What's on your mind?"

"Come on, let's take a lap," Damon suggested.

On the walk Dodger brought up Doogy's bill. These old niggas weren't slow by far. They'd basically peeped us from the moment we all showed up in the yard. Which was abnormal. I explained the situation to Damon and Dodger and they appeared to understand. Of course, they'd both ride or die for Doogy no doubt. But, they respected men and knew right from wrong. And Doogy was dead wrong. Damon and Dodger expressed to me that they weren't trying to get off into no gangster shit over no crumbs. Because there was no money in war and nobody ever truly won. In the end, Damon assured me that, Dodgy would pay Pole and informed me that, in the future, should there ever be another situation like that one. It was best to let the dude speak up for himself so it wouldn't appear as if he had someone else fighting his battles. "At the end of the day, men respect men, soldier," Damon said before we all shook hands and went our separate ways.

"Fuck them old niggas hollering about?" Bugeye inquired the moment I walked back over to the bleachers.

"They say Doogy going to pay. Something about his sister getting in an accident." I confessed. "But, yo, them niggas were all over us." I continued. "They know that we don't ever all be in the yard. So, in the future niggas gotta remember that because them old niggas be playing for keeps."

"So, what now?" Pole asked.

"Just wait for yo, to give you your money. It shouldn't be no more than a few days." I repeated what Damon told me. "Whatever you do, don't pull him up or nothing though. I don't want you to fuck around and spook these old niggas."

***

Two weeks had passed and Pole still hadn't heard a word about the four hundred dollars owed, but he wasn't saying nothing and I was starting to think that he wasn't trying to represent the situation. I kept telling L.A. and Bugeye that I thought Pole was scared, but they felt differently. Who knows? I could've been wrong. I was hanging from the pull—up bar working out with Red Burn and Outlaw when L.A. and Bugeye approached. I could tell by their body language that something was up. Plus, I thought about what Damon had said about all of us being in the yard at the same time.

"I'll be right back." I put down the bar, wiped the sweat off my face with my towel, and began to walk toward L.A. and Bugeye.

"Nah man, get your last set." Red Burn instructed going up on the pull-up bar.

I held my finger up to signal for L.A. and Bugeye to give me a moment. Then, I climbed up on the dip bar and completed my tenth set of dips before following L.A. and Bugeye over to the bleachers. "What y'all niggas up to, man?"

"Yo, you know what time it is." Bugeye smiled, and I instantly knew we were about to get into some bullshit. "That nigga Doogy still ain't paid up."

"Where's Pole at?" I questioned.

"Still on his visit," L.A. informed.

We sat on the bleachers and rapped until Pole came of his weekly visit. Whole time, L.A. and Bugeye were mad about the shit with Doogy, I was observing the chaotic order of the big yard. It amazed me how murderers, hustlers, cowards, snitches, snakes, stick-up boys, and booty-bandits could all co-exist in such a small space and only every so often, step on each other's toes.

"Over here Pole!" L.A. got his attention before he could get past the bleachers and go into the gym to jump on the phone or play pool.

"What's up, yo?" Pole gave everybody some love.

"Ayo, what your people say about that four?" Bugeye get straight to the point.

"What four?" Pole responded like he was caught off guard or playing dumb.

"The four hundred from Doogy, nigga!" Bugeye snapped aggressively. "You know what the fuck I'm talking about."

"Oh, nah, my mind was somewhere else. I'm still waiting on that, though," Pole admitted, like he didn't really want to talk about it. "But like Dak said, I'ma give it a couple days."

"That was two weeks ago!" L.A. fired.

"Yeah, and I changed my mind after that nigga didn't pay last week," I confessed. "So, that nigga's getting hit today."

"Did you holler at Damon and Dodger?" Pole asked me.

"For what? I already hollered at them niggas once. I'm done talking. Whatever happens now, happens. Them old niggas know the law of the land better than we do," I replied.

After putting Red Burn and Outlaw on point, so they wouldn't get jammed up with their joints, I pulled up on Doogy and Dodger and got them to follow me and Pole into the music room. Bugeye had already slipped Pole some steel after he said he wasn't strapped and tried to use that as an excuse to stall. My whole thing was Pole had to kick it off. After all, it was his bill.

Everybody else was ready to push. The plan was to trap Doogy and Dodger inside the music ream and tear their old asses up the moment Bugeye walked in. L.A. was supposed to hold the door down just in case anybody tried to get in our business.

When we got inside the music room, Doogy started running them slick ass, old dope-fiend lines. Calling Pole his nephew and shit, saying he was a soldier and all that. Dodger was standing there like me, listening, waiting. It was no doubt in my mind that he thought they were walking out of there untested. When Bugeye strolled in, I expected Pole to go to work. I mean, after all, that had been the plan. But, this nigga Pole just kept running his mouth.

After a while, Bugeye and I started looking at each other, trying to figure out what to do next. But Bugeye, being Bugeye, just stepped forward and punched Doogy square in the mouth while he was talking, forcing Pole to draw his knife.

The situation escalated so quickly that before I realized it, Doogy had taken Pole's joint and stabbed him with it. "Get him, yo!" Pole cried out as Doogy got on his ass.

Bugeye and I both whipped out our joints and assisted Pole before Doogy could slaughter his ass. I pushed Doogy into a large speaker and got ready to work. The next thing I knew, Dodger's joint was out and he was stabbing me. From that point on, shit was gruesome.

In the midst of all of the knife slinging, this bitch ass nigga Pole breaks out of the music room. When L.A. peeped in and saw that Dodger and Doogy were jive getting out on us, he ran in to assist us.

When it was finally over and we were all drug out of the gym to medical, they called another code up on the west wing, and about five minutes later, I saw the nurses rushing past with Pole laid across the stretcher and smiled. *Bitch ass nigga!* I thought. Somebody had tore his ass up bad. It literally looked like he was bleeding from twenty different large holes. I heard one of the COs say Damon's name and shook my head respectfully.

I couldn't wait to go down lockup and tell L.A. and Bugeye about his work. I could just hear Bugeye now, though, 'That's what that whore ass nigga get for trying to duck that rec." And I definitely wouldn't disagree with him either. Especially since it was Pole's beef to begin with and he was always talking that gangster shit! That wasn't the kicker, though! The kicker was that my man, Michael Sligh, had to come to the medical room to talk me into accepting medical attention from the nurses, because I thought by admitting that I'd been stabbed was equivalent to snitching, and I'd rather die than be labeled a snitch.

I could still remember Michael Sligh's words the moment the nurses and guards stepped out of the medical room. "Everybody know you a soldier, *joe*! And everybody knows what happened. You got hit. So, keep your mouth shut, get patched up, and get your get-back. That's how it goes, *young*."

Chapter 33

The Life of a Gangster

When I first found out that Chanae was pregnant, I was crushed. Not just because it wasn't mine. But also, because she didn't even have the courage to tell me herself. I was like, 'after all the shit we'd been through, all the working on our relationship' I had to find out from the streets. What hurt the most was she continued to allow me to believe that she was just getting thick, until she couldn't. Then, she just started making all kind of excuses why she couldn't visit. In the end, I realized that she was just scared.

When I finally got over the fear of whose child it may be, and got up the courage to question Chanae about the pregnancy over the phone. She didn't deny it, but she didn't admit it either. She fired back with some shit like, 'Why? Is that going to change something if I am?' I was like, 'Hell yeah! If you're pregnant you belong to your baby's father.' Then, I hung up with plans to never call her ass again. After all, she'd crossed me to the highest degree. She'd laid down and let a nigga knock her up. Wasn't no coming back from that. Like I said before, 'My honor had always been bigger than my heart.' However, Chanae had other plans. Two weeks later, I got a letter requesting a five-minute phone call. I called, we argued, we cursed, we made up. And I was glad we did, because on April 30th 2000—my grandmother's birthday—my angel, A'myiah Cashae Johnson, came into the world and changed everything I thought I knew about love. I was in love from the first moment I held that little girl in my arms.

I only received thirty days on lockup because it was my first infraction. But, I was still transferred over to the Penitentiary-Annex where Frank was along with Damon, Dodger and Doogy. Both Bugeye and L.A. remained over The Cut and Pole remained in the hospital. I was ready for whatever. Niggas were going to have to kill me before I bitched up. But, as it turns out, Doogy and Dodger were Frank's uncles, Marlow and Timmor, rap buddies. So, the beef got squashed. Honestly, niggas respected that I'd even had the balls to go up against '3D.'

Them old niggas weren't to be played with. Niggas said we'd been lucky to have had survived, let alone make it through without losing at least a limb. But, I assured them that Dodger and Doogy were just as lucky after fucking with us. I was hearing the names of a lot of Park Heights legends and gangsters. Niggas who had all but been lost in the system for years, almost forgotten on the streets. Of course, there were always the exceptions when you considered men like Little Dinky, Zimbabwe, Percy Pair, Darryl Hill, Big Yock, Butt-Butt, Cookie-Man, Corey fox, Little Peety, Jerry Johnson and Frank Nitti. Men I'd grown up looking up to. There were some popular Park Heights suckers floating around too. But that was another story.

The Penitentiary-Annex was a hell of a lot different than the 'Cut.' The CO's were less tolerant. The space was a lot tighter. Especially, considering the fact that it took you some time to get a single cell. The movement was more restrictive and there were virtually no programs. So, the prisoners were more violent. I mean, it was like everybody was strapped. Because every time things seemed to escalate, the knives came out. It didn't matter if it was a card game or over a simple argument. The knives always came out. There were rarely fist-fights like over the 'Cut.' When it went down in the Penitentiary-Annex, niggas got sent out and not just in the ambulance or on the helicopter. Child's play my ass! The Penitentiary-Annex was five times as dangerous as the 'Cut' and ten times as treacherous. One thing about the Penitentiary-Annex that didn't differ was the fact that, rats were still considered weak, rapist were outcast, homosexuals were social rejects and the Cherry Hill niggas basically controlled everything. I mean, these niggas had their hands up everybody's skirt.

Another thing I found funny were the old heads who blamed the young boys for everything and tried to impress you with some shit they'd done twenty years ago. You had both young and old suckers in the system from all parts of town and every walk of life. There were only a few men real to the core. And that was whom I respected. I didn't care if they were young or old. Drug free or dope boys. A gang member or a member of a religious organization. As long as they were a man, I'd shown them respect until they proved unworthy of that respect.

Everybody in the joint couldn't go for bad. I even respected the homo-thugs. The real ones! The ones who were open about what they were into with their family, friends, and females. What I hated was the undercover, down-low dudes who went uptown acting like they were super gangsters on the yard. When they were really taking the dick or doing some shit their peoples would disown them for. My motto was, a nigga shouldn't do nothing in the joint out of desperation that he wouldn't do uptown. You had niggas marrying women they wouldn't even look at on the streets. You had so-called men writing love letters to homosexuals out of either loneliness or greed. Fuck that! A man should never allow his situation to dictate his actions. I would never settle for things in the joint that I wouldn't go for on the streets. In a nutshell, I respected men who were exactly who they presented themselves to be, because that's what I was.

I was in D-building, on A-tier, working in the kitchen. Frank and I had just lost our direct appeal. So, the fight for freedom would take a little longer than I'd originally thought. But, it hadn't killed us. In fact, I honestly think it made us stronger. Of course, a lot of so-called friends and family for that matter turned their backs and left us for dead because they thought that we were finished. The same ones who claimed to love us the most. But, it was all good. The hate, frustration and hunger would not allow either one of us to give in or give up. Not until we were back on top. We had a jailhouse lawyer name Walter Lomax showing us the ropes. On top of that, my brother Antauwn came home looking into everything for me. So, I felt like it would not be too long before we found a loophole to get back in court. We just had to hope that the courts played favor and respected their own laws.

"Damn, yo! Put some cut on that shit!" my cell buddy, Moon, fired from the other side of the homemade curtain hanging across the cell to block him from being able to see me, while I was using the bathroom or taking a birdbath. "You jamming!"

"Nigga, I know you're not talking as much as you been fucking the spot up." I reached back to give him a courtesy flush, laughing.

Usually Moon and I weren't in the cell together. I worked in the kitchen during the day and he worked down lockup at night. But, due to the recent gym incident, we'd been tight for three days.

I fucked with Moon. First of all, he was a fucking goon. Secondly, he was Red Burn's cousin. So, just like Red Burn, he was sharp and calculated. Finally, I admired how he surrounded himself with fall guys. Gangsters, but fall guys nonetheless. He fed them just enough to keep them loyal. Yet, he kept the spoon long enough to make them expendable if anything ever went wrong. I had witnessed a few niggas take the charge for Moon because they felt like they owed him. Hence the reason why we were currently locked down. Moon and his man, Kenny-Mac, another Cherry Hill psych, had severely butchered a nigga in the gym's bathroom. Hit him close to one hundred times and got another nigga to carry the weight.

"Nigga, I always give a courtesy flush!" Moon retorted. "Every time something come out, I put that cut on it."

"That don't mean it don't stink, nigga!" I continued to laugh before flushing again to try to keep the smell down.

"I hope you wash your hands when you finish too, nigga! 'Cause I know how y'all dirty little Park Heights niggas get down."

"Dirty?" I repeated. "Nigga, don't get the neighborhood mixed up with the people," I added, knowing that Park Heights had some of the cleanest niggas in and out of prison. "Especially when we all know y'all Cherry Hill niggas don't wash y'all asses. That's why all the bitches run up Park Heights."

"Yeah a'ight," Moon fired as if he caught an attitude. "Just light an incense or something over there, nigga."

***

When I got word that Murdock was in the jail, I immediately sent him two equalizers down E-building because I knew how he got down. I was fucked up when I found out that the judge had hit him with life plus fifty for the felony murder conviction, but I wasn't surprised. Them courts weren't playing. Them bitches were giving out death sentences like it wasn't nothing. Fat Relly popped up too. But, there wasn't no beef. We decided to leave that shit over the city jail, where your manhood is or should be tested so weak niggas couldn't slip through the cracks. I'd once heard an old head say that, 'if you could make it over city jail as a respected, stand-up man, you could make it anyway.' But, I didn't care about none of that shit when I got word that Little Ray's ass was down on lockup. I sent word down F-Building to Little Phil and he straight out ten grams of dope on Little Ray's head. The price of life was cheap in prison. So, ten grams of blow just showed how personal it was.

Delmont Player

Chapter 34

Gangster Practice

"What's up?" Antauwn asked Jamaine as he climbed into his brand-new Range Rover.

"I need you, bro," Jamaine confessed honestly. He knew Antauwn had come home and jumped right back in the streets. Niggas were already talking about how Antauwn and his cousin, Tony, were flooding the city. So, Jamaine was trying to get plugged in. "I'm trying to get some work," Jamaine revealed.

He'd already hollered at Urtle a few times, but he kept running the he's not in the game 'no more' play. Antauwn stared at Jamaine for a moment. He didn't want to turn him down. First of all, he was like a little brother. Secondly, he'd sat him out when he first came home. Antauwn could still remember how the little, young bitch Jamaine had turned loose on him tried to fuck him into submission. Jamaine had told the little bitch to treat him right and she only replied, 'yes daddy' and then went to work. Finally, Jamaine had turned him and Tony on to a coke strip in South Baltimore, which was where he'd met and instantly fell in love with Samone, who just so happened to be the cousin of a female Dakaron used to be after.

"What are you looking to get?" Antauwn inquired.

"At least a brick." Jamaine wanted to see the kind of numbers the coke was doing before he invested his entire savings.

"I got you." Antauwn nodded. "But look, I'ma need you on top of something for me too."

"Anything," Jamaine assured.

"Tony had some static with an Edmondson Village bitch who'd took him off for some scratch back in the day."

"What kind of static?" Jamaine wanted to know so he knew how to approach the situation.

"He slapped her and she said she was going to get some kid name Poochie. I think he's her baby father or something. I told Tony to leave that shit alone, but that's how he is about his money."

"What do you need me to do?" Jamaine searched Antauwn's face.

"You still deal with the dude you was telling me about from up Edmondson Village?" Antauwn had an idea.

"Yeah, my man Jeff Ebb-Banga. But, he's from Uplands," Jamaine replied.

"Man, see if you can get him to hook you and Poochie up, so you can squash that shit!" Antauwn explained. He'd seen too many niggas get caught up over a nothing ass female, and he didn't want to see his cousin fall victim to the same fate. Especially not when they were about to invest in the strip club industry and go legit. "Niggas don't need to be out here beefing over no bitch."

"I'm on it." Jamaine assured. He needed to holler at Banga anyway.

"What are you doing around the second week of next month?" Antauwn had another idea.

"Man, I don't even know what I'm doing tomorrow," Jamaine laughed. "Why? what's up though?"

"Nah, why don't you come out to Atlanta with me and Tony?"

"The A-T-L?"

"Yeah, you know they got some of the baddest strippers in the world. And I need to recruit some dimes for the spot Tony and I are trying to open on Baltimore Street."

"You already got the building?"

"Well, not really," Antauwn replied after a long pause. He really didn't want to count all of his eggs before they hatched. "But the deal will be closed soon. We got two more spots we're working on also. One in Portsman, Virginia and one in Brooklyn, New York."

"That's what's up, yo, get that money."

"Yeah, a nigga can't play in these streets forever, you feel me?"

"I don't know about all that," Jamaine mumbled. "I do need to get the fuck out of the city though."

"A'ight then nigga, bring your A-game." Antauwn leaned over the armrest to give Jamaine some love.

"I'ma do you one better, nigga. I'ma bring my B-More game," Jamaine exclaimed before climbing out of the truck to head back to his car.

Delmont Player

Chapter 35

You Must Love a Gangster

"Stop playing nigga, before I fuck your little ass up!" Little Phil snapped as we sat at one of the many tables in the Penitentiary-Annex dining hall at work.

"Nigga, stop crying, damn," I retorted, rubbing his bald head again. "You always on serious time."

"What other time is there to be on, Cuzzo?" Little Phil challenged. "It be too much going on around here to be slipping."

"Whatever," I said, not paying Little Phil any mind.

"Nah, though Cuzzo, you know who she reminds me of?" Little Phil continued to flip through the photos of the new, college, county girl our cousin Sabrina had hooked me up with.

"Who?" I asked curiously.

"What's the CO girl name that you always be talking about?" Little Phil looked at me. "The one you like?"

"What girl?" I raised my eyebrow in wonder.

"The one that work over the Cut in H-dorm. The pretty ass one you were always chasing."

"Ohhhhh, you talking about Turner," I revealed, smiling. "Yeah, she could pass for Lakeria's sisters," I agreed, nodding.

"Yeah, they got them same pretty smiles and big ass titties," Little Phil added licking his lips.

"Stop playing nigga," I shot him a jab. "All jokes aside, though, they got the same, big ol', wide, flat butts too."

"Oh, them joints blossom when you bend them over, Cuzzo, don't get it twisted."

"Oh, I know." I confessed thinking about a few wide, flat butt chicks I had fucked. "Why you think Turner my baby nigga?"

"Nigga, if you wasn't hitting, and you wasn't. That's not your baby." Little Phil teased because it was a known fact amongst us and a rumor amongst others, that he damn near smashed something in every joint he touched.

"Turner my baby nigga! Believe that." I corrected knowing that if I ever ran across her sexy ass uptown. I could bag her. "But, I got Lakeria now. That's Turner two point zero."

"Shorty proper, she got that cute, little, chubby supermodel face like Turner too," Little Phil shook his head and smiled respectfully. "Sabrina came through."

"I know," I admitted. "Oh shit, I almost forgot. I saw Stuckey in the visiting room last night. He said John supposed to have made transfer. I think he said, he's going back over the Cut."

"That's a blessing. That nigga definitely don't need to come over this tight motherfucker after coming out of that supermax." Little Phil said. "Shid, honestly I wouldn't mind going back over there myself."

"You and me both," I declared thinking about Ofc. Turner for a moment. "I'd straight press Turner out this time. Grab her ass up by that dorm and put my tongue in her mouth."

"Nigga, you about to fuck around and go home." Little Phil instantly changed the subject as the first of several dudes walked into the dining hall to eat.

"Not if these bitches keep playing games." I winked at Little Phil to let him know I was focused. It wasn't personal. A nigga could just never be too careful. Especially in the Penitentiary-Annex. The walls had ears. So, if the cameras didn't get you. The inmates on patrol would. I mean, you had dudes telling for everything from extra visits to single cells. There were some niggas who would get you out of the way for a job.

"Why you say that? Ain't no way in the world the Court of Special Appeals not going to grant you and Frank that probable cause issue."

"Stupid ass public defender didn't even filed my certiorari in time, so I missed my forty-five-day deadline. Frank got his in though." I admitted still a little upset about the situation. After all, a nigga didn't get too many chances to challenge his conviction. So, he couldn't afford to just be missing opportunities.

"So what are you going to do now?"

"Wait," I replied. "I'ma see what happens with Frank before I file the post. That way I got some time to go over the transcripts again. while Detauwn finds me a good lawyer." I explained.

"What about the federal habeas corpus? You know you only got one year after your direct appeal or certiorari to file your post-conviction if you want to preserve it?"

"Yeah, I know. That's why I want to see exactly what this lawyer thinks."

"Don't let no lawyer tell you anything. Them bitches famous for that," Little Phil spoke from experience.

"You know I ain't going for that."

"You're definitely doing the right thing though. Studying your own shit.   Cause ain't nobody going to work on your case like you do. It's not that serious to them, you dig? I mean, every now and again, you'll find a lawyer with a sincere heart for the job. But, they're as rare as a cop in general population around here. Most of them bitches ain't shit! To them it's still just a job. They don't give a fuck that you're literally fighting for your life. They get to go home at night regardless."

"You right about that." I agreed knowing he was speaking nothing but the truth. "That shit ain't right though."

"Hell no, it ain't right!" Little Phil declared. "Our people already broke out there. Then, they go begging and borrowing to get that lawyer money up, only to get fucked over. I could give every last one of my attorneys an old fashion ass whipping for all the money they worked my mother out of." Little Phil laughed probably to keep from crying.

"Them bitches lucky a nigga don't come uptown and put that gun on their asses." I threatened thinking about all the guys in prison because a lawyer played with their lives.

"Seriously," Little Phil seconded. "That's why I always say that, a nigga would be a fool to walk around this motherfucker not studying his own case because he got a lawyer."

My belief was that a nigga got out what he put in. If a lawyer knew that you studied your case and they couldn't play with you. They went to work. But, when they saw that you simply relied on them and knew that they could tell you anything. They didn't work as hard. And why should they? I mean, if your freedom wasn't that important to you. why should it be important to anybody else?

"It's a known fact, that most of the dudes who get back in court, be the dudes who be working on their shit with or without a lawyer." Little Phil continued. "I mean, you got your exceptions. But, that's rare. The dudes who make it, be the dudes you see putting in work."

"That's why we putting in work, so we can be those guys." I encouraged with a smile feeling my cousin's pain. There were a lot of dudes wasting their families hard earned money, not studying, putting all their faith in the lawyers hands, getting high, etc. When they could just bullshit about going home for free.

"You crazy like that glue Cuzzo." Little Phil shook his head and we continued to talk until we had to wipe the kitchen tables off for the next line.

"A Cuzzo, let me ask you something." I requested as we sat down to eat after cleaning up. "I don't want to sound crazy, but, I have been thinking about this a lot lately."

"What's up?" Little Phil began seasoning up his food.

"Do you believe in love spirits and shit? Like reincarnated love from the past or something?"

"What?" Little Phil looked up from his tray. "Cuzzo, don't start that crazy shit." Little Phil warned. He always said I came up with some of the wildest ideas.

"Nah, I'm serious Cuzzo. Just listen to me. I feel like I been in love with Chanae forever. Like I can feel her in the pit of my stomach. And you already know that SweetPea is my gangster. But, this new girl, Lakeria, already got me falling for her." I tried to explain what I was feeling.

"What the fuck does that have to do with reincarnation?" Little Phil stuffed a piece of fish into his mouth.

"Just listen, Cuzzo! Think about it. Out of all the women Sabrina knows, why she put me on with Lakeria? Seriously, think about it." I tap my temple when I saw my cousin's face twist up. "What if I'm supposed to finish something that started before I ever met her?" I threw that at my cousin and waited for his response. I was really curious as to what he may think because I respect his opinion.

"My children's mother had me read this book about some shit like that before." Little Phil confessed. "It was a long time ago. But, I remember some shit where your spirit and a former lover spirit comes back together in another life time. I use to tell my wife about that shit."

"You don't remember the name of the book?" I questioned curiously, wondering for a moment if Lakeria and I were a reincarnated love. I mean, the way it seemed like we already knew each other for years had to mean something.

"Yeah, it's called ummmm...." Little Phil thought for a second.

"Shut your stupid ass up so I can eat my food!" Little Phil burst out laughing before taking a bite of his fish sandwich.

"Oh, that's fucked up Cuzzo. I'm trying to talk to you about some serious shit and you're over there clowning."

"Man, Cuzzo, all I know is that Chanae is your kryptonite and SweetPea's your Achilles heel. All them other females ain't about nothing," Little Phil mumbled through a mouthful of food.

"Man, I haven't even talk to Chanae," I reminded him, knowing he just didn't understand. "She's doing her and I'm doing me."

"Yeah, but who do you think she's looking for?"

"Oh, she'll never find that!" I assured, knowing that I was one of a kind. "That's her problem. She keeps looking for me in all the wrong places. I'm in here though."

"*Truesdole!*" One of the drop-slots above our heads slid open. "*Truesdole!*"

"Yeah, what's up?" I looked up at the sound of the voice, knowing exactly who it belonged to. A little ugly-faced, welfare bitch who I couldn't stand.

"You got a visit!" she disclosed like she had an attitude somebody still loved me in the streets, before slamming the drop-slot.

Why you mad bitch? You supposed to be happy somebody loves me. You sound like you wish I was written off in the joint, I thought, grabbing my sandwich as I stood up. "We're going to finish this conversation," I informed Little Phil, ignoring the CO bitch.

"Oh, that's how you doing it, huh? Back-to-back action. Who that, the new girl again?" Little Phil smiled.

"Nah, b-m," I confessed. "She's bring Delmonte down."

"Yeah nigga, Chanae might be M-I-A, but SweetPea gangster ass not." Little Phil stood up to give me some love before I left.

"Yeah, SweetPea cut from a different cloth." I broke the embrace and headed for the exit. "Catch up with you tomorrow, Cuzzo."

"A'ight nigga." Little Phil nodded. "And don't wear them kitchen whites down that hole, nigga!" I heard Little Phil laughing as I went out the door.

I shot back to the building, took off my work clothes, threw on some crispy white, leather New Balance, a pair of blue denim jeans and a white and blue Iceberg sweater. I was going to see my princess, so I had to get fresh. Plus, I knew SweetPea's little sexy ass was going to be checking me out.

***

"See, that's the problem around here shorty. Too many Indians and not enough Chiefs. See, I'm from that old school though. When anybody couldn't just play the game or hustle around this mother fucker. See, now y'all just call yourselves gangsters. But, you little niggas aren't putting in no work. You know what though..."

I was standing at the table in the dayroom, making a hook-up (tuna fish, cheese, boiled-eggs, cups of noodles, honey, onion and crackers), tripping off my old head -Black Dana, talk shit about the game. I was in an amazing mood after having just gotten some pussy at 'Family Day' a few days ago. The family was so thick out in that big yard. That my brothers had to come in under Moon's name. The first thing I noticed at 'Family Day' was the absence of men.

I kept asking Little Phil where all the men where? All the gangsters who claimed to keep it real? But, he said there were so few that even those who showed up in between didn't matter. It was the women who held shit down.

"...that's why I goes for your rap buddy so much. Shorty don't be with that wild shit! Soldier laid back, but he's gangster. I saw him bitch slap a kid--"

"Yo, they're calling a code!" somebody alerted, when all of a sudden, COs started running out of the building to an emergency. Everybody knew what that meant. Something was jumping off. Somebody was probably getting stabbed. As the tier—officer was ordering everybody on the tier to step into the dayroom. I heard his walkie-talkie crack,

"Ten-ten! Ten-ten on echo yard!"

Inmate on inmate, I thought as Black Dana and I slid over to the dayroom window to see who was getting it in. "Watch out, yo!" I pushed a few nosey ass lames out of my way so I could get a better look. Each building had its own small yard attached to the side of the building.

"Niggas out there pushing, soldier!" Black Dana revealed, taking his eyes off the yard to look at me for a second.

"Drop the weapon!" we heard a CO order as two bloody dudes with knives danced around in an imaginary circle. "Drop the weapon!"

"I think that's your man out there," Black Dana mumbled. "What's the little kid name you always be fucking with that work on the compound?"

"Murdock?" I exclaimed.

"Yeah, Murdock. That's him. Shorty just came in," he confirmed.

I looked closer and sure enough, it was Murdock. I couldn't make out who the other guy was because it appeared that Murdock must've stabbed him in his head a few times because his face was covered in blood. It took the COs a good five minutes to get the situation under control. "I don't even think Murdock sleep in E-building," I confessed out loud to no one in particular.

"Shid, an out of bounds ticket doesn't even matter when you're serious about getting your man," Black Dana spat. "Shorty put that work in too."

Murdock had definitely walked the nigga down. I mean, they both were hit. But, I could clearly see that Murdock had come out on top. I kept trying to see the dude's face as they lead him from the yard, but I couldn't.

Ten minutes later, a gang of police came on the tier, acting crazy, patting niggas down and locking us in. Black Dana tried to find out who'd gotten hit from a female who he claimed was sweet on him. But, she played dumb. I wasn't in the cell a good five minutes when I heard the all too familiar sound of the helicopter (Medevac). Which shit was ugly.

***

The next morning, Moon brought me a kite from Murdock on lockup. So, I immediately tore it open to see what was going on. *Love/loyalty/respect/understanding; D, all is well on this end. I'm good! Couple of stitches, nothing heavy, you dig? Anyway, I ran into your man, Lil' Ray from over the jail and showed him some love. You know me? I'm loyal to those who are loyal to me. So, whatever the outcome is, I'll live with it. Send me some music and candy down this bitch! Oh yeah, it's a crazy nigga named Money-Nigel Carter next door to me. He said he's your man. Yo, please send this nigga some coffee so he can shut the hell up! Slim a straight zapout down this bitch! Until next time, stay up and stay real. Poppa Dock*

I ripped Murdock's kite up and flushed it down the toilet. *Damn! That nigga Little Ray must've slipped off on me over the 'Family Day' weekend*, I thought. "Ayo." I touched Moon's arm to get his attention. "What all can you get down lockup?"

"Whatever you need, busta." Moon smiled, removing his head-phones.

"Yo, what I tell you about calling me a busta?"

"Man, I ain't trying to hear that shit, busta. What you need to get down there though? Candy bars, drugs, knife?" Moon asked over light echoing sounds of Tupac.

"Just candy right now," I said, shaking my head.

"That's all you going to send that man for putting in that work for you? That's how you treat a good nigga?"

"How the fuck you know he put some work in for me?" I questioned curiously. Murdock's kite had been sealed.

"You know I read that shit busta. I'm from Coppin Court!" Moon confessed, and I wasn't sure if he was serious or not. "How the hell else you think Cherry Hill stay on top around this bitch?"

I shook my head. Moon was crazy as shit. That was my nigga though.

"I got some earphones and weed for him too." I smiled knowing Moon was right. Had I stabbed Little Ray myself the hearing officer would've hit me with at least one hundred eighty days because I was already in a poor category from the shit with Doogy and them. So, I definitely had to do right by my nigga Murdock.

Chapter 36

I Am My Gangster's Keeper

Jamaine, Antauwn and Tony hit the ATL like the planes hit the world Trade Centers—hard. They got fresh and rented a 2002 black Bentley GT. But, big boy shit was everywhere. Ferraris, Porsches, Chargers, Navigators, etc. They even spotted rapper/producer Jermaine Dupri, hanging out of pearl white Mercedes Benz S500 stretched-Limo and Snoop Dogg and his crew in a couple of supped up Chevy Impalas.

"Damn, I didn't know Atlanta had bitches like this," Tony confessed, eyeing women of various shapes, sizes and color going up and down the block.

Antauwn slowly pulled up behind a silver 2002 Cadillac Escalade with tints. All they could see was a redbone chick with a big ass hand digging all up in her ass, making her cheeks visible at the bottom of her booty shorts, as she leaned into the driver's side window. "This silly ass nigga holding up traffic." Antauwn tapped the horn.

"I know his goofy ass iced out though," Jamaine said checking out the large ass, diamond glistering watch and bracelet around the nigga's arm as it hung from the window. "He's lucky we down this bitch on business."

"Man, just go around that dumb nigga!" Tony instructed realizing that his attention was on the half-naked red bitch, hanging on the door of his truck.

Antauwn laid on the horn again. This time the dude in the truck, threw his arm up and waved it forward, signaling for Antauwn to go around. "He should've been did that." Antauwn fired slowly pulling the GT around the Escalade.

As they got closer to the driver of the truck. Jamaine noticed the iced out, pinky-ring and arm-sleeve of the number 58 Baltimore Ravens Jersey. "I'd take that nigga truck and everything," Jamaine confessed, checking out the 26-inch, spinning Panther Elements Rims, chrome door handles, Pirelli Scorpion Zero tires, and Classic

Mesh Grill. What really fucked Jamaine up the most though was not the truck, but the nigga who was behind the wheel. "Oh shit!" Jamaine fired, nodding with a smile.

"You know big man?" Tony questioned.

"Yeah, that's Dak's man, Big Al, from over east," Jamaine responded, knowing Big Al was probably on a mission.

After driving about four or five more blocks. Antauwn located the 'Blue Flame' strip club and pulled into the parking lot. They had only been in town two nights and had already recruited three dime piece from a strip club called, 'The Diamond Trap.' Now they planned to stay an entire week.

Stepping out in the latest Sean John and Roca Wear gear, Jamaine, Tony and Antauwn made their way to the strip club's entrance VIP style. Inside they found a dark corner, ordered a few glasses of Hennessy and a bottle of Moet and waited for the next set to begin. The spot was packed and there were enough diamonds inside to give Jacob 'The Jeweler' a run for his money.

"Damn baby!" Jamaine fired, licking his lips as a fine ass glittered covered, stripper strutted by in nothing except a pink g- string with matching stilettos. Her skin was so dark chocolate that it almost appeared to be melting. Like she had been sitting under the hot sun, baking for hours. "I didn't know Atlanta had it like that." Jamaine added reaching for her hand.

"Stay focus Maine," Antauwn warned, stealing a look as the stripper blushed and kept it moving. "It's all business tonight. You can fine pleasure on your own time."

"It's all business for you nigga. I'm trying to get my dick wet!" Jamaine declared honestly. "I'm trying to see what that A-T-L head and pussy hitting for."

"Shorty was bad though." Tony admitted trying to steal another look before she disappeared into the crowd. "I like 'em chocolate like that too boy."

"That's how Dak is," Jamaine revealed. "That nigga would've went crazy over shorty."

"Look man, I need y'all niggas to stay focus. I'm trying to fine some girls for the club." Antauwn explained.-

"Oh, I'm definitely focused. But, I'm also with Maine on this one." Tony grinned making his position clear. "Everybody ain't got wifey at the crib waiting on him."

Antauwn just shook his head. He knew Tony was right. He was a lucky motherfucker to have found Samone. "A'ight man, at least after all the pleasure. Can y'all let me handle my business?"

"That's why we're here baby." Jamaine raised his glass. "To take care of business."

After about two hours of lap dances, stage performances and countless shots of Hennessy. Antauwn had recruited two more dime pieces and talked one into at least during a monthly featured show. Jamaine and Tony had disappeared to the Champagne Room with two stripper bitches that a nigga couldn't go wrong with.

"These niggas better hurry up," Antauwn said to himself signaling for the waitress again. He needed another bottle of Moet. "Would you mind bringing me another bottle of Moe?" Antauwn pulled out a knock of cash as she approached the table with her pretty Kool-Aid smile.

"Sure," She accepted the money.

"And do me a favor please," Antauwn handed her another fifty.

"Tell my friends that if they're not out here in ten minutes. I'm gone."

"You're talking about the two gentlemen you were with earlier?" She asked to be sure and Antauwn nodded. "I'll bring your bottle back and get right on it." She added slipping the extra fifty inside her bra.

"Thank you," Antauwn said just as the music stopped.

"Okay fellers, it's the moment you all been waiting for! The reason why the ladies sneak in and we can't get the fellers out!" The deejay began ranting on the speakers. "The reason you been saving all your big faces! It's about to get extremely hot up in here! But don't worry. The Atlanta Fire Department's already in the house!" the deejay announced, and a gang of guys near the stage held their drink up and started shouting.

"So, for all you new jacks who don't know any better and all the out of towners who are about to learn," the deejay continued as the waitress sat Antauwn's bottle of Moet on the table and headed for the Champagne Room. "Go ahead and dig deep baby because it's about to go down. Known to most as the A-T-L-bank breakers! Ladies and gentlemen, welcome to the stage, Japan and China!!!!" when the music dropped, Antauwn found himself moving toward the stage with everybody else as two bad body bitches walked onto the stage in nothing but heels and face masks and began going to work. They weren't five minutes into their routine when Antauwn knew that he needed them in his club. The way they worked the crowd was next level. They did this trick on the pole that fucked Antauwn's head up.

It was like Japan and China's was in the air forever. He had never seen no shit like that in his entire life. when they finally hit the stage -literally-and began their freak show. Antauwn almost lost it. China was working a double-headed dildo on Japan and he could literally see her pussy juice coating it as her body slowly moved like a snake to the beat.

"Who the fuck is that?" Tony walked up beside Antauwn with pure lust in his eyes as Japan removed her mask, pushed China's leg all the way back until her toes were damn near touching the money-covered stage and began to devour her pretty pussy right there in front of everybody as the crowd went nuts.

"Damn!" Jamaine came up on Antauwn's left to get a better look at the little Japanese-flick looking bitch. "Look how long that bitch tongue is."

"That's Japan," Antauwn disclosed looking from Jamaine to Tony shaking his head. "The one about to take her mask off now in China. I want both of them bitches at the club!"

"Me too." Jamaine licked his lips and placed his arm over Antauwn's shoulder as China removed her mask. "Yo, you gotta to be kidding me." Jamaine's whole mood seemed to alter.

"What?" Antauwn kept his eyes on the show.

"Business just got personal," Jamaine leaned over to whisper in Antauwn's ear. "That's China Doll. The bitch who set Dak up."

Antauwn's blood went cold. He knew that name well. He and Dak had talked about her several times on their visits. He had

224

wanted her dead, but Dak wanted to find out her real name for the lawyer. He even convinced Antauwn to hire a private investigator to locate a kid named Johnny Blocksome, who Dak once had calling China's house. But, it fell through after the private investigator discovered that Johnny Blocksome had been killed. "You sure that's her?"

"Man, that's that bitch!" Jamaine declared. He'd only seen China Doll once, but he would never forget her face. She'd gotten a little thicker, looked slightly older, and was now covered in a series of new tattoos. But, Jamaine was sure that it was her because she still looked exactly like Toni Braxton.

"Let's go back to the table before I snatch this bitch off the stage," Antauwn threatened, needing to clear his head because he had all kind of wicked thoughts running through his head.

"Maine, what's up with the big dude that was in the Escalade?" Tony inquired the moment they sat down at the table, ready to cover their tracks and tie up all loose ends if need be.

"What do you mean, what's up with him?" Jamaine questioned, confused.

"I mean, he knows we're down this bitch," Tony retorted. "So, I need to know if we're going to have to take a trip over East Baltimore when we get home."

Jamaine burst out laughing. "Nah yo, Big Al solid. All that shit you saw was a front. Big feller down here lurking. He gonna leave something dead and stinking, trust me. He ain't never seen us."

"Sounds like my type of guy," Tony confessed, bringing his attention back to Antauwn. "So, how do you want to play this, Cuz?"

"That bitch set my little brother up. It's only one way to play it. Bodymore Murderland style." Antauwn picked up the bottle of Moet and began to drink.

Chapter 37

Walk Slow, Think Fast, Stay Gangster

It was a week after New Year's when my brother Antauwn came to see me about the China Doll situation. Around the same time I'd started having these strange ass dreams about getting old, being killed or just dying in prison. The one that involved my cell flooding up with my own blood seemed so real that I'd awake in cold sweats. I knew prison had broken the minds of some of the strongest. But, I was determined not to fall victim. They would never find my body hanging from a light fixture. Never catch me in the cell talking to myself. I couldn't see myself cutting magazine photos out for my photo album, so that I could create my own family. And I prayed to the gangster God's that I never became one of those dude who sat in the cell, faking themselves out, thinking that every woman was on me and every man was after me.

I talked to Chanae about the dreams. She was having dreams too. But, they were of me, coming to make love to her and things like that. So she couldn't understand. Little Phil and I were still working in the kitchen and Frank was on lockup for jerking off on a female guard name Miss Sellmen. Shekey Sellmen to be exact. I mean, jerking off on women wasn't my kind of thing. But, if it was, Miss Sellmen would definitely be my first choice. She was hands down bad. A sexy little, chocolate, bow—legged thing with a blue stud in her left eyebrow and a matching tongue-ring. I was on Miss Sellmen and she knew it. But, I wasn't jumping out of no trees, peeping around no corners or pressing my face into no crack to prove it. Yeah, I looked at girl magazines and imagined fucking some of the female staff too. Especially since most of them walked around in skintight uniforms with their ass, titties and phat pussy prints on display. But, there were still certain things I just wouldn't do. Certain levels I would not stoop too. I would rather stick to chasing good movies, wild tv shows, girl magazines and freak novels. Still, my motto was 'to each his own.' I never knocked the next man's game.

"So the whole time. This bitch ass nigga was fucking China Doll too?" I stared at my brother in a daze after he explained to me how the whole China Doll situation had played out. According to Antauwn. He, Tony and Jamaine's phony ass had been in Atlanta scouting strippers for his club, when Jamaine recognized China Doll on the stage. At that point, Antauwn planned to grab the bitch and do something drastic. However, unbeknownst to them, China Doll had spotted Jamaine during her set and immediately approached them afterward with security in tow.

China Doll explained how Monique had gotten her to set me up without her knowledge. She even told Antauwn that he'd paid her to keep her mouth shut and tried to convince her to go to the police. Monique wanted her to say that she'd witnessed me and Frank shoot Darryl Diggs. She didn't know why, instead though she took the money and moved. In fact, she moved out along the Eastern Shore near Johnny Blocksome. And when he got killed and Monique showed up, she just skipped town. My cousin Tony still wanted to knock her noodles out, but by then, China Doll had convinced Antauwn that she was worth more to me alive then she was dead. And she was right, with the information she provided, she could easily got our case overturned on post-conviction.

I couldn't wait to run that shit by Frank. But, I knew that we were going to have to keep China Doll under wraps and out of sight until we knew for sure, our other ducks weren't lining up.

"That's basically how she explained it to me." Antauwn admitted. "That nigga, Monique, treacherous bro. The only way to deal with a nigga like that is to knock his head off." '

I knew Antauwn was right, but that didn't make me feel any better. Monique was hiding out and nobody seemed to know where to find his bitch ass. "Man, just stay on top of China Doll." I instructed ready to change the subject again. I had learned a while ago that I could only talk about Monique for so long before my head started hurting. There was nothing worst then coming to terms with the fact that for as gangster as I had claimed to be, I had been stupid and careless when it came to protecting myself from harm.

"I got her bro trust me." Antauwn replied confidently.

"Did you talk to Cuzzo?" I wondered thinking about Little Phil.

"Nah, but I talked to Michelle, so I know that he goes to court next month for his post right?"

"Yeah." I shook my head. "That's what I was going to tell you."

***

"Man, fuck all that bullshit you talking. When I hit them bricks. I'm busting with that seven-forty-five. The gold joint." Little Phil fired as we sat in the kitchen at work.

"Nah Cuzzo, you got grab a truck. You got the build for that shit." I stressed. We'd been going back and forth for a minute.

"I don't know yo," Little Phil looked down almost as if he was checking himself out. "I feel like a big body, coup nigga!"

"I can see that," I smiled. "You ready though, Cuzzo?"

"You better know it." Little Phil replied without hesitation. "I ain't got too much more of this shit in me Cuzzo. I can't keep giving these bitch ass lawyers money I don't have, you feel me? Niggas out there not going to be in the streets forever."

"You right about that," I admitted. "That's why I respects Lomax so much. Yo, got like thirty in and he still rumbling with the system. I would've been out of my mind around this bitch! Shid, I'm not even good for ten. I just ain't got it in me Cuzzo. They're going to have to kill me around this bitch," I declared seriously. "That's why I be saying, if I don't give this shit back. It's on, I'ma be stabbing and robbing everything!"

"You're crazy like that glue Cuzzo." Little Phil waved me off. "What about the family? what about Delmonte and A'myiah? what you going to tell them?"

"I love the family and you know that my daughters are my world. I mean, I'm not committing suicide or nothing. But, I don't want to see my mother still coming down this bitch trying to see me when I'm sixty, seventy years old!" I explained unable to fathom it. "I want freedom Cuzzo. Worldly or heavenly. I don't want to be like Lomax. Down twenty- five, thirty years still fighting, faking myself out, hoping I get to see the streets again. Nah, fuck that! I'ma face reality early on."

"Sounds like you're laying down to me."

"Oh, I definitely ain't laying down." I retorted. "I ain't letting nobody take shit from me! I ain't letting nobody disrespect me! I ain't letting nobody put their hands on me! And I damn sure ain't walking around this bitch until I fall over and crock!" I knew that if I started running wild a lot of people would think that I wasn't trying to come home. But that wasn't the case. Prison was predatory and a man couldn't afford to be weak. Not if he wanted other men to respect him. But I knew that my family wouldn't understand that no more than they would understand me making peace with the fact that I may die in prison.

"Man, I'm not fucking with you. Shit ain't never over!"

"Shid, After the post-conviction, it's game over Cuzzo." I said. "Some niggas don't like to face reality. So they get old dreaming. Not me! These bitches don't let me go. I'm make em' famous, mark my word!"

Little Phil and I continue to go at it until we got lost in our own thoughts. It's wasn't that I couldn't survive prison. I was a Truesdale. I just couldn't see myself submitting to some motherfuckers who didn't give two cents about me after being a gangster all my life. Disregarding the law and shit. Even disobeying my parents. Nah, I was too prideful. So, if I was still behind enemy lines ten, fifteen years from now. I would either be dead, on death row or hitting the gate.

"What's on your mind Cuzzo?" I interrupted Little Phil thoughts after the silence began to get to me.

"You just got me thinking about what I'm up against." He confessed softly.

***

"That judge was full of shit!" Antauwn snapped walking out of the courthouse after Little Phil's hearing. "All that hidden evidence, what they called it again?"

"The Brady violation." Tony revealed.

"Yeah, the Brady violation." Antauwn nodded. "If they know there was a Brady violation. Why not just rule on that shit today? why the judge got to go over this and that? when it's plain as day. That shit don't make no sense to me."

"Yeah, it don't make sense to me either. But, you know how them folks are. They make it easy to get in, hard as a motherfucker to get out." Tony explained knowing a little bit about the system from having studied his own case. "I think he's going to make out though. The lawyer ate that shit up! Especially that ineffective assistance of counsel issue."

Antauwn hoped Tony was right.

After stopping at the mobile vending machine just outside the courthouse. Antauwn and Tony headed on over to parking garage to pick up Antauwn's Range. "So, what are you about to get into?" Antauwn asked as they climbed into the Range.

"Damn, nigga, what are you trying to get rid of me?" Tony joked.

"Nah, I'm about to go chill with Samone," Antauwn disclosed.

Little Phil's hearing had made him a little stressed and he only knew one way to relieve it. Go home and lay up in some good pussy.

"A'ight, take me back to the club so I can get my car." Tony requested. He knew how excited Antauwn was that Samone was pregnant with their first child. And he knew how important it was for Antauwn to enjoy that feeling. It only came once.

"I got you." Antauwn said gassing the Range Rover up as Tony began fidgeting with the sound system.

Delmont Player

Chapter 38

Black Gangster Family

The next couple of months went by slow and before anybody knew it another year had slipped by. Little Phil's post-conviction was denied for some bullshit, so he was on heavy study time. Murdock was off lock- up and on the tier. Both of my brothers had babies on the way again and Jamaine was still running around lying, telling niggas that he was getting to me. Which had Tony and I at odds because I couldn't figure out how he continued to deal with Jamaine after I told him how that nigga had left me for dead.

Chanae was in and out. It was almost like whenever another nigga broke her heart she'd come running to me to get repaired for the next nigga. I guess she figured that I'd always take her back. And I did because I loved her. I always would, but time, prison and distance was really starting to play on our relationship. I was beginning to get tired of being a rebound that Chanae could always count on even when I couldn't count on her. I was really coming to terms with the fact that things between Chanae and I may never be the same again.

It took a different kind of strength to survive a bad verdict, maintain a good prison relationship and endure a long prison sentence through all the ups and downs. A lot of motherfuckers didn't make it. Most women lost their faith and slowly began to fade away within the first two years. I mean, it takes more than love to truly stand by a men in prison. It takes respect, honor, commitment, understanding, honesty, and some more shit. And the truth is, a lot of woman just don't have it in them. That's why they say that, 'when you're doing a bid, the only people who will be there the entire time, are mother's and true lovers.' Now, I understood why dudes went uptown on some bullshit.

Don't get me wrong. You got some family members that will hold shit down. And it's a proven fact that a lot of men have met their soulmates while behind the wall. But women who stuck by the men they loved regardless of the circumstances were considered diamond's in the rough. They just weren't born very often.

"I don't think f-building out here yet." Murdock confessed as we strolled into the yard war ready -hoodie, knife and cell-made vests. Murdock had gotten word from a reliable source that some shit was supposed to go down with my cousin Little Phil and I wanted to be there when it did.

"Them niggas out here though." I exclaimed instantly spotting a group of hyenas huddled up in the back of the yard with workout gloves. A dead giveaway, especially since they weren't working out. It was also a sign that they didn't plan to get away though. But hyenas never did because they only attacked in packs.

"So, what's up? What you want to do?" Murdock questioned always down to push first and politic later.

"Let's wait for Cuzzo." I replied looking around. The deck was definitely going to be stacked against us. But, I didn't give a fuck and I knew Murdock didn't either. He was all heart and guts. Plus, I knew that once we got to slinging them knives out that bitch. A lot of them niggas were going to have a change of heart. They always did. The stand-off only looked good. But when it was time to conduct business only the true businessmen showed up. That's why Murdock always called his joints 'the equalizer.'

"Cuzzo, what's up?" I stepped straight to Little Phil and his man, Boy Gant, the moment they entered the yard and knew something was definitely in the air. *So Murdock's man was right*, I thought. "You about to work?"

"I don't know," he confessed. "Joe Louis knocked two of them gang kids out in the dayroom last night. And you know if he go, me and Boy Gant going."

"Bet." I nodded. That was all I needed to hear because if my cousin got to rocking in the yard. Murdock and I were rolling wasn't no ifs, ands or buts about it. "What you need me to do?"

"Hold up, here come Joe Louis now." Boy Gant interrupted.

Joe Louis was a tall, pot-bellied, dark-skinned joker I liked to call the 'Black Bomber' because he was nice with his hands.

"Where them niggas at?" Joe Louis walked up ready to get the party started.

"Wait until the police lock the gate." Little Phil instructed knowing that most niggas tried to take flight when they got hit. Once the yard gate was secured and the lines where clearly drawn. Little Phil, Boy Gent and Joe Louis made their way across the yard to see if there was going to be some slow singing and flower bringing or just another rap session.

"How the hell we suppose to know if we should start hitting these niggas?" Murdock inquired before Joe Louis and them had walked off. "What's the signal? Thumbs up, thumbs down, what?"

"Oh, you're going to know it's time to start working out this bitch if you see me pull this Bethlehem out," Boy Gent fired.

"And that's for sure." Joe Louis seconded.

It didn't take long for things to get iron out after niggas put their pride to the side. The leader was a seasoned knife slinger and well-known man, but it wasn't dying to go up against Joe Louis because he knew how ugly it could get. In the end, it was settled the usual way, with simply words and future agreements. That's why I loved being my own man and paying my own way in prison. It just separated you from the rest when you earned your spot at the top with your own blood, sweat and tears regardless of the odds. Regardless of the consequences. It meant that you didn't have to answer to nobody for nothing you did. It meant respect. It also meant danger. Danger because it made you a threat to the prison status quo. But, I could live with that because niggas knew that if they fucked around and didn't finish me, I would surely finish them. Putting in work had never been a problem for me in prison. It was knowing when to stop that always seemed to be my issue. I always went over board and most guys weren't built or willing to go to that extreme.

**

"This bitch definitely ride smooth," Antauwn admitted pulling up to the red light on Edmondson Avenue listening to Nas's latest album, *God's Son*, in Tony's brand-new, sky-blue 2003 Lexus

SC430. "Plus, I like the sound' system." Antauwn added wondering if he should jump on something new. Especially since Samone had turned his Range into a family minivan after their second daughter was born.

"I told you this motherfucker was like that!" Tony exclaimed. He'd been bragging about the Lexus since he'd copped it, trying to convince Antauwn to take it for a test drive.

"Look out!" Tony screamed suddenly over the music as a hooded figure ran up on the car aiming a gun.

Doom, doom, doom, doom, doom.... Antauwn froze up for a second as bullets tore through everything in their path—glass, metal, flesh, and bone. Then he heard Tony ordering him to go and stepped on the gas and went flying across the intersection until he was fish-tailed by a school bus into a complete three-sixty. When the car finally stopped, there was blood, bullet holes, and glass everywhere. A crowd quickly began to gather around the car. Antauwn could hear the faint sounds of whispers and police sirens in the distance.

"Help," Antauwn managed to mumble as he was losing consciousness.

The last thing Antauwn heard was somebody say, "Watch out! That's my nephew's car!" a moment before the car door swung out and him felt someone going through his pockets.

Chapter 39

Only A Gangster Can Judge Me

I was just about to get into the shower when a soap-covered white boy came speed balling out, looking crazy. A second later I noticed a well-known faggy peeping out of the shower from behind the curtain with a smile on his face. *I don't know what's up with these gumps around here,* I thought to myself making a U-turn to head on to the shower upstairs. I don't know why I was trying to play the downstairs shower anyway. I knew better, that shit was for jerk-off artist and suckers. I was just being lazy because I'd been at work, booting licking all day.

"Fuck going on down there yo?" My neighbor -a lame who should've been showering downstair questioned being nosey.

"Don't know, don't care." I assured. I just wanted to mind my business and take my shower, so that I could lock in and lay down. Little did I know how involved I would actually become.

About an hour later I rolled over half asleep and saw the same soap-covered white boy standing at the door, talking to my cell buddy, Moon and wondered what the hell was going on. Moon was solid, through and through. And he despised bustas, so I can't understand what they could be talking about. Whatever the case, within seconds I was out like a light bulb.

"Ayo, why the white boy down the tier just offer me a pound of Arizona to holler at that big gump nigga, Walter Hall that sleep upstairs in cell five eighteen," Moon exclaimed the moment I got up to use the bathroom.

"Oh yeah?" I yawned and looked at him like he was crazy. It was no secret that if you wanted a nigga touched in Jessup, rather for some shit he did on the streets or in the system. Moon was the man to see. I mean, any of them Cherry Hill niggas really. Them boys were getting it done on all levels. Plus, they had a stronghold on everything from lockup to f-building. If food was moving they were eating.

"Yeah." Moon shook his head as I began to take a piss. "Yo said Walter Hall tried to suck him off in the shower earlier," Moon explained.

So that's why that nigga came flying out that shower, huh? I thought. "Man, fuck that white boy. Let him run down on that faggy ass nigga himself," I argued. Everybody in the system knew that Walter Hall was a coldblooded homosexual who ran around the penitentiary, having his mother put money on dudes books so that he could suck their dicks. His prison history was legendary. It started when he had gotten gang raped for three days straight over the Baltimore City Jail back in the eights. Then, while he was in the Supermax. He became famous for sucking niggas off through the feed-up slots. But, if that wasn't enough to give him a household name. He'd been caught by a female captain giving the Chief of Security head in the warden's office and she got fired.

"Nah, I'ma get that pound up off that basta." Moon declared. "Of course, you know I'm not going to do nothing to that bitch myself. I'ma holler at City and Big Gorge and get them to put one of them little DC niggas on that bitch. But, I'm getting that weed."

The next morning when we came out for breakfast I could just feel the tension in the air. Plus, I already knew that some shit was going to happen because Moon and I had been up all night, smoking that good ass Arizona. "Slow down some," I whispered to Murdock as two little DC flunkies breezed by like they were on a mission. "What they say, youngin and 'em about to work," I warned. I knew Walter Hall was up ahead. Not only had I heard his voice. But, I knew that he came out for breakfast every morning because he worked in the wood shop. Which was funny in itself. *A gump working in the wood shop*? I busted out laughing.

"Fuck is you geeky about nigga?" Murdock stared at me curiously.

"Nothing," I lied. "Just stay on point nigga."

"I'm always on point." Murdock retorted and I knew he was right. Even when there wasn't nothing in the air that nigga was on point. "I'm tripping off dog though. I can't believe yo, letting niggas put that battery in his back."

"Are you serious?" I looked at Murdock in surprised. I was honestly shocked because he of all people knew that half of the jail was battery operated. "That nigga look like the Energizer Bunny."

"What the hell does that mean?"

"That means, he's just like most of these crash-dummies walking around here, waiting for one of their big homies to push their bottoms."

"Oh, that's fucked up! That's my little guy too." Murdock confessed just as the two flunkies caught up to Walter Hall and started tearing his fat ass up. That had to be one of the funniest things I'd ever seen in prison. A big, fat ass, grown man, who'd prayed on social, running down the compound, screaming for his life as two little paint sized kids stabbed him everywhere except his legs.

Oddly enough, when we got back to the cells. They locked us down. I guess nobody was supposed to assault the Security Chief's head doctor. It was crazy because as soon as the shift changed. The shakedown crew rushed the tier and began tearing our shit up. Niggas were going off. All this disrespectful shit about a dick-sucking gump?

In the end, nothing was found. No knives, no drugs, nothing! Unless you consider the homemade wooden dildo that was recovered from Walter Hall's cell. The Chief of Security went off. He wasn't trying to hear nothing. He wanted somebody to fall for Walter Hall's assault. So he sent the shakedown crew back on the tier to tear our shit up again. Then, he ran the cameras back for two days and watched all the video footage. From that point it was over. He saw the white boy run from the shower. Then, he saw Walter Hall peep out.

Later, he saw the white boy standing at the cell, talking to somebody through the crack of the door. After that, he sent the SRT squad to grab all of us. They came deep too just in case we bucked. After a little back and forth, Moon and I were packed up and marched down the compound to the administrative lockup building. I was mad as shit! I didn't want my name attached to nothing that had anything to do with no punk. That's how shit always got twisted. When it was all over, said and done through. It turned out to be a   blessing in disguise because two days later my property was boxed up and I was walked back over to the 'Cut.'

Chapter 40

Definition of A Gangster

It took Antauwn a week to slip out of his coma. But, once he found out about Tony he was ready to slip out of the hospital. However, after taken seven of the thirty-two slugs fired into the Tony's Lexus that was just impossible.

"So what do you need me to do bro?" Detauwn questioned standing beside Antauwn's hospital bed. Finding out who'd tried to kill him was his only concern. "Find the niggas who did this to me."

Detauwn stared at his brother. After barely escaping the last murder investigation, Detauwn had vowed to never pick up a pistol again. He didn't want to be like so many others. Trapped off in prison while their children grew up without them. But, his family was everything to him. Especially his little brothers. So, the moment he heard about the shooting. He started calling in old favors. Edmondson Village had once been his old stomping grounds. "I'm already on it." Detauwn revealed. "What you know about a kid name Poochie?"

Antauwn thought for a second. Poochie was the bitch Tony slapped boyfriend or something. "Are you talking about the kid from the Village?"

"Yeah, niggas been saying yo may have had something to do with it. They say he went through the car after the crash too."

"Oh yeah." Antauwn grinned. He'd felt somebody running his pockets.

"Tony used to fuck yo' old washed-up ass bitch! She took him off for scratch back in the day." Antauwn remembered Tony telling the bitch to go get the kid. "But, Jamaine supposed to have straightened that shit out. He came back like everything was good. He acted like he may have fucked the bitch. He said she had the little kid Poochie's nose wide open and she was going to handle him. Plus, his man Banga knew the kid personally. So I thought that shit was over."

Detauwn just shook his head. Jamaine was a big disappoint-ment. First, he left Dakaron high and dry. Then, he left Antauwn in the blind. "I think I'm go see that little nigga too." Detauwn spat. He never truly liked Jamaine anyway. Dakaron had kept him off of Jamaine before when he'd put his hands on one of their female cous-ins. To Detauwn, Jamaine was one of those phony niggas who were only with you when there was a benefit to be had.

"Nah bro," Antauwn shook his head. Even after all the bitch shit Jamaine had pulled. He knew Dakaron still had love for him. "If this kid Poochie went rogue, it was out of Jamaine's hands," An-tauwn justified. He just didn't believe in his heart that Jamaine would knowingly leave him and Tony in harm's way.

"Bro, the fucking doctor saying you may not walk again. Some-body gotta answer for that!" Detauwn raised his voice.

"Since when we started believing doctors?" Antauwn laughed. "Just find out if that nigga Poochie had something to do with that shit! If he did—"

"If he did, he won't have nothing to do with nothing else, be-lieve that!" Detauwn cut him off.

"I love you, big bro," Antauwn confessed with watery eyes. When it came to family. There was nobody in the world he de-pended on more than his mother and brothers.

"I love you too, nigga," Detauwn countered. "Now let me go find this bitch, Poochie."

Antauwn simply nodded his head as Detauwn headed for the door.

"Send Samone back in too."

"Sucker for love ass nigga!" Detauwn teased, exiting the room, making Antauwn laugh so hard it hurt.

***

I had been trying to catch up with Detauwn for days. I knew how he was when drama hit the home front and didn't want him to do nothing that could come back on him or the family. But, he wasn't answering his cellphone. *What the hell is the purpose of" having a phone that you can carry with you if you're never going to answer the motherfucker?* I wondered slamming the jail phone down, making niggas look at me like they wanted to say something.

I knew dudes don't play about the phone in prison. It was like our only life line. But, I also knew that niggas respect that look. The look that said now is not the time. I thought about calling Jamaine or my cousin, Urtle, Tony's brother. Maybe I could finally get one of them niggas to come through for me? However, my pride wouldn't allow me to do. And to be honest, it was hard to point a finger when you lived your life in sin. But, after all the let downs and lies. I just didn't have no faith in Jamaine, nor Urtle and that was the worst thing for a man in prison to lose. Because without faith, there could be no trust, no respect, no understanding. Which ultimately meant, no relationship.

"Boy, you know your brother is going to be okay." SweetPea encourage across the visiting room counter trying to calm me down. I'd asked her to come see me, so that I could find out what was going on out there and as always, she showed up. "He's a Truesdale and all y'all motherfuckers fighters!"

I knew SweetPea was right, but my concerns weren't Antauwn. All he had to do was recover. It was Detauwn that I was worried about. Because he was the one running around the streets looking for a nigga, who obviously wasn't as rusty as he was when it came to playing with that burner.

"Yeah, I know," I agreed noting really wanting to get into. "That shit just hit too close for comfort." I added as that feeling of helplessness washed over me again. "And I wish I could do something."

"You can," SweetPea assured. "Be there for your mother right now. She needs you because she has two sons not talking to her right now."

SweetPea was right. I could only imagine what my mother was feeling. Because I knew that neither one of my brothers were telling her what she wanted to hear. "That's why I love you so much," I admitted thankfully.

"No, that's one of the reasons why you love me so much," SweetPea corrected.

"Yeah, you ain't lying about that," I agreed, biting my bottom lip, thinking of quite a few other reasons.

"I told you, I got you."

***

Detauwn was sitting in a stolen car in the middle of the afternoon, dressed in all black, patiently waiting for Poochie to show his face outside of the Uplands Apartment Complex. First, he got confirmation that Poochie was his man. Then, he crept up on Jamaine's slimeball ass anyway and got all the information he needed to locate and destroy Poochie and his old dick-eating bitch. Detauwn couldn't believe that Poochie hadn't done his homework. But, that was the problem with most young niggas today. They don't know who they are up against. Maybe they didn't care, but they should. Because had Poochie did a little digging. He would have realized that after he ran down on Tony and Antauwn he'd have to answer for his attention rather he went to prison or remained free. Instead, he now had Detauwn outside his apartment with a chrome Bulldog .357 waiting to knock his socks off, because he had crossed the point of no return.

***

Antauwn was laid back in the hospital bed upset after the homicide detectives departed. He couldn't stand them bitches. All they ever wanted to do was lock a nigga down and throw away the key or kill him off like an animal in the fucking street. They didn't care about the facts.

You good, baby?" Samone gently rubbed Antauwn's cheek concerned. She could always tell when he got tensed.

"I'm just ready to get the fuck out of this hospital!" Antauwn snapped with a huge vein shooting across his forehead like a lightning bolt.

"Don't worry, baby. We'll be home soon." Samone leaned forward and kissed him on the top of his head.

***

"Bingo!" Detauwn exclaimed to himself as he saw who he believed to be Poochie and his bitch stumble out of the apartment building hand and hand. He knew it had to be them because they looked just like Jamaine had described. Tall, slinky, poppy-eyed, brown skin nigga with a wild bush and pretty, older, redbone bitch with blond hair and a phat ass. Detauwn wondered just how much the bitch was involved with Poochie's actions as she smiled and laid her head on his shoulder.

"Yeah, you're with it." Detauwn mumbled before slowly pulling his mask down and getting out of the car. It always felt good to deceive the deceiver.

Detauwn jogged across the street with his eyes locked on his targets. "Poochie!" Detauwn called out raising the .357 as he emerged from the darkness. The moment Poochie looked up Detauwn shot him in the chest and knocked him into the wall. The female stood in shock and began screaming. "This for Tony, bitch!" Detauwn silenced her with one mean head shot and watched her body crumble to the ground. Then, he carefully walked over to Poochie as he laid there on the ground, leaned up against the apartment building, wide-eyed, trying to stop the bleeding from the hole in his chest with his hands, fighting to breath.

"That's not going to help yo, the hole too big," Detauwn squatted down next Poochie as blood seeped through his fingers. "That's why I love the bulldog so much." Detauwn took a moment to analyze the .357 the way he used to do before he sealed an enemy's fate. "All I got to do is hit you once above the waist."

Poochie was shivering like a fiend going through withdrawal as Detauwn pressed the .357 Bulldog against his head. "If you run across my cousin Tony, I suggest you apologize." Detauwn grinned and blew Poochie's brains all over the apartment building wall. Then, he stood up over top of Poochie and the bitch and shot them both in the head again to be sure the deed was done before running back to the car and driving off into the night.

***

The first thing Antauwn did when he was discharged from the hospital was go to Tony's gravesite. He wanted to tell him personally that Detauwn had gotten the nigga who had gotten the drop on them. He also wanted to thank him, because had he not talked him into driving his new car. He'd have been the one in the passenger's seat who ended taking the head and chest shots after warning Tony. Antauwn knew he had to make sure his cousin's children were taken care of. After all Tony had basically traded *his* life for his.

"I'm done, Cuz," Antauwn declared after Samone had rolled him over to Tony's headstone and back away to give him some privacy. "I'm finish with this shit! No more playing the fifty. I'm going complete legit."

Antauwn continued as tears began to fall from his eyes. "I wish we could've did this shit together, Cuz. I miss you so much already nigga! We were supposed to do this shit together. But, I'ma do that mother fucker for us, Cuz, just watch and see. I love you, nigga! Always."

Knowing that Samone was waiting for him in the car, Antauwn looked up into the cloudy sky and said a quick prayer. Then, he tossed a single green rose on Tony's headstone, backed up, and tried to rolled away.

Samone saw Antauwn struggling and went over to assist him. Samone had never witnessed a grown man cry before. Let alone the father of her children. But, for some reason, seeing Antauwn cry only made her love him more. She could not wait to tell him that she was already pregnant again.

"Thanks, baby," Antauwn said as Samone began pushing the wheelchair back toward the car.

Chapter 41

Gangster 4 Life

Being back over the 'Cut' was a blessing. I got to hook back up with my niggas again and finally hang out with John. All the old heads showed mad respect because of how I'd carried it after the gym situation when the investigators showed up. There weren't too many young niggas who got hit and kept their mouth shut. But, I didn't even yell down the tier. By the time winter rolled around things seemed to settle down.

Antauwn was in therapy trying to get his legs back under him. Chanae had another baby on me. A son name Darrien. I loved him to death too, but he was just another reminder of another opportunity some joker had taken from me. Another thing I could no longer give Chanae first. Our love could never change; but our relationship certainly did. The gap between us got wider and wider. I invested my energy in building some with Lakeria because she deserved it. She was something special. Something fresh, something that I'd never possessed before. I was used to gangster bitches, hoodrats and around the way girls. Damn near all my women with the exception of maybe one or two was streets. Lakeria was different though. She was soft spoken, kind hearted, intelligent, beautiful inside and out and independent. She was like the country, square version of Samone's cousin, Tinika.

I was also able to jump straight back in school because my teachers—a short, darkskin African named Dr. Vincent and a cute, heavy set, older woman with crazy freckles named Ms. Galzer—loved me to death. Even though I drove both of them crazy on a daily basis.

"Ayo, please tell me that you're strapped?" I interjected out of nowhere as Bugeye, L.A., and I were sitting up on the bleachers talking about my man Big Al being on the news for a rack of bodies.

"What's up?" Bugeye and L.A. looked around.

"Nah, y'all see that nigga right there walking with Anwar and Tyson?"

"Yeah, what about him?" L.A. inquired.

"That's the nigga that testified on me," I revealed as my heart began to pound.

"That's Monique!" Bugeye questioned to be sure.

"Yeah," I confirmed, never taking my eyes off him. It was bitter cold outside but for some reason I began to feel warm. My hands and head began to sweat. I couldn't believe my eyes. Monique was here, on the 'Cut' yard. In the flesh. I didn't know what to think. It had to be a setup because when I was sentenced, Miss Shakir had made sure that Monique was documented as my enemy so we'd never end up in the same institution if he ever decided to hold water and come to prison.

"But I don't get it. That nigga's on my enemy list."

"Didn't you say that they fucked up and spelled your name wrong?" L.A. reminded.

Oh shit! It's not a setup! It's an opportunity, a blessing, I thought to myself. "I'ma kill this nigga," I declared, standing up.

"Chill, yo." Bugeye pulled me back down "Hold up, that nigga don't even know you're here. We can bake him a real good cake."

"Nah, yo, Monique ain't like your average rat. He been through the system and a lot of niggas still respect him, despite the fact that he was telling, because they know he gets money," I argued, knowing I had to strike first and fast before Monique got armed up and surrounded himself with a crew. "I got to get at this nigga now!" I added, knowing that Monique would find out if me or Frank was on the yard the moment he got on that phone.

"So, what do you want to do?" Bugeye eyed me.

I thought about how Monique use to always say that, any nigga who showed up on the yard and didn't get set out was a lame. And I knew that Monique wasn't a lame. A rat, yeah, but not a lame, so niggas were going to set him out. "I want to kill this nigga!" I admitted sincerely, staring right back at Bugeye until he realized that I was serious.

"Say no more." Bugeye looked around cautiously before pulling a long ass, serrated-blade steak knife from his dip.

"What the fuck is that, a steak knife, nigga?" L.A. took the words right out of my mouth. I mean, Bugeye always kept a nice murder weapon on him, but the shit he'd just pulled out took the cake.

"If you can't kill that rat with that, there's no reason to set another trap," Bugeye warned earnestly, handing me the knife.

"I got that bitch," I assured quickly, sliding the knife in my hoodie pocket before getting up again. "Watch my work," I instructed, pulling my hood over my head before stepping off.

I kept my head low the first time I walked past Monique on the track. I could've stabbed his dumb ass, because he was definitely slipping. Standing there running his mouth to Anwar and Tyson. The only reason I didn't bust his ass was because it was against the prison man code. You never stabbed a dude while he was walking with another man, unless you didn't have no respect or concern for that man. It was blatant disrespect. And I had much respect for both Anwar and Tyson, so I bopped on by. I figured I could catch Monique on the next lap. After all, the phones had been acting crazy all morning. So, I didn't have to worry about him finding out that I was in the jail. However, before I could get around the yard again, I noticed that Anwar and Tyson were cutting across the yard and saw Bugeye and L.A. speed-walking around the track.

"Let me see you for a second, Ock." Anwar and Tyson walked over just as Bugeye and L.A. pulled up.

"What's up, Anwar?" I kept my hand on the knife just in case. They were cool, but I wasn't stupid. I knew how the game was played.

"That's what I'm trying to figure, Ock," Anwar confessed. "You just come past us like you had it on your mind."

"Nah yo, I'm chilling, getting my stroll on," I lied.

"Look, Ock, I'm not trying to be in your business or nothing, but I go for you. Plus, Little Phil is my guy," Anwar explained. "So, all I ask is that if you're about to hit one of my Muslim brothers, holler at me first."

"That dude y'all was talking to earlier Muslim?" L.A. questioned, making me mad as hell. Because it didn't matter if he was

Muslim or not. That nigga told on me and he was getting punished for it.

"Who? Monique?" Anwar started laughing. "Nah, Monique and I go way back. He just came in last night."

"So, what, that's your man?" I gripped the knife.

"Hell no," Tyson interjected.

"Nah, I don't deal with slim no more," Anwar answered for himself.

"So, that's what I was letting him know. Plus, my partner, Big Head, told me that he supposed to have told on some young boys about a bunch of bodies."

Anwar's facts were a little off, though his information was correct, which told me that he could keep a secret. "That bitch told on me and my right-hand man," I confessed, trusting that I was amongst men. Of course, I knew that Anwar and Tyson had lost their love for the game. They made that very clear. But, they'd never lost their morals and principles, and that's why they were still respected amongst men.

"You got the paperwork?" Tyson questioned.

"Yeah, but I'm not showing it until I hit that nigga!" I explained. I wasn't about to make the same mistakes other dudes had made. When they decided to expose a rat before exterminating it and ended up getting bit by the rat again. "I'ma tear the fur off his ass first!"

"Well, if that's the case, don't let your emotion override your judgment, Ock, that's how you make mistakes," Anwar warned.

"Yeah, ain't no sense in getting caught for something that you can easily get away with," Tyson seconded. "This is a big prison, you can catch that nigga anywhere. Plus, he can't fight what he don't know is coming, you feel me?"

"I hear you." I shook my head, thinking of ways to get away with killing Monique.

"It's always best to strike in the midst of confusion," Anwar added with a smile. "When there is no confusion, all you have to do is create some. But, as a Muslim, I say let Allah have His day because He is the best of knowers."

Bugeye, L.A., and I walked back over to the bleachers to try to come up with a plan to take Monique out of the game for good. I started thinking about all the shit Monique used to say about me being too nearsighted, never seeing the whole picture. The start as well as the finish. "You know the difference between those who succeed and those who fail isn't what they have. It's what they choose to do with their resources," Monique had said when we were still over the jail.

"I got it, yo!" I fired excitedly. "I know how to kill this bitch and get away with it."

Since Monique was oblivious to the danger that lurked about, we laid on him until he headed for the west wing showers. I made sure everybody knew what to do. When we got to the shower room, everybody went their own way. If a nigga had to be killed, the shower room was the place to do it. It was open, but escapable.

I waited until the shower was packed with about twenty-five niggas rotating under the six shower heads. Then, I gave L.A. the head nod and slipped in under the water all the way on the opposite side of Monique.

Bugeye was over fucking with the phone as if he was trying to get it to work. The CO on post was a New York wannabe who loved to play like he was down for niggas, but for real, he was just another sucker in a uniform looking to climb up in rank on the backs of the guys he played like he was cool with. Once I was about two shower heads away from Monique, Bugeye slammed the phone and cursed, giving L.A. the signal. L.A. began slowly walking toward the door. If anybody had really been paying attention, they'd noticed that I never soaped up my washcloth. I just kept it in my hand as I slid from underneath one shower head to the next. I saw an old head heading for the exit and got ready. I watched as L.A. intentionally bumped him. And when he turned to question L.A., he got hit square in the mouth, and it was on.

"Fight! Fight!" Bugeye screamed, getting everybody's attention as L.A. and the old head began clutching in the middle of the floor. In prison, niggas craved action. So, while the CO called the code for assistance and everybody was trying to get a good look at the action, I slid right up behind Monique. He, too, had been captured by all the excitement.

I knew my first hit had to count. So, I flipped the knife underhand, threw my hand over Monique's mouth, and slammed the knife into his back five or six times before he even realized what was happening. When Monique spun around and saw me, his eyes got big with recognition as his hand shot to his back. His mouth opened, but his scream never came out because I'd purposely stabbed him in his back to puncture his lungs and take away all his fight.

By now, L.A. and the old head were rolling around on the floor wrestling as the CO maced them and continuously ordered them to stop. I slung the knife again, cutting right into Monique's chest like butter as he stumbled back and fell behind the crowd. That's when I went to work.

I sat up on Monique's chest and held his head down. Then, I stabbed him repeatedly as he tried to fend me off. "Nah bitch!" I pushed his arm out of my way. "It's judgment day."

Monique looked at me as if he was seeing me for the first time. He froze. But eyes locked. I could see his fear. I could read his thoughts. He wished that we were still cool. He wished that he could've made it right. But, he knew that it was too late. His past actions had doomed any chance we had of doing anything but killing each other if we ever crossed paths again in the future. What seemed like minutes was only seconds. I forced Monique's head to the side and jammed the knife into his neck. By now, the shower room was beginning to fill with corrections officers. I left the knife in Monique's neck and got up off of him. I quickly got back underneath the shower head and began rinsing off. Two dudes backed up and damn near tripped over Monique's body. That's when everybody got on point and started rushing out of the shower. Nobody wanted to be caught with a dead body whether they did it or not.

"Let's go, gentlemen! Grab your shit!" one of the COs screamed, walking around the shower room.

I moved quickly as Monique's blood began to mix with the shower water and go down the drain. I slipped on my boots, flipped my towel over my head, and walked right on past the CO doing all the hollering.

I had just gotten out of the shower room when I heard one of the guards call for medical assistance over the radio. "We need medical assistance in the west wing shower area!" she repeated, but death was in the air and there was nothing that she was going to be able to do to stop it. "Take everybody's ID who's not locked in!" was the last thing I heard as I sped down the west wing stairs and tried to make it back to my cell.

To Be Continued...
The Birth of a Gangster 3
Coming Soon

Lock Down Publications and Ca$h Presents assisted
publishing packages.

BASIC PACKAGE $499
Editing
Cover Design
Formatting

UPGRADED PACKAGE $800
Typing
Editing
Cover Design
Formatting

ADVANCE PACKAGE $1,200
Typing
Editing
Cover Design
Formatting
Copyright registration
Proofreading
Upload book to Amazon

LDP SUPREME PACKAGE $1,500
Typing
Editing
Cover Design
Formatting
Copyright registration
Proofreading
Set up Amazon account
Upload book to Amazon
Advertise on LDP Amazon and Facebook page

***Other services available upon request. Additional charges may apply
Lock Down Publications
P.O. Box 944
Stockbridge, GA 30281-9998
Phone # 470 303-9761

Submission Guideline

Submit the first three chapters of your completed manuscript to <u>ldpsubmissions@gmail.com</u>, subject line: Your book's title. The manuscript must be in a .doc file and sent as an attachment. Document should be in Times New Roman, double spaced and in size 12 font. Also, provide your synopsis and full contact information. If sending multiple submissions, they must each be in a separate email.

Have a story but no way to send it electronically? You can still submit to LDP/Ca$h Presents. Send in the first three chapters, written or typed, of your completed manuscript to:

LDP: Submissions Dept
Po Box 944
Stockbridge, Ga 30281

DO NOT send original manuscript. Must be a duplicate.

Provide your synopsis and a cover letter containing your full contact information.

Thanks for considering LDP and Ca$h Presents.

<u>NEW RELEASES</u>

TIL DEATH by ARYANNA
IT'S JUST ME AND YOU by AH'MILLION
QUEEN OF THE ZOO 2 by BLACK MIGO
THE HEART OF A SAVAGE 4 by JIBRIL WIL-
LIAMS
THE BIRTH OF A GANGSTER 2 by DELMONT
PLAYER

STRAIGHT BEAST MODE III

De'Kari

KINGPIN KILLAZ IV

STREET KINGS III

PAID IN BLOOD III

CARTEL KILLAZ IV

DOPE GODS III

Hood Rich

SINS OF A HUSTLA II

ASAD

RICH $AVAGE II

By Martell Troublesome Bolden

YAYO V

Bred In The Game 2

S. Allen

CREAM III

THE STREETS WILL TALK II

By Yolanda Moore

SON OF A DOPE FIEND III

HEAVEN GOT A GHETTO II

By Renta

LOYALTY AIN'T PROMISED III

By Keith Williams

I'M NOTHING WITHOUT HIS LOVE II

SINS OF A THUG II

TO THE THUG I LOVED BEFORE II

IN A HUSTLER I TRUST II

By Monet Dragun

QUIET MONEY IV

EXTENDED CLIP III

THUG LIFE IV

By **Trai'Quan**

THE STREETS MADE ME IV

By **Larry D. Wright**

IF YOU CROSS ME ONCE II

ANGEL IV

By **Anthony Fields**

THE STREETS WILL NEVER CLOSE IV

By K'ajji

HARD AND RUTHLESS III

KILLA KOUNTY III

By Khufu

MONEY GAME III

By Smoove Dolla

JACK BOYS VS DOPE BOYS II

A GANGSTA'S QUR'AN V

COKE GIRLZ II

By Romell Tukes

MURDA WAS THE CASE II

Elijah R. Freeman

THE STREETS NEVER LET GO II

By Robert Baptiste

AN UNFORESEEN LOVE III

By **Meesha**

KING OF THE TRENCHES III
by **GHOST & TRANAY ADAMS**

MONEY MAFIA II

LOYAL TO THE SOIL III

By **Jibril Williams**

QUEEN OF THE ZOO III

The Birth of a Gangster 2

By **Black Migo**
VICIOUS LOYALTY III

By Kingpen
A GANGSTA'S PAIN III

By J-Blunt
CONFESSIONS OF A JACKBOY III

By Nicholas Lock
GRIMEY WAYS II

By Ray Vinci
KING KILLA II

By Vincent "Vitto" Holloway
BETRAYAL OF A THUG II

By Fre$h
THE MURDER QUEENS II

By Michael Gallon
THE BIRTH OF A GANGSTER III

By Delmont Player
TREAL LOVE II

By Le'Monica Jackson
FOR THE LOVE OF BLOOD II

By Jamel Mitchell
RAN OFF ON DA PLUG II

By Paper Boi Rari
HOOD CONSIGLIERE II

By Keese
PRETTY GIRLS DO NASTY THINGS II

By Nicole Goosby
PROTÉGÉ OF A LEGEND II

By Corey Robinson
IT'S JUST ME AND YOU II

Delmont Player

By Ah'Million

Available Now

RESTRAINING ORDER **I & II**

By **CA$H & Coffee**

LOVE KNOWS NO BOUNDARIES **I II & III**

By **Coffee**

RAISED AS A GOON I, II, III & IV

BRED BY THE SLUMS I, II, III

BLAST FOR ME I & II

ROTTEN TO THE CORE I II III

A BRONX TALE I, II, III

DUFFLE BAG CARTEL I II III IV V VI

HEARTLESS GOON I II III IV V

A SAVAGE DOPEBOY I II

DRUG LORDS I II III

CUTTHROAT MAFIA I II

KING OF THE TRENCHES

By **Ghost**

LAY IT DOWN **I & II**

LAST OF A DYING BREED I II

BLOOD STAINS OF A SHOTTA I & II III

By **Jamaica**

LOYAL TO THE GAME I II III

LIFE OF SIN I, II III

By **TJ & Jelissa**

The Birth of a Gangster 2

BLOODY COMMAS I & II

SKI MASK CARTEL I II & III

KING OF NEW YORK I II,III IV V

RISE TO POWER I II III

COKE KINGS I II III IV V

BORN HEARTLESS I II III IV

KING OF THE TRAP I II

By **T.J. Edwards**

IF LOVING HIM IS WRONG…I & II

LOVE ME EVEN WHEN IT HURTS I II III

By **Jelissa**

WHEN THE STREETS CLAP BACK I & II III

THE HEART OF A SAVAGE I II III IV

MONEY MAFIA

LOYAL TO THE SOIL I II

By **Jibril Williams**

A DISTINGUISHED THUG STOLE MY HEART I II & III

LOVE SHOULDN'T HURT I II III IV

RENEGADE BOYS I II III IV

PAID IN KARMA I II III

SAVAGE STORMS I II III

AN UNFORESEEN LOVE I II

By **Meesha**

A GANGSTER'S CODE I &, II III

A GANGSTER'S SYN I II III

THE SAVAGE LIFE I II III

CHAINED TO THE STREETS I II III

BLOOD ON THE MONEY I II III

A GANGSTA'S PAIN I II

By **J-Blunt**

PUSH IT TO THE LIMIT

By **Bre' Hayes**

BLOOD OF A BOSS **I, II, III, IV, V**

SHADOWS OF THE GAME

TRAP BASTARD

By **Askari**

THE STREETS BLEED MURDER **I, II & III**

THE HEART OF A GANGSTA I II& III

By **Jerry Jackson**

CUM FOR ME I II III IV V VI VII VIII

An **LDP Erotica Collaboration**

BRIDE OF A HUSTLA **I II & II**

THE FETTI GIRLS **I, II& III**

CORRUPTED BY A GANGSTA I, II III, IV

BLINDED BY HIS LOVE

THE PRICE YOU PAY FOR LOVE I, II ,III

DOPE GIRL MAGIC I II III

By **Destiny Skai**

WHEN A GOOD GIRL GOES BAD

By **Adrienne**

THE COST OF LOYALTY I II III

By Kweli

A GANGSTER'S REVENGE **I II III & IV**

THE BOSS MAN'S DAUGHTERS I II III IV V

A SAVAGE LOVE **I & II**

BAE BELONGS TO ME I II

A HUSTLER'S DECEIT I, II, III

WHAT BAD BITCHES DO I, II, III

SOUL OF A MONSTER I II III

KILL ZONE

The Birth of a Gangster 2

A DOPE BOY'S QUEEN I II III

TIL DEATH

By **Aryanna**

A KINGPIN'S AMBITON

A KINGPIN'S AMBITION **II**

I MURDER FOR THE DOUGH

By **Ambitious**

TRUE SAVAGE I II III IV V VI VII

DOPE BOY MAGIC I, II, III

MIDNIGHT CARTEL I II III

CITY OF KINGZ I II

NIGHTMARE ON SILENT AVE

THE PLUG OF LIL MEXICO II

CLASSIC CITY

By **Chris Green**

A DOPEBOY'S PRAYER

By **Eddie "Wolf" Lee**

THE KING CARTEL **I, II & III**

By **Frank Gresham**

THESE NIGGAS AIN'T LOYAL **I, II & III**

By **Nikki Tee**

GANGSTA SHYT **I II &III**

By **CATO**

THE ULTIMATE BETRAYAL

By **Phoenix**

BOSS'N UP **I , II & III**

By **Royal Nicole**

I LOVE YOU TO DEATH

By **Destiny J**

I RIDE FOR MY HITTA

I STILL RIDE FOR MY HITTA
By **Misty Holt**
LOVE & CHASIN' PAPER
By **Qay Crockett**
TO DIE IN VAIN
SINS OF A HUSTLA
By **ASAD**
BROOKLYN HUSTLAZ
By **Boogsy Morina**
BROOKLYN ON LOCK I & II
By **Sonovia**
GANGSTA CITY
By **Teddy Duke**
A DRUG KING AND HIS DIAMOND I & II III
A DOPEMAN'S RICHES
HER MAN, MINE'S TOO I, II
CASH MONEY HO'S
THE WIFEY I USED TO BE I II
PRETTY GIRLS DO NASTY THINGS
By Nicole Goosby
TRAPHOUSE KING **I II & III**
KINGPIN KILLAZ I II III
STREET KINGS I II
PAID IN BLOOD **I II**
CARTEL KILLAZ I II III
DOPE GODS I II
By **Hood Rich**
LIPSTICK KILLAH **I, II, III**
CRIME OF PASSION I II & III
FRIEND OR FOE I II III

The Birth of a Gangster 2

By **Mimi**

STEADY MOBBN' **I, II, III**

THE STREETS STAINED MY SOUL I II III

By **Marcellus Allen**

WHO SHOT YA **I, II, III**

SON OF A DOPE FIEND I II

HEAVEN GOT A GHETTO

Renta

GORILLAZ IN THE BAY **I II III IV**

TEARS OF A GANGSTA I II

3X KRAZY I II

STRAIGHT BEAST MODE I II

DE'KARI

TRIGGADALE I II III

MURDAROBER WAS THE CASE

Elijah R. Freeman

GOD BLESS THE TRAPPERS I, II, III

THESE SCANDALOUS STREETS I, II, III

FEAR MY GANGSTA I, II, III IV, V

THESE STREETS DON'T LOVE NOBODY I, II

BURY ME A G I, II, III, IV, V

A GANGSTA'S EMPIRE I, II, III, IV

THE DOPEMAN'S BODYGAURD I II

THE REALEST KILLAZ I II III

THE LAST OF THE OGS I II III

Tranay Adams

THE STREETS ARE CALLING

Duquie Wilson

MARRIED TO A BOSS I II III

By Destiny Skai & Chris Green

KINGZ OF THE GAME I II III IV V VI

Playa Ray

SLAUGHTER GANG I II III

RUTHLESS HEART I II III

By Willie Slaughter

FUK SHYT

By Blakk Diamond

DON'T F#CK WITH MY HEART I II

By Linnea

ADDICTED TO THE DRAMA I II III

IN THE ARM OF HIS BOSS II

By Jamila

YAYO I II III IV

A SHOOTER'S AMBITION I II

BRED IN THE GAME

By S. Allen

TRAP GOD I II III

RICH $AVAGE

MONEY IN THE GRAVE I II III

By Martell Troublesome Bolden

FOREVER GANGSTA

GLOCKS ON SATIN SHEETS I II

By Adrian Dulan

TOE TAGZ I II III IV

LEVELS TO THIS SHYT I II

IT'S JUST ME AND YOU

By Ah'Million

KINGPIN DREAMS I II III

RAN OFF ON DA PLUG

By Paper Boi Rari

The Birth of a Gangster 2

CONFESSIONS OF A GANGSTA I II III IV

CONFESSIONS OF A JACKBOY I II

By Nicholas Lock

I'M NOTHING WITHOUT HIS LOVE

SINS OF A THUG

TO THE THUG I LOVED BEFORE

A GANGSTA SAVED XMAS

IN A HUSTLER I TRUST

By Monet Dragun

CAUGHT UP IN THE LIFE I II III

THE STREETS NEVER LET GO

By Robert Baptiste

NEW TO THE GAME I II III

MONEY, MURDER & MEMORIES I II III

By **Malik D. Rice**

LIFE OF A SAVAGE I II III

A GANGSTA'S QUR'AN I II III IV

MURDA SEASON I II III

GANGLAND CARTEL I II III

CHI'RAQ GANGSTAS I II III

KILLERS ON ELM STREET I II III

JACK BOYZ N DA BRONX I II III

A DOPEBOY'S DREAM I II III

JACK BOYS VS DOPE BOYS

COKE GIRLZ

By Romell Tukes

LOYALTY AIN'T PROMISED I II

By Keith Williams

QUIET MONEY I II III

THUG LIFE I II III

Delmont Player

EXTENDED CLIP I II
By **Trai'Quan**
THE STREETS MADE ME I II III
By **Larry D. Wright**
THE ULTIMATE SACRIFICE I, II, III, IV, V, VI
KHADIFI
IF YOU CROSS ME ONCE
ANGEL I II III
IN THE BLINK OF AN EYE
By **Anthony Fields**
THE LIFE OF A HOOD STAR
By Ca$h & Rashia Wilson
THE STREETS WILL NEVER CLOSE I II III
By K'ajji
CREAM I II
THE STREETS WILL TALK
By Yolanda Moore
NIGHTMARES OF A HUSTLA I II III
By King Dream
CONCRETE KILLA I II III
VICIOUS LOYALTY I II
By Kingpen
HARD AND RUTHLESS I II
MOB TOWN 251
THE BILLIONAIRE BENTLEYS I II III
By Von Diesel
GHOST MOB
Stilloan Robinson
MOB TIES I II III IV V VI
By SayNoMore

The Birth of a Gangster 2

BODYMORE MURDERLAND I II III

THE BIRTH OF A GANGSTER I II

By Delmont Player

FOR THE LOVE OF A BOSS

By C. D. Blue

MOBBED UP I II III IV

THE BRICK MAN I II III IV

THE COCAINE PRINCESS I II III IV V

By King Rio

KILLA KOUNTY I II III

By Khufu

MONEY GAME I II

By Smoove Dolla

A GANGSTA'S KARMA I II

By FLAME

KING OF THE TRENCHES I II

by **GHOST & TRANAY ADAMS**

QUEEN OF THE ZOO I II

By **Black Migo**

GRIMEY WAYS

By Ray Vinci

XMAS WITH AN ATL SHOOTER

By Ca$h & Destiny Skai

KING KILLA

By Vincent "Vitto" Holloway

BETRAYAL OF A THUG

By Fre$h

THE MURDER QUEENS

By Michael Gallon

TREAL LOVE

Delmont Player

By Le'Monica Jackson
FOR THE LOVE OF BLOOD
By Jamel Mitchell
HOOD CONSIGLIERE
By Keese
PROTÉGÉ OF A LEGEND
By Corey Robinson

BOOKS BY LDP'S CEO, CA$H

TRUST IN NO MAN

TRUST IN NO MAN 2

TRUST IN NO MAN 3

BONDED BY BLOOD

SHORTY GOT A THUG

THUGS CRY

THUGS CRY 2

THUGS CRY 3

TRUST NO BITCH

TRUST NO BITCH 2

TRUST NO BITCH 3

TIL MY CASKET DROPS

RESTRAINING ORDER

RESTRAINING ORDER 2

IN LOVE WITH A CONVICT

LIFE OF A HOOD STAR

XMAS WITH AN ATL SHOOTER

Delmont Player